THE RED QUEEN

MARGARET OF ANJOU
and the
WARS OF THE ROSES

THE RED QUEEN

MARGARET OF ANJOU
and the
WARS OF THE ROSES

By

Ruth S. Perot

Copyright © 2000 by Ruth S. Perot

All rights reserved. No part of this book may be reproduced, stored in a retrieval system, or transmitted by any means, electronic, mechanical, photocopying, recording, or otherwise, without written permission from the author.

ISBN: 1-58721-233-1

1st Books-rev. 02/25/00

About the Book

This novel, ***The Red Queen***, covers England's *War of the Roses,* 1444-1475. Fascinating characters abound in that period. There are, in addition to Margaret, who was married at age 14:

Henry VI, her husband, who was "fitter for a cowl than a crown."
Cardinal Beaufort, who pushed the marriage.
The Duke of Gloucester, who opposed it.
Warwick the Kingmaker, Margaret's greatest enemy.
The Yorkists and Lancastrians who tore England apart.

Margaret was a strong woman more suited to our own times than her own. Overlooked, it is time she is reintroduced as a heroine for today's readers.

CHARACTERS

Margaret of Anjou, daughter of Rene and Isabel of Anjou.

Henry VI, son of Henry V and Katherine of France.

Humphrey, Duke of Gloucester. Uncle of Henry VI.

Henry Beaufort, Cardinal Winchester, uncle of Gloucester and great uncle of Henry VI. Descended on bastard side.

Suffolk, William de la Pole. Adherent of Cardinal.

Richard, Duke of York. Traces descent from Edward III through second and fourth sons.

Cecily Neville, wife of Richard of York.

Edmund Beaufort, 2nd Duke of Somerset. Nephew of Cardinal.

Henry Beaufort, 3rd Duke of Somerset. Son of 2nd Duke.

Edmund Beaufort, 4th Duke of Somerset, brother of 3rd Duke.

Edward, Earl of March, son of York and Cecily.

Rutland, George of Clarence, and Richard. Other York sons.

Salisbury, Cecily's brother.

Warwick, son of Salisbury.

Isabel and Anne Neville, daughters of Warwick.

Lancaster adherents included **Henry Percy**, 2nd Earl of Northumberland; Exeter; Stafford (Buckingham); and Wiltshire.

Charles VII, King of France, uncle by marriage of Margaret.

Louis XI, son of Charles VII, and cousin of Margaret.

CHAPTER ONE

1444

The Council Chamber held only five people. The attendants had been dismissed except for a page who tended the logs in the great fireplace. The flames leapt and crackled and cast a warm light on the arras which had been drawn across the windows against the icy winds which forced their way into the room.

More heat came from the argument which flared at the heavy oak table where four men were seated. Two of them were among the most powerful in the kingdom. The third was a hard-bitten veteran of the French wars.

The fourth man could have been, should have been, mightier than the others but his nature was such that he shrank from exerting his own will on these men who had long been his mentors.

This young man was England's King, the Sixth Henry. Few would have picked him out of a crowd, for instead of the silks and brocades favored by young gentlemen, Henry wore a simple black, wool gown. On his head was a felt cap which covered his hair and framed his face.

Now he wavered between the proposals put forth by his uncle, Humphrey, Duke of Gloucester, and his great uncle, Cardinal-Bishop Beaufort. As the arguments between the two men grew more and more heated, Henry's stomach roiled and an iron band tightened across his neck and shoulders. He fought back tears of frustration.

The old Cardinal saw his nephew's distress. He lay a gentle hand on Henry's arm and asked, "What is *your* wish?"

"The Princess Margaret," came the low answer.

Gloucester, his face empurpled, shoved a parchment and a painting away with an oath. He stood and pushed back his heavy chair so violently that it fell over with a crash which reverberated against the stone walls.

"You've not heard the end of this," warned the red faced

man as he strode from the Council chamber. He was, as usual, in a temper when things weren't going his way, as they surely weren't today.

Neither the Cardinal nor the other man, Earl Suffolk, was much upset by the Duke's anger. Henry, however, blamed himself, all because he had agreed to marry a French Princess despite his uncle who had other hopes.

After the Duke stormed out, the tension in the room lifted. Cardinal Beaufort smiled and nodded almost imperceptibly to his friend, Suffolk. It had been a stormy session but it looked as if they had won.

The Earl had a less sanguine view. Was it a real victory or just another skirmish in an everlasting struggle for power? The two older men were always at loggerheads. Humphrey of Gloucester, younger brother of dead King Henry the Fifth, detested his Uncle Beaufort. The feeling was returned. When the Sixth Henry was crowned at nine months, the men had begun their contest for control of the young King and his kingdom. Suffolk thought of the old warning, "Woe to the country whose King is a child."

When Henry mastered himself, he reached over and retrieved the portrait which Beaufort had commissioned and which had so angered Humphrey. It was of Margaret of Anjou, thirteen-year-old niece of King Charles of France. She was lovely, no question about it, even if the court painter might have exaggerated, as they were wont to do. Yes, lovely. If he had to marry, and it seemed he must, she would do.

"Yes." He cleared his throat and said firmly, "You may tell people that it is our wish that you, Suffolk, with Lord Moleyns and Lord Wenlock, go to Tours to arrange for our marriage to the Princess Margaret. You will be our ambassador extraordinary, empowered to do all things you deem necessary." Suffolk started to object but was silenced by a quick gesture from the Cardinal who said, "Your Grace has made a wise decision."

"It seems my Uncle Gloucester does not agree."

"Oh, he will come around. It is just that he is unused to no longer being Protector. It is hard for a man of his nature to relinquish power, and he had his heart set on an Armagnac marriage."

"Well, I did not and I am tired of his eternal nattering of Armagnac. I shall marry whom I wish."

"You are completely right, my Lord. Now, at 22, it is fitting for you to make your own decisions."

Henry smiled, his dark blue eyes clearer now, his lips no longer taut in his long, slender face. "It is too bad that Gloucester is not pleased with my choice, but if I waited till everyone was pleased I should never be wed ... and then my people wouldn't be pleased. They are always at me to marry. First it was the daughter of the King of Scots, *to keep the peace in the northern marches.* Then they thought we could better hold our French crown by marrying France's daughter. And when my other uncle, Charles of France, did not reply to that, then comes Uncle Humphrey with the idea that we ally ourselves with Charles' enemy, Armagnac. When that, too, came to naught, great Gloucester blamed me. By Saint John, I did my best. Sometimes I feel like I'm being pulled asunder. People expect too much of me; I can't please everyone, and I'm tired of uncles." He was close to tears again.

Beaufort bent over the young man and laid a gentle hand on his shoulder. "My boy, you do not need to please everyone, nor even anyone ... you are the King. And," in a lighter tone, "I hope you are not tired of all your uncles."

"Wh ... wh...what? Oh, oh, no. You did not think...?"

"Henry, you must not fret. *You do not have to please. You are the King.*"

"Yes, I am the King and my Uncle Gloucester had well take heed of the fact." He drew himself up so that his sometimes rounded shoulders showed their true breadth. His eyes flashed with a sudden hardness and determination that reminded the older man for an instant of his father, that other Harry, now in his tomb these twenty years. Then Henry's expression softened and he added, "Yet I must beware of the sin of pride. I shall go now and pray that our dear Lord smooth our way to the Lady Margaret's heart." He shrugged his simple black robe closer about his shoulders, and fingering the gold chain he wore about his neck, walked slowly and thoughtfully from the room.

When he had gone, Cardinal Beaufort voiced his concern to Suffolk. "He is right; I fear we ask too much of him. Sometimes I worry about his heritage ... his mother, Katherine, with her mad father. But I am an old man and belike I worry overmuch. Perhaps it is only natural that Henry withdraw from the many demands on him. He is too thoughtful, too kind ... when he disappoints someone he, himself, is hurt. I wish for his own sake that he were more like his father. Why," he mused, "I can remember when Harry ..." He shook his white head. "Ah, but no matter; right now we must plan what you are going to do at Tours."

"No," said Suffolk, a short, stocky man with grizzled, closely cropped hair. He spoke with the directness of an old soldier. "I am not going to Tours."

"Not going? Great Heavens, man, here we have planned and worked to advance this Angevin marriage and now Henry himself is willing, and you say you're not going? Have you taken leave of your senses?"

"No, I'm being very sensible. You know that her father, Rene, and his brother-in-law, French King Charles, will insist on a treaty in exchange for Margaret."

"Of course. That's one reason it's a good match."

"The people won't like it."

"The people don't know what's good for them."

"Parliament won't like it," insisted Suffolk. "If I come back and tell them that I've committed us to peace with France --on French terms -- it will be as much as my head is worth."

"We need peace, whether the people will admit it or not. Nobody will pay the taxes to win the war. They don't even want to man our garrisons over there any longer."

"That's all well and good, but every time Gloucester says *to retreat is to betray our heritage,* the crowds throw their hats in the air and cheer *Good Duke Humphrey!*"

"I know. I wish their purses were as open as their hearts and mouths."

"Can't they realize that Henry is King of France in name

only? That when Charles was crowned by Jeanne d'Arc we were through?"

"Look you," persisted Beaufort. "You must go; we need you to negotiate, to see that Charles doesn't rob us blind. England needs an end to this war, as well as a firm hand to guide her. We have agreed that this Angevin marriage will bring peace, for a while at least, and perhaps the Lady Margaret will help strengthen Henry. I have heard good report of her. She should be an excellent wife for Henry, and she is pretty into the bargain. Poor soul, he deserves a good wife. Her mother, Isabelle, is notable for her courage and good sense."

"But her father, Rene?"

"Yes, there is always the chance she might be like Rene."

"Heir to half a dozen duchies and countries that fell into his lap and unable to get or hold any of them. Suffolk grimaced.

"He's intelligent, though," the Cardinal pointed out. "Margaret is said to have his intelligence and her mother's spirit. She is young but we can help her grow - understand? I tell you, Suffolk, if we plan well, we can all benefit ... the country and we, too. It never hurts to have the Queen favorable to one. The next move is ours; for God's sake, let's use it wisely."

In spring, the thirteen-year-old Princess was summoned to the French court in Tours with her mother, Isabelle, and her father, Rene.

Because her portrait had been commissioned by an Englishman, Margaret believed that her uncle planned to marry her off to someone from that country. But to whom? She wished she knew more about their dukes and earls. Who might be needing a wife? She hoped it wouldn't be some old man whose wife had died childless and who needed an heir. Surely her parents and the King wouldn't send her off to someone of the lesser nobility ... unless to someone of wealth. Wealth would count. Which was why, of course, she couldn't look very high. Her father had inherited titles aplenty. He was not only Duke of Anjou and Count of Provence, but also styled himself King of the Two Sicilies, Jerusalem and Hungary. Empty, worthless titles, of no use in marriage negotiations.

And worse, there was no wealth, only debts. Debts of honor still owing.

I have no dowry to take a husband and no chance of getting one. Uncle Charles will never give a sou he doesn't have to.

It was a puzzle. Neither Rene nor Isabelle could -- or would -- tell her what the King planned.

I think Father has some idea -- he keeps smiling.

When the day of the court appearance arrived, the Princess, accompanied by her mother, was escorted into the royal presence chamber, the very room where King Charles had received Joan of Arc after raising the siege of Orleans. Margaret had better things to think about than a war which had been fought before she was born.

When she entered the room, her father and uncle were chatting, Rene standing only a step below the royal platform, was smiling broadly, as was his brother-in-law, the King.

Charles beckoned Margaret to approach. Puzzled and a little diffident, for she had only rarely seen her uncle in her thirteen years, she walked slowly over the rich carpet laid upon the stone floor. She was conscious that the men and women about the King had stopped talking and were watching her. In the quiet she could hear the sputtering of the candles set into niches along the thick walls. She wanted to take her mother's hand but Isabelle stayed behind her so that she walked alone. She stopped before her royal uncle and bowed low.

He leaned forward and said, "My child, we have obtained for you a glorious place. You will be elevated to a position second only to that of our Queen."

A murmur went through the crowd but she had no idea what he was talking about.

"What's the matter, Margaret? Have we not won for you a magnificent prize -- *non?*"

"But, Sire, what ...?"

"Don't you know, girl? You are to wed English Henry. You will be Queen of England!"

The court attendants gave a cry of approval.

It was too much to take in. A dozen thoughts warred for place in her head.

So they aren't going to pawn me off on some nobody -- but the King? How can that be? Our family isn't that high and I have no dowry. Surely the English will require some price -- a great family or a great fortune --and I have neither.

Isn't the English King our enemy? He and Uncle Charles claim the same French crown.

The word *Queen...Queen...Queen* reverberated. Never, ever, had she imagined... What was back of this? She couldn't find the words to say.

The King was chuckling at her discomfiture. "Don't I deserve a little thanks?"

Rene, standing next to Charles, laughed. "Brother, our daughter is overwhelmed by your generosity and her good fortune. Margaret, find your tongue and thank your uncle."

"Oh, yes." She curtsied low and, finding her voice, stammered, "Your Grace has done me much honor. I owe you all my gratitude."

"Good. We will speak of this later. Now you may go."

Margaret bowed again and left the presence chamber, followed by her mother. Rene stayed behind.

As soon as they were in the solar, Isabelle enfolded her daughter in her arms. "Isn't it wonderful? We didn't tell you until we were sure." Then an afterthought. "Though we shall be sorry to lose you."

Margaret hadn't had time to think of that. If she went to England she probably would never see her mother again. Sudden tears pricked at her eyes. Leave home? Her mother and father? Her friends?

"I'm not sure I want to marry the English King."

"Don't be silly. Of course you want to. Besides, if Charles and your father want it, you'll be wed, want it or not."

Margaret hated to be told what to do. She wiped away her tears, put back her shoulders, and said, They can't make me marry anyone I don't want to."

"No, they can't, but if you don't you may find yourself in a nunnery in short order. But enough of such foolishness. You have been granted a wonderful opportunity that any other girl would jump at."

The opportunity was a long time coming. The court waited for an English delegation to complete the political negotiations. Margaret had decided she really did want to marry the English King, and waited with the impatience of youth while Isabelle used the time to gather the meager possessions that would go with her daughter. But the Duchess was in no hurry to see Margaret set out on her new life. Despite what she had told her child, she was not at all sure that the English marriage would be *wonderful.*

Looked at practically, it couldn't be an unmixed blessing. Henry's father may have won France, but the English grasp was tenuous, at best, evidence that the young King was probably ineffectual. Well, her own husband was ineffectual and yet both she and his people loved him. Perhaps the match with Henry would turn out all right. In the meantime, she welcomed the long wait.

With the first news, Margaret's friends and attendants had gathered around her, hugging her and voicing their wishes for a happy future. Isabelle said they sounded like a flock of twittering birds.

"Yes," teased Rene, "Magpies."

Some of the ladies reminded Margaret of their devotion and begged to accompany her. To be a lady-in-waiting to a Queen would be a grand adventure. Life in Anjou was boring.

Slowly, as little more was heard of the possible nuptials, some so-called friends fell away and an envious few were heard to suggest that either there never had been a marriage offer or that Henry had declined to marry a nobody like Margaret of Anjou.

She refused to show how this cruel spite hurt her but her nerves were stretched by the suspense and she grew sharp with her family and attendants.

As the days turned to weeks, Margaret's excitement waned and her impatience grew. Though at first she had hated the idea of being forced to marry with no say in the matter, sometimes the idea was appealing and she dreamed of being so exalted that no one would dare malign her, and the hateful gossips would sue for her favor again. These days she ached to be a Queen.

She chose a bad time to share her thoughts with her mother.

"Just think, when I go to England I'll be a Queen - a real Queen."

Isabelle snapped, "Yes, a real Queen; not like the poor Queen of Sicily, an empty title with no power."

Margaret colored and looked down. "You know I did not mean it that way."

"That's what I heard."

"You are always doing that -- making me sound thoughtless."

"Well, weren't you?"

"But Mother, you know I wouldn't hurt you."

"I know you wouldn't hurt me purposely, and I wasn't really hurt, but you must learn to guard your thoughts and tongue. It is a hundred times more important in a ruler than in a subject. You must train yourself to think again and again before you speak. A Queen cannot afford to be impetuous." She looked at her daughter closely. "Are you sure your really want to be a Queen?"

"Yes, yes!" the girl cried. "I mean -- I think so."

"Ah, Margaret, I know your head is filled with dreams. You would be the mother of Kings ... true Kings. You would have a legitimate title, not one you would have to be forever defending as we have had to." She paused, praying that her daughter would listen and take her words to heart. "It has not been easy. I know it sounds wonderful to you, and it will be, too, but do not dwell on it too closely. Remember, our house is rich in little but honor, and for all we know, the English may not accept a dowerless Queen, however pretty and whatever their King has decided."

"Is not the King the master? Cannot he do as he wishes?"

"Goose! Have we not taught you better than that? There are always those about Kings who seem to wield more power than they, and to whom they must listen. Particularly, a King as young as Henry."

"Then I hope those people will want me." She grew grave, thinking of three other marriage alliances which had fallen through. "Do you think I might be fated never to be wed?"

Isabelle looked at her daughter's promising, soft, slim body and lovely face and could not suppress a light laugh. "No, I do not think that will be your fate, though your marriage might not be the one you wish. It is for your father and your uncle to marry you where it will do the most good."

Margaret pouted but Isabelle added, "Don't worry. They love you and will have a care for you. Whomever you wed, I am sure it will be all right. However, if the good Lord willed it that you never did marry, then it would be for you to accept it with grace and thanks."

"Thanks?"

"We must thank *le bon Dieu* for all he sends. As for marriage, it is not always a blessing. Even the best brings with it pains and worries that the unwed never know. When children come, they are another pain and worry. For rulers it can be the worst of all, for their subjects are as their children and multiply their woes.

"Well, I would risk those pains and worries and woes to be the Queen of England."

"Hush, girl. Mind your tongue lest God think you speak from vanity and ambition. Vanity goes before destruction and those who reach the top of Fortune's wheel often cling there but briefly before they fall and are crushed by it as it turns. Remember your light words when you are with your ghostly confessor so that he may give you shriving penance."

Though Margaret nodded her head submissively in dutiful obedience to Isabelle's words, she scarcely heeded them. Much more interesting than one of her mother's little sermons filled with words of parental wisdom was the enchanting prospect of the English marriage."

"You understand, Margaret?"

"What? Oh, oh yes, Lady Mother. I shall try to do better."

"Fine." Isabelle put her hand on her daughter's shoulder. "Ah, child, perhaps you are right to dismiss these words of mine."

"But ..."

"No, no. I understand. It is natural for youth to dwell on happiness ... would that age could do the same."

Margaret curtsied low as her mother left the room. She stood there a while, still musing about England and its King. From childhood she had heard tales of the fame of his father, the great Henry Plantagenet of England who had come smashing and slashing through half of France to win a throne and a French Princess for his bride. Surely, the Sixth Henry, son of that King and his lovely Queen, would be a most powerful knight, and he and his wife would live as happily-ever-after as any fairy tale King and Queen of whom her father's troubadours sang. So she dreamed and hoped.

All the same, a tiny fear flickered at the edge of her mind. Would the English, old enemies of France, have her or, having her, would it be with mistrust and hate because of all those years of war between them? And Henry ... was he like his father or, she scarce dared let herself think of it ... was he, as fleeting gossip whispered, timid, but half a man, fitter for a cowl than a crown?

She shivered, then crossed herself and went out into the warm, French sunshine.

CHAPTER TWO

1444

"I tell you, Adam, I do not like this. I knew I shouldn't have come; Henry should have chosen someone with more talent for bargaining. England will lose more than she gains from any treaty with Charles of France. Read this last message from King Henry." Suffolk handed the parchment to Adam Moleyns who took it over to the light from the narrow window set deep in the stone wall. Sir John Wenlock and the other men in the room crowded around to read it.

"Indeed, my Lord," said Moleyns, "From this I would say there is little we can do but try once more for some new compromise."

"Compromise!" snorted Suffolk. "How can you speak of such when it is all so one sided? They demand all and offer nothing -- save the lady."

Wenlock put in, "We have little choice, though, for it seems that King Charles and his advisors argue from power."

"Aye," agreed Suffolk. "Charles and his advisors. Not for nothing is he called the 'well-advised.' I am beginning to think that Henry will go down in history as the 'ill-advised.' To order us to secure a marriage agreement at all costs -- it is madness!"

"Let us not speak of madness," cautioned Moleyns. "It is said that the Princess Margaret is fair beyond measure, and Henry is an eager young man. He wants this marriage now that he has made up his mind."

"Fair she may be," retorted Suffolk. "But the people of England want to keep their Norman lands. Won at such cost, what do you think would happen to anyone who lightly traded them away?" Involuntarily, his hand crept up and he rubbed the back of his neck. "No," he said suddenly, "I will not do it no matter what Henry says. Poor lad, such an action could topple him from his throne."

"With his uncle, Humphrey of Gloucester, ready to ascend it," added Wenlock.

"I shall try again for a better bargain." Suffolk strode to the doorway and summoned a page. "Tell their Graces that we have received a further message from our lord and are ready to wait upon them when they desire."

The page left and Suffolk let fall the hangings. "Their Graces -- I feel as if I were being smothered by feather beds. I am an old soldier, not a diplomat to scrape and treat with nuances, and exchange tidy terms. I could have handled Rene alone, I think, but the devil take that tricky Charles."

When Charles and Rene next met with the English delegation, Suffolk suspected that the French King had a shrewd idea of what Henry's message had been. The Englishman had examined the parchment rolls carefully and found the seals undisturbed, but secret messages had been read by prying eyes before and Suffolk put nothing past the French.

Charles repeated his demand that the English give up their claims to Normandy and Aquitaine. Suffolk refused to sign any agreement that involved such a concession. It would, he said, be a shame for the marriage negotiations to fall through, but there it was.

"Surely our cousin England desires peace," urged Charles.

"Naturally, my Lord, for all men of good will desire peace, and our King is most devout and pious, but I can offer no more."

The proceedings were at a standstill again, and Suffolk was given leave to withdraw. He was disheartened for he had failed; not only failed, but gone directly against Henry's express orders. No betrothal and no end to the ruinous war.

"I know how to treat with men on a battlefield," Suffolk complained to his companions, "but I have no experience negotiating these ceremonial matters. I have neither the skill nor the stomach to cope with these Frenchmen. I thought they wanted the marriage -- why in God's name have us here otherwise? --but it seems they don't." He threw the papers he carried down on the table in disgust. "I say, let's go home."

But the French had not given up. Charles needed an end to the war even more than the English, and both Charles and Rene wanted the marriage. Rene did not care a great deal about the problems of his brother-in-law, but he viewed the proposed marriage as a feather in his own cap. His daughter, Margaret, the English Queen --what a dream -- married to the flower of chivalry -- for surely the son of the great Henry of Monmouth must be that epitome -- no matter if sly tongues sometimes whispered unpleasant rumors. What an alliance for the house of Anjou! Rene was lost in a vision of his own importance while Charles and his advisors were pondering Suffolk's stubbornness.

Pierre deBreze said, "There are factions in England who are ever ready to foment new battles, and the rabble will follow them -- until their purses are pinched."

Dunois, the King's chief military advisor, broke in, "Let us move slowly, Monseigneur. More than once I have driven back the English, and I can again, but I must have time. The wheel will turn, but slowly. Just give me time."

"You may be right," mused Charles. Our treasury will grow fatter in the fullness of time, too. How long do you need?"

"At least two years, Sire."

"All right. You shall have it. Now call back our English cousins. Meanwhile," he turned to Rene who was now paring his nails with a silver knife. "I think we should get *a little* land, at least, in exchange for my fair niece. Listen well, Rene..."

Suffolk was mystified when Charles summoned him once more and in an apparent about-face, said, "We have thought well on all that you have said, and always desirous of peace with our Cousin England, we have decided that we should cease this petty quarrel over Normandy and Aquitaine. We cannot agree as to who legally holds the provinces, and as neither of us wishes to burden our people with the mighty charge of winning them by arms, let us at least stop bickering over them."

"We will not withdraw," insisted Suffolk.

"We do not ask it, Milord. At least, not entirely. Let us say you might reduce your garrisons a bit, though, since we will pledge our sacred honor to reduce ours, too. Say -- for a period of two years."

"And after the two years, your Grace?"

"Aha!" Charles winked broadly. "Perhaps after two years our problems will all be solved by God's good grace." He clapped his hand sharply and, accompanied by a loud fanfare, Rene entered the chamber leading Margaret. The pair stood silent, the father with full face beaming and the daughter, after a deep curtsey first to the King and then to the English ambassadors, looking at the floor. She was dressed in a very plain but expensive gown of green silk which had been supplied by Rene's sister, the French Queen. Margaret's red gold hair, ornamented only by a simple circlet of pearls, was unbound and fell almost to her waist.

She is truly lovely, thought Suffolk with a start he could not hide, while Charles watched him covertly from beneath lowered lids. The Earl had seen Margaret's picture but one naturally expected such a portrait to flatter. In this case, the girl was far more beautiful than the painting.

Charles laughed coarsely and continued, "I think in two years time our troubles may be over, for our brother England will no doubt by then have engendered lusty boys on this lady. She looks like a breeder, does she not, Milord?"

The men, with the exception of Suffolk, laughed and Rene nudged Wenlock in appreciation of his monarch's rare joke. Suffolk saw how the Lady Margaret colored and bit her lip to hold back tears of chagrin and anger. Lady -- nay, child, for her embarrassed confusion at being the butt of such a vulgar speculation proclaimed her youthful inexperience. While the men's laughter rang through the great audience chamber, Margaret looked up, hurt, to Suffolk, the only one who was not smirking.

He saw a look, not of resignation so much as of determination, cross her face.

Yes, he thought, she'll be the one to stiffen Henry. His brief feeling of pity for her was mixed with his own realization that if he could make a friend of Margaret her goodwill would bolster his own position at court.

He smiled at her, trying to signal his concern.

Then he forced his attention back to the King who was saying, "In time, perhaps the issue of this union can hold the provinces in peace. Would it not be an easy solution to a knotty problem?"

"It would, your Grace," answered Suffolk. "It is our fervent prayer that heaven will bless such a union and because of this I urge that the proposed marriage articles be signed." But, he thought, it didn't work the last time or Henry the Sixth would now sit on the throne of France instead of this vulgar Charles with his crude jests.

"First the truce," said Charles. "Then the marriage articles. And, Milord, knowing your great wish for peace, we have already had the treaty drawn up." He indicated a parchment. The Englishman picked up the document and studied it, then passed it to Wenlock and Moleyns. He wished he could see into the future. Was there a trick in the treaty to entrap his country?

He had a growing sense of foreboding, both for himself and for England. He tried to drive away such thoughts. Had he not had the foresight to obtain letters patent from Henry and the Parliament before he left? Letters that absolved him beforehand from any blame or punishment for troubles that might arise from any arrangements he had to make?

When the other men had finished studying the treaty, they nodded and he turned to the King. We are agreed, your Grace. It shall be signed."

This done, the marriage contract was produced. The English embassy was already well acquainted with its provisions and prepared to sign it, too, although it was a most unusual document, without precedent, for the bride brought no dowry; Henry would provide everything, even her clothing and the expense of the wedding entertainment. Margaret's gift to Henry was deemed to be the affection in which she was held by the French court and her softening influence on any warlike thoughts her uncle, Charles, might have. As Suffolk bent to put pen to the paper, Rene interrupted blandly, "Hold a minute, Milord."

Suffolk stopped, the quill in his hand.

"My dear Earl Suffolk, much as I desire this noble union

between my most virtuous daughter and the great King of England, and as much as it would please my brother France, I find I cannot allow it."

"What --" Suffolk threw down the pen.

"Oh, it grieves me; you have no idea how it grieves me, for I have taken comfort in the fact that my dear Margaret, my dove, though wrenched from the bosom of her loving father and mother -- and uncle," he added, smiling at Charles, "would be tenderly cared for by his most Christian Highness, Henry, but I cannot do it."

"Cannot do what?" asked Suffolk from between clenched teeth while he thought to himself ... God's nails, what now? I am a poor ambassador -- I cannot stand the gabblings of this French fop. What does the rascal want now?

I cannot; you understand, it would be unseemly, inconsistent with my honor, even the honor of my great house, to bestow my daughter, my treasure, on the usurper of my hereditary domains."

"But --"

"I know, I know -- a father's foolish pride, perhaps. But there it is. I could not possibly let go my lovely jewel unless Henry were to relinquish his claim to my rightful fiefs of Maine and Anjou. Of course, they are very small in Henry's eyes, I am sure, and they would still be in the same family, as it were. But there it is. I cannot help myself; it is the way I am made, " Rene finished, his lips smug as a merchant who has set his terms for a hard bargain and means to win.

A hundred arguments rose in Suffolk's mind but he stifled them at the sight of the girl who was still standing there while her father haggled over her.

"Your Grace," said Suffolk rashly, "take as a small gift from England's Henry those two provinces of Maine and Anjou. Let it be set down in the contract." He would show them that England would not stoop to bargaining to win a Queen. Henry was no French peasant, eternally weighing and grasping, but a generous, open-handed monarch.

"Ah, Milord, I am so touched by your kind understanding that to show my rich regard, I will add to my daughter's portion my appanages of Majorca and Minorca. Let this, too, be set down." He smiled expansively.

So it was that by the Treaty of Tours, England and France declared a two years' truce in the Hundred Years War, and the marriage contract of Henry of Lancaster and Margaret of Anjou provided that England cede to Rene the old, blood-won duchies of Maine and Anjou in exchange for an empty, unquiet title to two small, unimportant and distant islands.

CHAPTER THREE

May 1444 - February 1445

The relief was almost palpable after the agreement was signed.

Rene had restored his fiefdom without a struggle. King Charles was a step closer to regaining the territory lost to the English. Suffolk and his delegation had fulfilled their chief objective, but at what cost he preferred not to think on.

Margaret's future was secure, or so she and her family thought.

To cement the pact, a betrothal followed in the Basilica of Saint Martin at Tours, Suffolk standing as proxy for his King. Though the Earl was a mere conduit for his Sovereign's promises, he vowed in his own heart to protect Margaret, come what may. His determination to safeguard the girl was a mixture of a fatherly benevolence and ambition. He saw nothing selfish in his desire to direct her actions to his benefit. He wished only the best for her. She was young and untried. He determined then and there to help guide her.

The vows exchanged, Margaret's family crowded around her with hugs and kisses. Then, in the first procession in which Margaret would be the center, they all moved off to the 200-year-old Abbey of St. Julian where a feast was waiting.

There, a chair had been raised at a great table in the center of the hall. "For you," they said.

Rene's sister, Queen Marie, laughed, "Now that you are Queen of England you must accustom yourself to great heights."

Her mother and aunt took their places at her right and addressed her as Queen. King Charles' own attendant brought the ewer to her and poured water over her hands before any of the others.

Although Margaret loved the attention, she had mixed emotions. Throughout her fourteen years she was used to treating her elders with deference. How could she change so quickly? She certainly didn't feel any different.

Queen Marie seemed to understand her niece's problem. "You'll get used to it, your Majesty," she whispered.

It would be easy to get used to it. How sweet the titles sounded. A few papers signed, a few words spoken, and the world had opened up before her. Queen ...Your Majesty ... Your Grace ... Madame ... Your Worship ... Queen Margaret ... Queen of England ... second only to the Queen of France and -- who knew, perhaps someday mother of a King of France. It was not beyond imagining. Margaret savored the attention and glowed with happiness at her unaccustomed importance.

All the fruits of the yards, fields, woods, rivers, and ocean graced the trestle tables where the noble guests had course after lavish course. They were served venison, beef, mutton, rabbit, wild boar - with the head still intact --, swan, heron, bittern, partridges, plovers, quails, larks and peacock. The peacock had been carefully skinned, the meat roasted, and the skin and head replaced, with the peacock's tail outspread.

There were jellies made of tenches, plaice, pikes, turbot, carp and eels.

Custards and fritters were decorated with leopards and fleurs de lis for England and France.

Each course ended with a subtlety, a device of sugar and paste. The first subtlety showed Saint Edward and Saint Louis. The second depicted King Henry and King Charles. The third was of Saint George and Saint Denis.

While the nobles ate in the Abbey, the merchants, masters and apprentices crowded into the building or clustered close to the doors where they were served with great cheer of meat and drink. The hall was lighted by hundreds of torches and tallow candles while the folk outside lit bonfires.

The guests were delighted by the exotic entertainment arranged by Rene, a display of two giants bearing trees, followed by a jousting match between two knights mounted on camels.

Shortly after the celebrations, Suffolk returned to England

with the treaty. He was apprehensive about how his embassage would be received.

He needn't have worried. Henry, who had been worked on by his Uncle Beaufort, convinced now that not only was it his duty to marry but that he really would enjoy that state, was pleased with Suffolk's report of Margaret. He was interested in the treaty only in so far as it meant peace.

The Cardinal had reminded him that blessed are the peacemakers. Henry was so grateful that he made Suffolk a Marquis.

The people, aware only that their King was finally betrothed, rejoiced. London turned out to welcome the new Marquis with the betrothal papers.

Duke Humphrey of Gloucester fumed and wondered what his enemies were up to. He was fond of his nephew and wished him well but he wanted to be the one on whom Henry relied. He was exceedingly unhappy to be pushed into the background.

In France, several times before Margaret went back home to Angers to wait for Henry to send for her, King Charles spoke with her. He told her plainly that her marriage was due to him and that she owed him and her native country her loyalty. It upset her when he hinted that her betrothed could easily be swayed. "We trust you to use your influence for the benefit of France."

She had mixed emotions again. She wanted to be a dutiful wife, to count on her husband and to follow his wishes but she was intrigued with the idea that her native country depended on her and that for the first time in her life her own views might be important.

With the betrothal behind her it proved harder than ever to wait for Henry's summons. However, anticipation and planning carried Margaret over the early period. Her English wedding ceremony was set for November, six months off, and days were filled with fittings and planning and supervising the packing of the heavy, iron-hinged sumpter chests she would take with her. Time and again, the chests would be packed, only to have

Isabelle say, "No, no, that won't do. Take it all out. Here, put these things on the bottom," as she indicated some bed linen, or, "I think the plate should go in with those hangings; they will travel better," and the servants would unpack the chests. Margaret, herself, took scant interest in her belongings. When Isabelle asked, "Don't you think that is better? That your things will travel more securely this way?"

Margaret replied, "I don't really think that it matters."

"And why not, pray?"

Oh, Mother, that plate is inferior, and those old linens and dresses are ... well ..."

"There's nothing wrong with them," snapped the older woman, tired and cross because Margaret was not paying proper attention to her possessions. Isabelle and her ladies had put in countless hours on the trousseau with little help from the bride.

"Of course not," Margaret said, "Nothing really wrong, but ... well, I can soon have better."

"That may be so, Madame, but it ill becomes you to say it. There have been many sore, stiff fingers and many a burning eye spent in embroidering these poor garments and linens."

Margaret immediately regretted her thoughtless words. She threw her arms around her mother. "I didn't mean it that way. Please, don't let's quarrel. I'm sorry if you thought me ungrateful. I guess I'm too keyed up. It's so hard to wait."

Isabelle stroked her daughter's bright hair. "I know, I know. But time will fly before you know it." At that moment the chapel bell rang out. "Hear?" She smiled. "It is already time for another English lesson. How are they coming?"

"All right, I think. It is an odd language -- no rhyme or reason -- and it sounds so harsh to me, but I am determined to master it. I want Henry to be proud of me."

"I warrant he will be, "reassured her mother, turning back to the chests.

Isabelle insisted that Margaret learn the history of England as well as its language. She learned how the Norman Conqueror, William the Bastard, beat the Saxons and made England an appanage ... strange to think England once belonged to Normandy instead of the other way around. She learned how the country grew in strength; how Eleanor of Aquitaine brought that province as her dower to England. Margaret was a quick student, and she found this history engrossing. She marveled how the English claimed a right to the French throne through a woman. The lowliest varlet knew that the French crown could not descend through the female line. The English didn't follow the practice, either, for if they did ... she painstakingly traced out the lines down a chart ... When Richard the Second died (or had been murdered, they said), the children of his uncle's daughter's daughter ... or some such ... really, it almost made her head ache ... would be King instead of her Henry. The English had such strange laws and customs ... but, as any sensible people, they put practicality before custom.

She complained to the Abbot who gave her the lessons that it became too tedious to trace all those lines that sprang from Edward the Third. She wished Edward had had fewer children. But the Abbot insisted she work it out. If the English followed their own rules, then the Duke of York, who even now held a garrison in France, would be King. That was foolish, though, even to the English, for their Parliament sensibly enough had chosen ... years ago, Henry's grandfather, the popular Henry Bolingbroke, Duke of Lancaster, to be King, before any female cousin or her issue. How justified time had proven them! For from this same Henry, who was the Fourth, came mighty Henry the Fifth, and now his son, the Sixth of that name... She dreamt, and never, in the green summer and golden autumn of Anjou were her dreams troubled by the shadow of York, the descendant of that insignificant female cousin.

In England, unaccustomed activity seized the court. Henry summoned Suffolk's wife, Alice, from her home to London to help prepare for his new Queen. There was almost too much to be done. The royal palaces had fallen into disuse and decay. No wifely eye had seen to hangings, furniture, or even simple cleaning. Marchioness Alice took a hasty and ever more horrified tour of Henry's homes. Then she called in his chamberlain and treasurer and told them exactly what was needed.

The treasurer set up a wail, "But we can't; it would be much too costly."

"Nonsense," said the Marchioness, a small, soft, comfortable woman, but sharp and practical. "We can't let our new, young Queen and all France think we are barbarians. You have allowed these rooms to go to rack and ruin. Where's the money that should have been spent on upkeep? Either get some funds from the King's privy purse or else from your own where I'll venture some of it has already wandered."

The money was raised. The castles at Westminster and Richmond and the royal quarters in the Tower were readied. New stewards were appointed. Carpenters, joiners, armorers, saddlers, and masons were hired, along with grooms, cooks, ushers, and pages. Under the careful eyes of the Lady Alice, tapestries were renewed or replaced. Moldy and foul floor rushes were swept out and replaced with fresh ones, strewn with sweet smelling herbs. Mice and moths were dislodged when long-unused carpets were unrolled and beaten. Musty, equally unused halls were aired. She visited kitchens where kettles were scoured and hearths scrubbed. Chimneys were cleared of nests and leaves. Bolsters and comforters were stuffed with fresh down. Liveries were distributed to serving men and gowns to the women.

The treasurer added long columns and muttered that the French war had almost emptied the royal treasury and now it looked as if the French marriage would finish bankrupting Henry.

In France, the strain of the long wait was increased by a dispatch from England. Along with a list of English retainers going to attend the proxy wedding, the King's Council sent word that there was no need to include any French ladies-in-waiting in Margaret's retinue.

It was a heartsick Princess who told her ladies, including Katherine, her best friend, the news.

"If you can't go, then I won't go, either," threatened Margaret.

"Of course you will," said level-headed Katherine, her eyes welling. "You have to; you already promised ... and in Church."

"I'll be lost in a strange country without any friends."

"You'll make friends fast enough ... and anyway," Katherine brushed at her tears, "You won't need friends with a husband. With your new, important life you'll soon forget us."

"No, I'll never forget you, I promise. I'll always remember you."

"And I you."

When Rene learned that there would be no French ladies-in-waiting he ranted and raged and vowed he would never let his daughter marry such a barbarian. At Charles' suggestion, he had planned to place some observers in his daughter's court. He fumed until Isabelle reminded him of Maine and Anjou, Henry's princely gift. She could not so easily console the young girl whose dreams of a powerful knight were shattered and replaced by wonder that an English King could so lightly be ruled by his Council. It wasn't fair, Margaret said. He must not want her to be happy ... he could not love her ... she broke off in tears.

Isabelle scolded, "Do not be a greater goose than you have to. No one ever promised you that life would be fair. You must learn that Kings and Queens cannot do all -- or even much -- that they wish." She continued more gently, "As for love, I trow Henry will soon love you as much as we do if you are sweet and biddable to him. Now stop those foolish tears, for what cannot be helped must be endured. And pray to our blessed Lord and His gentle Mother that you never have cause to weep for worse than this simple disappointment."

The waiting grew more and more tedious. In the spring, people had said, "Your Grace," "Your Majesty," and "Madame Queen." Even her mother had sometimes deferred to her. Now it was only "My lady," or, from her family, "Margaret." Her friends grew bored with talk of a someday wedding and a few of them, disappointed because they weren't going to England after all, said, "What can you expect of an uncultured country?" and "My lady, I am so sorry that your fate has led you to this pass," or "No doubt the stories about the King of England are exaggerated ... of course it is always possible that where there is smoke ... but that is not necessarily so, my dear." A few of her closest friends wished her well, merely pressed her hand warmly and murmured, "I will pray for you."

In the daytime, Margaret made excuses, but at night she tossed in worry and often wept.

In November, Henry dispatched Suffolk to France. The Marquis carried instructions which read:

"As you have lately, by the divine favor and grace, in our name and for us, engaged verbally the excellent, magnificent, and very bright Margaret, the serene daughter of the King of Sicily, and sworn we shall contract matrimony with her, we consent and will that she be conducted to us over seas, from her country and friends, at our expense."

"At our expense -- it sounded good, but the time for the wedding passed. Henry could not afford a wife. He fretted and alternately railed at and pleaded with his Council. Suffolk worried. Rene seethed. Margaret was often in tears. Poor Suffolk, under the eyes of the bride's family, invented one excuse after another to postpone the wedding.

Across the Channel, Henry borrowed and pawned to pay the expenses of his wife's trip. In February, desperate for money with which to pay his bills and fetch his bride, he finally summoned Parliament. After a lengthy sermon by Henry's chancellor, the Archbishop of Canterbury, on "Justice and Peace have kissed each other," they heard for the first time of the cost of the King's betrothal and of the truce with France in which they had ceded so much. Stunned and bewildered, but glad that Henry was at last to marry and assure an orderly succession, they grudgingly granted him a half-fifteenth in taxes. Later, however, they were to remember this and hold it against the Frenchwoman.

CHAPTER FOUR

February - April 1445

Suffolk finally returned to France, this time accompanied by a large party of nobles with their considerable retinues, come to escort Margaret to England. There were 17 knights, 65 squires, 20 grooms, men servants, serving maids, and a military guard. Each of these received a stipend from Henry who could ill-afford it.

Charles and Rene were impressed by Margaret's escort and she was thrilled by the attention. In private, the French King shook his head. He had a good idea of his nephew's financial condition. *Bien*, he thought. *Bien, the more he squanders his substance, the better for us. Margaret is already helping us.*

The wedding party rejoiced when the day dawned crisp and clear. "Auspicious," they declared. "A beautiful day for a beautiful bride."

Margaret was gowned in white satin embroidered with gold and silver daisies - marguerites - her symbol. Her underskirt and sleeves were of cloth of gold. She was escorted to the Basilica of St. Martin's at Tours by her father and uncle.

Suffolk was next, there again as proxy for Henry, followed close behind by Isabelle. The rest of the bridal party crowded in behind them.

Margaret and Suffolk moved slowly down the nave to the altar where the Archbishop of Tours stood.

The air was fragrant with the incense from the censers swung by acolytes. Light poured in through the windows. The lovely chanting of the choir from the chancel praised God and all his works.

The crowd gathered to watch the ceremony was the most splendid the church had ever witnessed. King Charles and Queen Marie were seated near the altar as were the bride's father and mother, King and Queen of Sicily. In addition, there were four Dukes, seven Earls, 12 Barons, 20 Bishops and the Papal Legate who brought a dispensation because Henry and Margaret were related in the fourth degree. Their great grandfathers had been brothers.

How Rene preened himself upon such splendid recognition of his house!

Margaret was radiant in the warm light that poured in upon her through the tall windows of the cathedral. Despite her determination to remain humble and properly grateful to God, she exulted inwardly. She was on the threshold of both womanhood and a wondrous, promising new life. A resplendent future lay before her.

Isabelle fondly watched her daughter during the ceremony and Mass. It was she alone who noted that as the sun's rays crept from window to window during the long proceedings the light which fell upon the kneeling young girl changed from a soft glow to a harsh crimson so that for a moment it seemed as if Margaret knelt bathed in blood. Isabelle stifled a cry and Rene frowned. She was interrupting his dreams.

After the ceremony, the wedding party moved to Rene's castle for days of feasting, tournaments, and elaborate spectacles. Rene spared no ingenuity and little cost at English expense. The celebrations stretched out to eight days for Rene had had all too much time to make his elegant plans. He might not be able to win battles but he could show that he understood the requisites of French chivalry. A prince of Anjou would not send his daughter off without a show of *courtoisie.*

While festivities lasted, Margaret could not leave and Isabelle would fain keep her as long as possible. Margaret suddenly felt an odd, little girl tug to stay with the people she knew and loved. She did not urge a speedy departure. Even Rene felt an unaccustomed something in his throat and a pricking behind his eyelids when he realized that she would soon leave. The feasts and parties were fun and it was a ruler's duty to advance his house, but by Saint Louis, he would miss the child. After the third or fourth goblet of wine he would beg Suffolk to take care of his little girl.

When the day arrived for the trip that would take her daughter across France and to England, perhaps never to return, Isabelle sent the servants away so that she could bid her Margaret farewell alone.

"We have done all we can for you," she said. "You have been raised up in the sight of the world. I pray that we have done the right thing and that you will be able to maintain that place for the good of your country and yourself. It is up to God and you now. Kneel down, my dear."

Margaret knelt. Isabelle placed her hands upon the girl's head. "May our Holy Father bless and keep you." They embraced and then Margaret went out to where a new world awaited.

Rene rode with them as far as Bar. At their parting, neither father nor daughter spoke a word. The father and his knights stopped at a bend in the road. The knights trotted away while Rene spurred his horse to the top of a hill where he sat alone, watching the long train move slowly down the narrow road. Margaret turned many times to wave yet again to her father in his great, black armor, astride his horse, atop the ever more distant hill.

Now, despite her large English retinue, she was truly alone. There was a tightness in her throat and only by biting her lip and concentrating on the rider ahead was she able to keep the tears from coming. Suffolk's wife, Alice, who had been chatting with a friend a way back, noticed that Margaret rode alone now, her body stiff, looking neither to left nor to right.

The Marchioness guided her mount around the riders ahead until she pulled up beside the girl. She was cheery. "A lovely day, your Grace, surely a good omen for the start of a journey."

"I hope so," said Margaret solemnly.

"And better to come. It will be almost April when we get to England. Our winters are apt to be beastly but spring makes up for them. The whole countryside is in bloom then. As my grandfather said, 'when April with its sweet showers has pierced the drought of March to the root and the west wind has breathed on every grove and field, and the birds sing all night ...'Oh, yes, it is truly beautiful then. I know you will love our England."

Margaret smiled at the older woman's enthusiasm. "Your grandfather?"

"Geoffrey Chaucer, the poet. Do you know him?"

"I don't think so. Is he alive?"

"My goodness, no. I can't even remember him; he's been dead forty years. I meant, do you know his works?"

"I'm afraid not," admitted Margaret. "But I know many French ballads and songs. I am fond of poetry."

"At home I have a book with several of his poems. I shall be glad to lend it to you if you like to read."

"I do, very much, but as you can tell, I am not skilled in your language -- yet."

"Doesn't matter at all. If we have time, mayhap we can read together if it will help you. But Madame, you speak our language well already."

"You are kind to say so, but everyone talks so fast that I often have trouble."

"Then I, at least, will try to slow down, though I sha'n't find it easy -- it is my heredity, no doubt, that makes me so full of words," the Marchioness said, her eyes twinkling.

For the first time that day Margaret laughed.

That's better, thought the lady and she continued as they rode on, "My grandfather believed that a story shortened a journey. Let me tell you one of his ..."

What a nice woman, Margaret thought, comforted by the Lady Alice's friendly, cheery manner. The latter used the time to good effect. Her discerning eye was coupled with a sharp tongue as she described some of their fellows so that Margaret had to giggle. Thus the long days seemed shorter.

More important, was the opportunity to portray the nobles whom Margaret was going to meet when she reached England. Lady Alice, first cousin to Cardinal Beaufort, deftly painted her friends and enemies with colors of her own choosing. She thought she described them clearly and honestly, intending only to be of help to the new, inexperienced queen, but day by day Margaret heard that Humphrey, Duke of Gloucester, was intent on forcing his will on Henry, that he and his party were no friends of France nor her.

At Mantes, the party arrived at English territory. Here Margaret was welcomed by the Duke of York, Lieutenant of France, who was to escort her the rest of the way to the coast. York was cousin to Henry, and the third man in the kingdom. He was, Margaret remembered, that great grandson of old Edward the Third, the one descended through women. When Richard of York rode out to meet his new, young queen, he smiled on her and kissed his "Lady Cousin." The trumpets blared and the banners of his company stood out bold and beautiful in the fresh March wind.

Afterward, during a long, formal meal, sitting at the high table, she had ample time to observe both York and his Duchess, Cecily. Looking at the Duchess with her composure and assurance as she directed the serving, Margaret understood why she was called, as Alice had told her, "Proud Cis." But, admiring Cecily's raven hair, clear, honest grey eyes, and fair, almost translucent skin, Margaret thought that the other nickname she had heard became her more. Rose of Raby, the Duchess had been called, after the northern castle where she was raised.

After the lavish dinner, Margaret retired to the solar with her host and hostess. They were surprisingly informal. Tired from her journey, homesick for her loved ones, scarcely more than a child herself, she was enchanted by the York children. She tossed a ball back and forth with the five year old Anne, and jounced sturdy two year old Edward on her knee. She admired the rosy beauty of baby Edmund as he lay in his cradle. Edmund was less than a year old and Margaret could see that already another child quickened beneath Cecily's girdle. She saw the fond looks that passed between the Duke and Duchess. Cecily must be proud of such a fine family, she thought. She prayed silently that Margaret of Anjou might be as blessed by God as the Rose of Raby.

That night as she was being prepared for bed by her ladies, she told Marchioness Alice, "I like them. I like them both." She reached out and squeezed the lady's hand impulsively. "What nice people you English are. I know I shall love my new country."

The lady smiled as she unbound Margaret's golden hair. "And England is sure to love you. But ..." She searched for words. "Do not give your love too freely at first, my dear."

The seriousness of her tone troubled the girl. "Why, Alice, what do you mean?"

"It is just that some look higher than they should and ..."

"And what?"

"And desire ever more honors. York is always seeking more honors."

"Pooh. What honors they desire ... and earn ... why, those honors they shall have. Is it not the duty and pleasure of a good lord to reward and honor his faithful friends?"

"So they *be* faithful," the Marchioness muttered.

Margaret laughed. "Why, I believe you are growing jealous. Never fear, my friend; I know how well you and Lord Suffolk have served me, and are serving me every day. Do not think that Margaret will ever forget her first -- and best -- English friends. Why, I would be lost without you to tell me just who is who and to counsel me about these oh so many new things. Just because I like my new cousins, do not think I am so giddy as to forget old friends."

The next day, accompanied by York, the entourage continued its slow journey to Rouen. Here, as in most other towns, Margaret was greeted with acclamation by the lords, knights and squires as a promise that peace was at hand. The peasants and commoners enjoyed the festivities that accompanied the arrival of their Princess but they knew that her elevation to Queen of England would change nothing in their dull, daily lives.

Margaret was exhausted. She scarcely admitted it to herself but she was tired of all the celebrations, heavy feasts, religious services and endless speeches of welcome. She longed for the quiet and ordinary life of Anjou.

One last ceremony capped her visit to Rouen. It was not only Easter week, but also just a few days until her fifteenth birthday and she was obliged by custom to wash the feet of fifteen poor women as Christ had washed the feet of His Disciples. The women chosen for this rite were lined up in front of the Cathedral, waiting. They were jittery and jumpy but not as nervous as Margaret. The Sisters of the community had rinsed the dust off the women's feet. They gave Margaret a bowl of water and a towel. She did her best to be humble and kind but she was dismayed by what she saw.

Some of the feet were misshapen and all were engrained with grime and were cracked and callused. She, who had had warm baths with sweet smelling oils, had no experience or understanding of poor folks who had no water in their hovels and no soap. She had thought she and her family were poor. Poor meant debts, made-over dresses and so few treats that she had learned not to ask for any. Of true poverty she knew nothing. She could not commiserate with these poor creatures because there was no way she could understand anything about them. She would have been glad to give them money had she had any but she could scarcely bear to look at them, let alone touch them. To make it worse, she knew in her heart that she was neither humble nor Christlike. She had so much wanted to be caring but it was impossible right then. It was all she could do to keep from recoiling when one of the women, with a scummy green smile, reached out in gratitude to touch her and thank her. After she had washed all the feet - though not very well - she rose and turned away and drew her cape over her face. The onlookers murmured approvingly - she must have been overcome with pity, they said. In truth, she had hidden from them the fact that she was retching and fighting down nausea.

Lady Alice had watched her young charge and was disappointed at the girl's reaction. "I had thought she was tougher than that," she told her husband later. "She's bound to have much worse than that ahead of her."

It soon became apparent that more than a few dirty feet were troubling Margaret. She threw up several times and was blazing hot to the touch. She could not sit her horse nor could she stand the jouncing of a carriage. York suggested that she stay at Rouen until she was over her sickness but Margaret insisted that they press on. She just wanted to get the trip over. She was carried the rest of the way in a litter.

When they reached the dock at Harfleur, the Cokke John was waiting to take them to England. York saw Margaret and her company safely installed in the cramped quarters below deck, and then turned his horse and rode back to Mantes.

Still the ship did not sail.

The captain requested permission to speak to Margaret ... it was important, he insisted. Ill though she was, she had her ladies dress her so that she could receive him. He got to the point without delay. The sailors had not been paid since the vessel had been commissioned last fall. Many had left for other berths and he could get no new hands unless he could guarantee their wages ... the ship had a bad name by now.

"Surely my lord King will see that you are paid when the trip is over," she said. The captain shook his head.

"Madame, I told the men that, but they are for the most part ignorant -- and stubborn. They fear there will be no money and they will not sail without their back wages."

"But what about their loyalty?"

He spat. "Most of them own no loyalty to anyone ... neither king nor country. Loyalty fills no bellies."

"I see. If we get the money can we sail?"

"Yes, my Lady. But if you expect it to be today, it must be soon or we shall have to wait for the morrow. The tide will hold no longer than four hours."

"Thank you." She dismissed him. She summoned Suffolk and sent her ladies to their own quarters. They went reluctantly for they were agog to see what was happening.

Her appearance alarmed the Marquis. "Your Highness should lie down," he cried. "You are worse, I can tell."

"The news I have heard is enough to make me ill." Rapidly she sketched out what the captain had told her. "We must get the money from somewhere, and within the next four hours. Otherwise the ship will have to lay over and gossip will spread through the town, if it has not already done so, that England's King has no credit." She knew what lack of credit meant.

It was Suffolk's turn to shake his head. "It is a pity York has left. The best we can do is send a messenger post haste after him.

"How can it be that such a situation has been allowed? My Lord of England shall hear about it. Someone must have stolen the wages."

"Possibly, but I rather think that Parliament neglected to vote the taxes to pay them."

"Come, come, Suffolk, you do not mean that your Commons would have to be bothered over a few mariners' wages? Shouldn't they come out of the privy purse?"

"I am afraid the King's treasury is bare, your Grace. Parliament has been prorogued until later this spring, but we -- the Council -- are certain that when the people see you they will grant the King more than the half-fifteenth they last voted."

"But we need the money now." She was close to tears.

"My Lady, do not worry. I have some money I can advance. Of a certainty, King Henry will reimburse me in good time."

"My Lord, we will be forever grateful. Wait but one moment more." She spoke a few words to an attendant who knelt and unfastened one of the many chests piled along the wall. He displayed the contents: several pitchers, dishes, and bowls of silverplate.

"Here, Lord Suffolk, take these in surety."

No, no, your Grace. Your word is more than surety."

"You are most kind but I insist you keep the silver in pawn for I would not have it said that Margaret of Anjou came a beggar into England."

There was no time to argue. Suffolk bowed his head in acquiescence. He realized that Margaret could better brook the loss of her pitiful bit of dowry than the diminishing of her new stature. He bought something far more valuable than her paltry silver -- her never-to-be forgotten gratitude.

As he hastened to see about the wage, Lady Alice hurried into the Queen's quarters. She took one horrified look at her young mistress standing there so flushed, and ran to her, crying with alarm, "My dear child, what is the matter?"

"Nothing, nothing at all. Everything is all right now," Margaret whispered as she slumped to the floor.

Word spread rapidly throughout the ship that the Queen was gravely ill with an unknown malady. Suffolk decided that as Margaret had been so determined to sail they must leave without delay in spite of her illness.. Master Francis, a leech, was summoned to accompany them, and the ship slid out of the harbor with the turning of the tide.

Soon, most of the ladies-in-waiting, and many of the gentlemen and knights took to their own crowded quarters with sea-sickness. The sailors swore it was one of the worst crossings they had ever seen. Even those few who were not sick gave their mistress's room a wide berth for fear of contagion. The dread words 'pox' and 'plague' were whispered fearfully until the Queen was deserted by all but the doctor, Lady Alice and Suffolk.

The Marchioness sat by Margaret for hours at a time, chafing her wrists and applying wet cloths to her head. She held a basin for the young girl when she retched miserably, choking back the bitter bile that rose in her own throat from the heaving of the ship. When she was forced above deck to the railing to relieve herself, her place was taken by her husband.

Master Francis, whose skill was but slight, bled the Queen twice, and burned spices to purify the fetid air. He could scarcely move about because of his own queasy stomach and the rough sea so Margaret was spared the usual practices that might further have undermined her health.

The rough sea had presaged the storm that blew up as the Cokke John fought its way into Porchester. Despite howling winds and a cold, driving rain, crowds of enthusiastic and curious townsfolk lined the shore, eager to catch a glimpse of the famed beauty who was their new hope for a reign of 'peace and justice.' They were prepared for a holiday of pomp and pageantry, a change from their hard lives.

"Look. I can see people on the deck."

"Mama, I'm cold. Let's go home. I want to go home."

"Hush, Doll. The Queen's on that ship."

"I never seen a queen. Is she a fairy queen?"

"Naw, ain't no fairies. She's a real person, I guess. Like us, sorta."

"Hey, watch who you're shovin.' Mind you don't push somebody down."

"Mama, I'm cold. I wanna go home - I gotta pee."

"Just squat there. We ain't gonna go home now. We gotta see the Queen."

"I seen a king oncet but there weren't no queen."

"Look, look. They're puttin' sommat down."

"There's people comin'."

The pushing increased and the cries redoubled as the crowd pressed closer to the water, straining to see.

Suddenly, the waving, shouting onlookers fell silent as the worn and bedraggled company debarked with Suffolk in the lead, bearing in his arms the gravely ill child who was their new Queen.

CHAPTER FIVE

April - May 1445

The disappointed crowd broke up, with those farther from the shore calling, "What happened?" "Where's the Queen?" "Is she dead?" "What's the matter?"

Rumor passed from mouth to mouth as the people reluctantly trudged home.

"I seed her and she looked fair awful."

Those who were nowhere near heard the "awful" and took it up. "Is she dead?" became "She was dead."

There was speculation through the whole town of Porchester until a priest from the religious hospital, "Goddes House," where Margaret had been taken came out and announced to the crowd that because of the frightful sea voyage the pox had broken out upon her.

The word 'pox' brought fear and mutters of plague.

In the hospital, Lady Alice conferred with the nurses who were caring for Margaret. Together they decided that she was not suffering from the dread smallpox, but rather the chick pox which she might have gotten from one of the York children.

Henry, distraught, waited at Southwick. He was not allowed to go near his bride for fear of contagion. The first few days Margaret was so sick with fever and intermittent delirium that she knew little that went on around her. Later she had a hazy memory of the times she woke to find Lady Suffolk sitting beside her, gently rubbing her face and arms with unguents and salves so that she would not scratch at the scabs which itched so. Soon, though, she was mending, regaining her strength and it all seemed a dream.

Every day messengers were sent to tell Henry of Margaret's progress. Finally it was the day when both Master Francis and the King's own physician agreed that the Queen was well enough for Henry to claim her.

On the 22nd of April, 1445, a quiet nuptial Mass was

celebrated for Henry Plantagenet and Margaret of Anjou at Tichfield Abbey by William Ayscough, Bishop of Salisbury, Henry's confessor.

Henry was enchanted by his bride. She was pale from her recent illness and arduous journey, but bright and fair even beyond the promise of her portrait. She wore the same satin gown she had worn at her betrothal. Her bright hair was still unbound to betoken her maiden state.

Margaret had resigned herself for a marriage in which she had no say. For good or ill, she was already his sworn wife and she was determined to live the life that would become a Queen, wife and mother. She promised herself that she would make Henry and her new country love her.

Now, here in the Abbey, she tried to keep her eyes lowered as befitted a modest maid, well brought up, but Henry discovered as he watched her in open admiration that her gaze met his more than once and he thought he detected a sparkle in her eyes that bespoke a gay nature. He was more than pleased with his match, and a smile began to relax his usually tense mouth. Margaret, naturally curious, examined Henry as best she could without seeming to. What she saw pleased her, for he was a handsome, well built young man, albeit a trifle serious. The frank blue eyes that met hers promised an open heart. Both Henry and Margaret worked to keep their attention on the Bishop's words.

Ayscough, in a flat, grating tone, was going on, "Faith, that he may not break his conjugal vow -- Offspring, which may both be lovingly brought up ... and..." It seemed to the young girl that Henry actually blushed here. Henry, for his part, tried harder than ever to apply himself to the sermon but he had to give up the unequal struggle for the sight of Margaret with her smiling eyes drove all religious and pious thoughts from his head.

Throughout the bridal feast, the bride and groom were nervous. They exchanged the customary goblets of wine and replied to the well wishes of their guests but said little to each other. Despite the many courses of which they took but sparingly, before they knew it, before either of them wished it, it was time for their bedding. Margaret was prepared by her ladies and installed in the great bed with its rich velvet hangings of

Lancastrian blue and white which had been brought along in the royal train. Henry was escorted to the private chamber by laughing, jesting courtiers, and prepared for bed by his body servants. The press of lords and ladies about the bridal bed, and the crudeness of the jesting was less than usual for such a royal bedding in deference to Margaret's recent convalescence and to Henry's habitual solemnity and devoutness. When one knight laughed that he hoped the King was "up to it," he drew only a few snickers.

When the last of the crowd had withdrawn to the outer hall, the two who had first met but a short time earlier were alone together in the bed. Margaret, on one side, looked over at her uneasy husband who was sitting, stiff, far over to the other side, his eyes down while he plucked nervously at the cover. He spoke, his voice low so that Margaret could scarcely hear him.

"Are you well? Would you like me to leave you?"

"No, no. I mean ... that is ... I am all well now, my Lord."

"Oh."

There was no sound in the room but the soft whisper of the flickering torches set at intervals along the wall, and a subdued mutter of voices from the outer chamber, punctuated by an occasional sharp laugh. The two young people sat there, the bedclothes drawn up around each of them, tension growing between them. Then Margaret reached out and tentatively touched Henry on the arm. He started, but then laid a hand on hers.

"Would ... would you like to know about that ring?" he asked, pointing to the fair ruby he had placed on her finger at the morning's ceremony.

"Why, yes, my Lord."

"I had it made for you from the ring which my dear Uncle Beaufort gave me long ago when I was crowned in Paris. I wanted you to have something important to me. It was the ring with which I was consecrated King of France."

Margaret was uncomfortable with this reminder that she was likely to be torn between two loyalties - to her native and adoptive countries. She pushed the thought away. *Not now. Not now.*

She held her hand out and turned it so that the firelight played upon the stone. The ruby glowed like a great drop of blood upon her white hand. She drew her hand back and thrust it under the covers.

"I shall cherish this gift always, my Lord."

They were silent once more, neither touching the other.

"Margaret ..."

"Yes, my Lord?"

"Margaret ... I have never known any woman."

She said nothing. There was nothing she could say. Her mother had spoken to her of the duties of a wife ... explained about men, but the words had not prepared her for a timid suitor.

Suddenly Henry turned to her and buried his head in her lap. She stroked his head. They said not a word. She put her hand on his shoulder and patted it.

"Margaret," he cried, and she heard in his voice a mixture of passion and fear. "Margaret, help me. Please help me."

Gently she moved away from him, rose, and pulled the heavy hangings close about the bed. Then she climbed back in beside him and drew him to her.

The newlyweds spent the next month getting to know each other. They passed the month of May leisurely with few official duties, dividing the time between Henry's castles at Shene and Eltham. They rode and hunted in the King's forests which were a glory of green and white and pink, sometimes stealing off for hours by themselves to enjoy the rare delight of privacy. Margaret found herself falling deeply in love with her husband which puzzled her for she had to admit that neither her marriage so far nor Henry were what she had dreamed. Where she had envisioned strength and forcefulness, she found only gentleness and tenderness. Where she had thought to cling and to submit to Henry's wishes, she discovered she was fortifying and leading him. This was not what she had wanted, yet an awakening sense of power was not unpleasant. She remembered her mother's words, "What cannot be helped must be endured." Since Henry was not what she had fancied him to be she would have to make the best of what he was. This was not hard to do, for he was kind and loving to her, almost to the point of adoration.

One of the things which bothered Margaret, though, was Henry's piety. It troubled her that he spent so much of his time in his chapel. One day when she had felt a tug of homesickness, she went looking for her husband with plans to go riding out to picnic beside their favorite stream. She was melancholy and wanted cheering. She found him on his way to the chapel.

"Come on," she begged. "It is such a lovely day that we should be outside enjoying it."

"Later, dear. Right now I feel the need to spend some time in contemplation." He continued on his way.

"Oh, Henry," she cajoled, running beside him to keep pace with his determined stride. "Would you rather meditate with your long-faced churchmen than go riding with me?"

"Sometimes, yes."

She stopped and tears sprang to her eyes. She said, "Oh," in a small voice and stood alone as he went into the chapel. *Is that all I mean to him?*

Later, when she was still pouting and hardly speaking to Henry, he broached the subject. "I am sorry you were disappointed when I didn't go with you this morning." He waited for her to reply. When she did not, he pleaded, "Please don't be angry with me."

"I'm not angry ... but--"

"But what?"

Her words came in a rush. "I'm not angry, though I was disappointed. But it's not that. I really think you spend too much time in church."

"How could anyone spend too much time in church?"

"It's not ... not natural..."

"Come, now, surely you don't mean that. What could be more natural than to spend time with concerns of one's soul? Much as I like to enjoy myself with you, I have a higher duty to be with my Savior."

"Is not the Lord with all of us -- at all times? And not just in church?" she countered.

Henry laughed. "I see my Queen has a legal wit ... You are full of wonderful surprises."

He grew serious. "Margaret, you must understand that I have need of frequent contemplation. It is not easy to be a King -- at least not for me. There are so many duties and decisions that I often feel my strength is draining out of me. In church, at Mass, just being in that holy place, helps renew me. It is something I need. Can you understand?"

She could *not* understand. She wanted to cry out that he could renew himself from her love, but she felt guilty about being jealous of her husband's reliance on something apart from her -- especially church --. She was accustomed to going to church at prescribed times, to being educated by clerics, to praying for favors, to thanking God for favors granted, to confessing her girlish sins. She even understood that the church could be used as a political influence, but she never thought much about religion, had never let it intrude on her nature. Henry's reliance on religion made her uncomfortable. It was beyond her experience ... she was suspicious of it. She feared his emphasis on the other world was not good for him. ...*How can I explain to him how I feel?* she wondered, and remained silent.

Margaret wanted to try to share all of Henry's life, even the religious part, which she was beginning to resent. She tried going to Mass with him more frequently but when the service dragged on with tedious homilies and sermons, she whispered, "Forgive me, dear, but all of a sudden I feel so weak ... my recent illness, I imagine." She rose to leave. Would he follow her?

Henry reached out to squeeze her hand reassuringly. Smiling, he said, "I shall offer up an extra prayer for the well being of your body as well as of your soul." He allowed Margaret to leave the chapel accompanied only by her ladies. Outside, her weakness left her and she stalked back to her chamber, her back stiff with anger.

Except when he was occupied with religious activities Henry was thoughtful and solicitous of Margaret in all things. When Lady Alice mentioned one day that Margaret's wardrobe was a bit wanting for a Queen he sent a valet riding hot for London to bring back a tiring woman with chests of rich materials. The dressmaker fashioned several bliauts and kirtles of linen and silk, and houppelandes and cloaks of brocade, velvet, cloth of gold or damask. Unfortunately, the treasury and the privy purse were empty again, and to pay for this new extravagance, Henry had to pawn a rich collar to his uncle, the Cardinal. Expenses mounted. In a burst of enthusiasm, Henry had Margaret's badge, the daisy, engraved on all of his plate and embroidered on the castle hangings. He gave her a lion for her amazement and pleasure, as a symbol of the strength of his love. Housed in the Tower zoo, the lion ate enough to have fed several men-at-arms. But in the springtime of awakening, growing love, there were no worries. It was a lover and his lass.

Henry's servants marveled that the Queen was able to entice him away from his study of abstruse philosophy and theology, his old wont, to the reading of romances and poetry which so delighted her. She would come laughing into the room, all sunshine, and tug at his sleeve.

"Come, my Lord. You will become stiff and cramped sitting here. It is too nice a day to be mewed in this gloomy hall. Come out with me; I need your help. I find your Master Chaucer most pleasant reading, but difficult since I am so new at your language. You read to me and I can ask you questions."

"Oh, Margaret," he chided, "Chaucer, God rest his soul, is so frivolous."

"Nay, at least not always. Lady Alice ... did you know he was her grandfather? ... says there is a world of deep lessons in his books. Come, let us go out into the meadow and I shall put my head on your lap and you shall read to me. Please?"

He usually acquiesced. Though it troubled his conscience to be reading worldly books he did it for Margaret's sake and found he enjoyed them, a thing which he later admitted to his confessor. That ghostly advisor gave him a short penance, privately glad that the young ruler had finally something to confess, harmless though it was. Ayscough, a wise man, knowing the sometimes dark recesses of Henry's mind, was of the firm opinion that one can be too good for one's own good.

He and the others about the King who loved him were pleased to see how Margaret was drawing him out.

As Henry's affection for Margaret increased he seemed to grow younger, to act more like any other young man of twenty-three. Margaret taught him to play hide and seek with her and her ladies. His happy laughter made his attendants smile.

In their private talk, Margaret called him her knight -- *mon chevalier.* Henry called her his flower -- his Daisy -- for that is what her name meant.

When Margaret wove a length of the flowers, he looped it around her neck and said, "See, I have captured my Daisy and I will chain her to me." Then he stopped, suddenly serious. "These flowers will die, the chain will break...."

Margaret was quick to sense the change in her husband's mood. "No, no, *mon chevalier,* not break. I shall press this chain and keep it safe with my most precious belongings. When we are old I will bring it out and we will show it to our children and remember this happy day."

As May drew to a close, Margaret's coronation day approached. On May 28, she was introduced to the people in a triumphant procession. The countryside turned out to see her, flocking to the route of the parade. Everyone came wearing daisies. Margaret rejoiced at the shouting, waving throngs that lined her way. Laborers, young maidens, burghers, old men, children perched on their fathers' shoulders, and babies held up by cheering mothers; apprentices, beggars, craftsmen, clerks: all, all were there to see their Queen.

The mayor, sheriff, and aldermen of London, clad in scarlet, with other dignitaries in blue, were waiting to accompany the procession through Southwark to London. When they came to London Bridge, they saw a device of two moveable figures, Peace and Justice, who were made to kiss each other. Along the way, they were entertained by pageants representing Peace and Plenty. Children strewed flowers in Margaret's path and men and women sang, wept, and shouted for joy. All London was tipsy with love and with the red and white wine which ran in the conduits. The English did not yet know that they had traded two dukedoms for a Duke's fair daughter.

Along with the commons, knights and lords who journeyed to London to greet their Queen was Henry's uncle, Humphrey of Gloucester, second man in the kingdom. Stubborn and high stomached though he was, he could recognize a *fait accompli.* He had tried to prevent this marriage; now he would make the best of it. His intransigence had cost him. Had he agreed when the rest of the Council allowed Henry his bride, he could have sent his own representatives with the royal escort, but he had heedlessly thrown Margaret into the hands of his enemies, the Beaufort party. However, the game was not over; he still had a few moves.

And so, on that bright May day when all London wore daisies, Humphrey rode out to meet his new niece and Queen. In order to do her full honor, he said, he came with a company of five hundred retainers who wore his livery and badge. She could interpret this as a good will gesture if she wished. She could also see this small army as a tangible reminder of Humphrey's power, a warning that he was no man to discount.

Margaret did not miss the message. "How comes it that your uncle keeps a larger bodyguard than you?" she asked her husband.

"Does he? I hadn't noticed."

"Doesn't it worry you?"

"Why, no. Why should it?"

"It's just that it doesn't seem right for a baron to show more strength than his sovereign. I'd think it would weaken the royal power."

"Maybe, but they all do it. It doesn't hurt me, though; I've all the power I need. Now, come, let's talk about something else. You shouldn't worry your head over men's matters."

But Margaret did worry. When she asked the Cardinal about it she received a less reassuring answer.

"In the old days, only those who owed him service wore the livery of the lord of the castle. And they all went to the aid of the king when he called them. Nowadays, the lord puts his badge on everyone he can gather, whether they owe him fealty or not. In return for this, he protects them."

Margaret protested. "I don't like that."

"Actually, it's against the laws; has been since the time of Richard the Second, but it's more and more widespread. Many of the barons can call out armies larger than Henry's."

"Can't he forbid it?"

"I don't think that would be wise. Suppose Henry issued a decree against the practice ... and couldn't enforce it? He'd be worse off than if he ignored it. What do you think?" He peered at her closely.

She mulled over his question. Well, I think I would try to find out which of my most powerful lords favored me and I'd endeavor to bind them to me with ties of love and loyalty."

The old man nodded, well pleased with her answer. ...*She'll do,* he thought. *She'll do.*

Humphrey had arranged to entertain the royal entourage at his great house in Greenwich. Here, in the heart of his holding, amidst his numerous, loyal friends, he thought to impress the penniless Angevin Princess with his wealth and importance. He was always his expansive best in or near London where the people called him "the good Duke Humphrey." He proudly welcomed Margaret to his lovely home where her quarters were ostentatiously hung with rich tapestries and cloth of gold, of a quality finer than any she had ever seen, even at the French court. He displayed his halls, his gardens, stables, his fine library, and muniment room stocked with glittering weapons. But the constant evidence of wealth and power with their unspoken warning behind them did not intimidate the young Queen. She knew that he had sought to prevent her marriage ... there were plenty ready to tell her that. The daughter of "Good Duke Rene" was better able than many to see through the show of the "Good Duke Humphrey."

As the hours passed, her petulance grew. Finally at dinner, with the rashness of youth and inexperience, she said to him in a voice loud enough to be heard by most everyone in the lofty hall, "Uncle of Gloucester, we are both amazed and pleased to see your lovely home. But what a pity that you have no wife to share and grace your table."

The lords and ladies who had been chatting stopped their talk in mid sentence and the servitors drew back against the wall. Henry reached out his hand in a nervous gesture and said, "My dear, my dear..."

Humphrey rose abruptly, blood suffusing his face, his thick neck swelling, and almost put his hand on his dagger. But impetuous as he was, he managed to master his feelings and sat down again. Margaret looked about her, her large eyes even wider than usual at the sensation she had caused. She whispered as in distraction to Henry, then turned to Gloucester with a smile and said, "Uncle, please, I do not know what wrong I have said ... or done." She gestured helplessly, so that her great ruby ring flashed in the light. "Believe me, as you have shown me love, just so I would not wish you harm. If I have done something bad, it is only because I am ignorant and do not yet know the ways of your ... of our ... country. If I have haplessly offended, I beg you, please forgive me."

Humphrey, his fists still clenched, although he was unaware of it, nodded his head slightly and said, "Madame, it is nothing, believe me. Please continue your dinner ... and ... no one would ever think your gracious Majesty was ignorant."

Margaret bowed her head a little, but not enough to hide a trace of a smile. The others at the table resumed eating, silently at first, and then venturing to whisper to one another until the hall was filled again with the steady sound of a score of conversations. Occasionally, a curious glance was cast toward Humphrey or Margaret, and a snicker or quiet laugh even broke from some of the bolder ones who had no love for the good Duke, but the rest of the meal passed without incident.

Later there were those who maintained that the Queen had spoken unwittingly but Gloucester's friends insisted that she spoke either from malice or spoiled peevishness. No one ever, any more, who had any sense or courtesy, mentioned either of Humphrey's wives. He had been married twice and it was a matter of debate which of the marriages had been more disastrous. His first marriage had alienated Burgundy, England's greatest ally. Then he eloped with Eleanor Cobham, his wife's chief lady-in-waiting. Henry's displeasure at this was increased a hundred-fold when Cardinal Beaufort uncovered evidence that Humphrey's new wife, in hopes of putting her husband on the throne, had enlisted a witch and an astrologer to cast spells against Henry. The witch and the astrologer were executed while Lady Humphrey was sent to finish her days on the Isle of Man. She still lived there, abandoned by Humphrey, whose last wish was to call attention to either of his wives.

No one, not even his brashest enemies, ever mentioned them to him. Now, for the childish satisfaction of a few moments of heedless spite, the young Queen had turned Humphrey of Gloucester into an implacable and dangerous adversary.

CHAPTER SIX

1445 - 1446

On May 30, all the bells of London rang for Margaret. From the outlying towns, streams of people crowded in over London Bridge and through Billingsgate, Aldgate, Bishopsgate, Moorgate, Cripplegate, Aldersgate, and Ludgate.

Dressed in white again, riding in a litter of white cloth of gold, borne by two horses trapped in white damask, sprinkled with gold, with gilded hooves, she went through the noisy, crowded streets from the Tower where she had spent the night, to Westminster Abbey to her crowning. The Londoners thronged narrow streets, enjoying the holiday and eager to see the Queen, an event to tell their children's children. The citizenry shouted their love that day. At the Abbey, the great barons of the realm stood about Margaret of Anjou, now Margaret of England, and swore undying love and fealty to their new Queen.

She felt a swelling in her chest as if her heart would leap out. This was the culmination of the strenuous journey and all those months of waiting. It was all worth while. *I am a true Queen now, a real Queen.* She remembered her words to her mother, along with Isabelle's warning about Fortune's wheel but she pushed that thought away to glory in the adulation of the people -- her people. How she would love them!

Henry had invited his nobles to a celebratory feast held in the great hall of his Palace of Westminster. For the first time she would meet the magnates from the far reaches of the kingdom. She was seated at the high table in the raised seat of honor under the royal canopy with Henry, happy and proud on one side of her and Cardinal Beaufort on the other. The nobles with their wives were seated alternately, left and right, in accordance with their importance. The hall steward was as close as he had ever come to being a nervous wreck sorting out the ranks and seat order. Luckily, all went well that day. Curiosity about their new Queen overcame their usual fractiousness.

After they were all settled at the long trestle, the ewerer poured rosewater over their hands from a silver aquamanile. Next following a tedious blessing by Henry's chaplain, came the procession of servitors led by the nervous steward. Following him was the pantler with bread and butter, and then the butler and his assistants who poured the wine. The lesser knights and squires in attendance who sat at lower tables were served ale. Finally, the kitchen assistants brought in the first course and the company began to eat.

Many of the guests were awed by the variety of food but Margaret was accustomed to the rich choices. This meal was not a great deal different from the ones her father served when he was showing off. She had long ago learned to take but polite samples. Some of the food she left on her trencher. After dinner, the almoner would collect these slabs of bread and distribute them to the poor.

The company was served with a whole roast sheep and a whole suckling pig, complete with head. Whole calves' heads were gilded and silvered. A variety of roast birds were served with their feathers. A good cook could flay a bird as small as a starling, roast it, and then stuff it back into its original skin.

For those who liked fish there was cod, salmon, spiced lamprey and eels and tunny.

One special course was entrayle - sheep's stomach stuffed with eggs, vegetables, bread, cheese, and pork.

Luckily for both Henry and Margaret, he preferred a simple diet. He paid no attention to costs and his own wants were modest, but he wanted to display his wife and express his love.

The feast, which even included rare oranges and lemons, cost hundreds of pounds which he did not have.

Between courses, Cardinal Beaufort was happy to point out the most important guests and eager to tell her about each of them.

"Uncle," she said, "I shall never remember them all -- there are too many strange faces and names."

He reassured her. "For the most part it will not matter, for they return to their holdings and you will not hear from them from one year to another." He lowered his voice, "But be gracious to them all --"

"How could I do otherwise since they are all my loving subjects?"

The Cardinal went on as though she had not spoken. "Because these same lords, especially the ones who live far from London, choose which of their locals come to sit in Parliament...and it always helps to have a friendly Parliament. Now, let's see ... whom should you know? Yes, see that fellow over there?"

"You mean the blue-eyed one with the strong chin?"

"Yes. Henry Percy, the Earl of Northumberland. He's very important. Holds the northern marches for Henry."

"I met him earlier. He's awfully hard to understand ... he has an accent and he used words I didn't even know."

Beaufort chuckled. "That's the way with those Northumbrians. They pride themselves on their differences ...their speech, their bravery, too. His father was called the Hotspur of the North. They're all great fighters ... comes from those border forays by the Scots. As I say, the Earl of Northumberland is very important. He doesn't always get along with the Duke of York though he's his brother-in-law. There's a lot of argument over who has certain rights in the north. There's also friction with Salisbury who holds extensive lands there."

She asked, "Can't Henry keep the peace between his nobles?"

"Easier said than done," the prelate replied, signaling for his goblet to be filled once more. "Henry's a saint but it would take God himself to keep the peace among the marcher lords. Look, now, next to Lady Percy, further down ...that scowling fellow."

"Yes, I see."

"That's John Mowbray. He'll be Duke of Norfolk. He's also a nephew of the Duke of York."

"Is everyone related to the Duke?"

"Just about. I am, too, in a round about way. Actually, it isn't Richard to whom we're related, but his wife Cecily."

"I met her in France, you know," said Margaret enthusiastically. "I liked her ever so much."

"Yes, one of my nieces. My sister Joan, whom God assoil, was the second wife of Ralph Neville and they had so many children it would take a Garter King of Arms to keep track of them ... there were fourteen ... and he already had nine by his first wife. There's one of my nephews, there, Richard Neville, now Earl of Salisbury, the one who doesn't get along with Northumberland. He's the eldest of my sister's boys ... not really a boy, of course, getting along in years, and very level headed. You'll see a lot of him because he's a member of the Privy Council."

"Who's the young man carving for him?" asked Margaret with interest.

"His eldest son, another Richard. There are several more boys at home. Salisbury is almost as prolific as his father. The upshot of it is that wherever you go you'll find Nevilles. This one, the one serving, will probably inherit the Earldom of Warwick through his wife. Some of the richest lands in the kingdom will drop into that lad's hands."

She studied the young Richard Neville who was attending his father. He was scarcely more than a year older than herself so more interesting to her than older, more important nobles. She saw a tall, rather handsome stripling who held himself well. He was deferential to his elders while maintaining an air of self-assurance. His clothes appeared to be of fine material but his doublet was longer than the modern style. His dark hair was short and straight. But it was the important faces she had to learn and she doubted she would have anything to do with the young man.

Her head was well nigh to reeling from all the family histories the old Cardinal was recounting, all the information he was crowding into a few hours. She tried to pay attention but she was tired from the long ceremonies. Her head ached from the weight of the Queen's crown and her stomach was queasy from the rich menu of course upon course. Drooping with fatigue, she turned to Henry but he merely smiled, happy as a child at a party.

"Is this not pleasant?" he asked. "All our nobles about us to do you honor ... it is a great day."

She smiled in return, happy in his pleasure, patted his hand, and turned again to the Cardinal, ready to resume her lesson. He continued down the table.

"The next man is Humphrey Stafford, Duke of Buckingham. His wife is another of the Neville girls so he's brother-in-law to York, Salisbury and Northumberland. He's the peacemaker in the crowd and a very useful man in the Council. I'd say he's one of the few who values his loyalty to the crown more than his own advancement. Now, on down the table ..."

So it went during the long meal, Margaret trying to sort out the names and faces while she graciously answered all who spoke to her, and lovingly attended to Henry's pride and pleasure.

The feasting, along with shows and tournaments, lasted throughout the week. After the entertainments were over, the King and Queen were glad to take up quieter and more usual activities, as well as a new one for Margaret, who began to attend Council meetings at her husband's request. The first time Duke Humphrey hurried into the Council chamber to find her seated upon the dais beside Henry, he stopped in mid-stride, his mouth open.

"Greetings, Uncle," said Henry. "You come behind times. We were afraid we would have to start without you."

Humphrey resumed his course and went over to Margaret where he bowed to her and Henry. "I am sorry I am late, your Grace, but through some oversight I was not notified of the Council meeting. It was by merest chance that I learned of it. However, I see that I have been fortunate enough to arrive in good time, after all, since our lady Queen has not left yet. Perhaps she will favor us with her presence again ... after we have concluded our dull meeting."

"Fie, Uncle Gloucester," said Margaret. "You belittle yourself and the other lords -- or else me, for I am sure that anything that pertains to England will not be 'dull' but of deep interest to her Queen."

"But, Madame --, Humphrey began when Cardinal Beaufort interrupted him. "Oh, sit down, Humphrey, so we can get on with it. The rest of us have asked the Queen to attend."

The Duke looked around the room. Most of the men nodded their approval so he bowed once more and, fuming silently, took his seat.

Margaret played no role in early meetings. She watched her husband closely and noted that he was prone to be influenced by whichever councilor had last spoken. He was reluctant to hurt anyone's feelings and, with his Council made up of opposing factions, this led to vacillation and inaction. Besides this, Henry usually put off even the most pressing decisions until he had prayed over them with maddening procrastination.

While Gloucester, with the Earl of Salisbury and others of his friends were at a dead end in advancing any of their plans with the King, Beaufort and his faction worked on him through Margaret. The Cardinal prided himself that he had chosen the right wife for Henry. She was able to cut straight to the heart of a matter with practical dispatch. Neither was she one to be swayed by every comer. She was loyal to those who had shown themselves to be her friends, and the Cardinal knew she counted him as one.

After a specially stormy Council meeting at which the rivals had pulled and pushed at Henry until he took to his bed with a blinding headache and a churning stomach, Margaret sat at his side with cool cloths for his head and a soothing cup of well watered wine in which she had steeped chamomile and a sprig of yarrow.

Henry reached up and stroked her hand. "You are so good, my dear, to sit here in this dreary room with me when you could be out with your ladies."

"Silly. What is a wife for if not to ease her lord?"

He smiled, contented, the pain indeed less. Then he sank back, relaxing against the pillows while Margaret picked up a lute and played and sang softly a song of old Provence. Henry was almost asleep when a messenger came into the room with word that the King was urgently needed to settle a dispute between Northumberland and Salisbury. At once, lines of tension and anguish reappeared on Henry's face.

"They are at it again," he muttered.

"What is the matter?" she asked.

"This constant quarreling will drive me mad. Both men are claiming the same piece of land and I don't know what to do about it."

"Which of them is right?"

"I don't know. Both? Neither? I cannot choose between them," he despaired, the heels of his hands pressed against the sides of his head to relieve the returned pounding.

Margaret feared that he would be ill again. "Lie back down. I have an idea... I am only a woman and know little of statecraft but perhaps because I *am* a woman the Earls will calm themselves in my presence and you will have more time to make a decision -- or, perhaps time itself will provide a solution."

Henry leaned back against his pillows, grateful for the respite and willing to let his wife share his burdens. "Do what you think best."

Before Margaret summoned the quarrelsome lords, she consulted with Beaufort. "Can you tell me the background of this argument that so troubles the King? I fain would help arbitrate it fairly, and I trust your wisdom."

"My child, it would take the wisdom of Solomon himself to arbitrate that matter. Since time out of mind the Percies of Northumberland and the Nevilles have kept the northern counties in turmoil. It is a feud stretching back beyond the memory of man. Each family vies with the other to see who can amass the larger holdings. And to complicate matters, there is a good deal of intermarriage between them so that property lines are not always clear. Salisbury's sister, Eleanor, is wife to Percy, for example ..."

"Wouldn't that make them friends?"

"Hah! Salisbury resents the dower his sister carried with her and, I understand, the lady is so ambitious that she goads her husband to surpass her own kindred. The Nevilles were ever a contentious brood as are the Percies."

"What people! There must be some solution; they must not be allowed to trouble Henry's peace. I wish we could find a sensible way of settling this. Who holds the most land?"

"Northumberland."

"Then wouldn't it be practical to award the land to Salisbury? To match them more evenly?"

"A wise suggestion, were that all. But there are other factors."

"Yes?"

"Salisbury's son Richard will almost surely inherit his niece's Warwick lands ... I have heard she lies near death ... and then Neville will hold more than Percy. Another consideration ... the Exchequer owes Percy many thousands of pounds that the Earl has loaned for pursuit of the French war ... an expense behind us now, I hope, but Henry is indebted to him."

The Queen pondered, then said, "I thank you, Uncle, for your counsel in this. I think I know what to do."

When she called the fractious lords before her, she spoke to them with an assumed air of regal assurance, hiding the uneasiness she felt at facing these mighty barons on her own. But she had resolved to help Henry and her determination would carry her through.

"We are right happy to have you answer our summons so promptly," she said, smiling with an assumed cheerfulness. "It speaks well of your love for our lord, the King. We know, therefore, that you will accept his judgment in this troublesome affair."

"Yes, your Grace, but where is the King?" asked Salisbury bluntly. "We had thought to have heard the *judgment* from him."

"Of course, but my Lord has been taken ill ... oh, nothing serious; however, his physician orders him to stay abed and even rulers must be overruled by their doctors. Anyway, so that this may be settled now, the King has decreed that you, Salisbury, remove your wrangling retainers from this land to which he has adjudged Northumberland holds the title."

Percy's long face was broken by a grin of satisfaction and Neville narrowed his eyes in anger.

She continued in an even voice, "However, since you, Northumberland have been a party to disturbing the peace of this realm, you shall pay a fine of one thousand pounds into the King's treasury."

It was Salisbury's turn to grin at his brother-in-law's discomfiture.

Later, in the fastness of his northern castle of Alnwick, Northumberland laughed when he recounted the story to his young sons, Henry and Egremont. "By God, Madame Queen is a sharp one! She maneuvered that land right away from Richard Neville and made him like it, his thinking I'd have to pay a fierce fine."

"But won't you? A thousand pounds?" asked Egremont.

"When the King owes me twice ten times that amount? I just took it off the bill ... which I'll never be paid, anyway. I've the land and am not a whit the worse off because of it." He roared with laughter.

Salisbury, in his castle at Middleham, also had second thoughts. "I'll warrant it wasn't really Henry's idea; it was too clever. Well, I sha'n't forget it."

The Cardinal was well pleased with the way Margaret had handled the Earls. He was feeling more and more satisfied with his choice of a wife for Henry. He was truly fond of the young couple, and he invited them often to his great house in Waltham Forest where he kept a room designated as the Queen's Chamber, fitted with elegant hangings of cloth of gold of Damascus. Margaret was so enraptured by this unaccustomed luxury and beauty that Beaufort, pleased to have made her happy, left the hangings to her in his will. He also left 2000 pounds, a veritable fortune, to Henry. Two thousand pounds, for which no pleas nor accountings need be made to Parliament, and Henry turned them down. When the old man came to die, Henry said he had already received sufficient kindness from his great uncle during the prelate's lifetime. The dumbfounded executors of the estate, who must finally have believed that their King truly *was* an innocent, pleaded with him. Eventually he agreed to accept the bequest but only with the proviso that it be turned over immediately to Eton and King's College, his foundations, and this for the repose of the Cardinal's soul. But while the Cardinal was alive, his soul still in his own care, his estates offered Margaret a place to hunt, a pastime she loved, while Henry spent most of his time in contemplation.

It was at the Cardinal's that Margaret met Edmund Beaufort, Duke of Somerset, the prelate's nephew who had just returned from France where he held the post of Captain General of France and Guienne. Somerset's grandfather had been one of the many sons of Edward the Third but like his uncle, he had no claim to the throne because he was descended on the bastard side.

He was firmly in the peace camp so the Cardinal did his best to cement his friendship with Margaret. This was not hard for he was a handsome, vigorous, friendly man, and also ambitious. Besides the Queen was beautiful. The Duke couldn't help wondering how satisfactory was her marriage to Henry, whom he regarded as an *old stick* despite his youth.

"My uncle says you have graced the Council meetings and have given them wise counsel."

Self conscious, she demurred. "He is too kind. He is the one with wisdom. Will you be attending the Council?"

"No. I must return to my post in France."

"That is too bad. I don't know anything about military matters but I imagine your work must be very important." Margaret was more interested in finding a topic that would interest a soldier than in learning anything about *military matters*. Somerset was more interested in keeping the conversation going than in revealing any secrets when he admitted his work was not so very important because the garrison at Guienne was undermanned. And she was just trying to think of something interesting to say when she wrote her family about Somerset and the little garrison.

They both would have regretted the afternoon's conversation had they remembered it. King Charles did not forget his niece's interesting letter.

In July, a French embassy waited upon the English King. The ambassadors had instructions from Charles to extract from

Henry a written agreement to surrender Maine in exchange for a permanent peace treaty. There were rumors aplenty flying about London that Maine and Anjou had been the price paid for Margaret but nothing definite had been admitted. Both Beaufort and Suffolk feared such an admission. They understood far better than Henry or Margaret the fickleness of their countrymen. The same crowds who cheered their Queen one day were capable of cursing her another if they thought she was responsible for losing their territory. Henry was incredulous of the idea that his people might turn, but his Council convinced him that the Commons must be gradually prepared to accept the news. If the people could enjoy for a while the prosperity resulting from peace, they might accept the loss of their French possessions with better grace. However, Charles would not ratify the treaty without the immediate cession of the counties earlier promised him, while the English, in their turn, insisted on further delay. At an impasse, the ambassadors returned empty handed to France.

Margaret and her friends made several bad mistakes then. In the fall, they talked Henry into recalling Richard, Duke of York, from his post as Lieutenant of France. The Beaufort faction was still trying desperately to hide the bargain with the French until their peace party had consolidated its position. With Richard of York out of France, the way was paved for Beaufort's nephew, Somerset, to take over command of all the English forces in France. Somerset liked Margaret and would support her side in any quarrel so her friends rejoiced in what seemed a clear advantage.

York, home, turned out to be an unexpected danger. Although he preferred to be in England where he could keep his eye on those he believed were his enemies, he was incensed at his summary dismissal from the post he had held so long and honorably. He was appalled to find that his cousin Henry was more than ever withdrawn, and allowing others, including Margaret, still but a young girl, to grasp the reins of government.

"What can Henry be thinking of?" he asked Humphrey.

"He isn't thinking. Our uncle, the Cardinal, and that French woman are making the decisions for him. They and Suffolk just about run the Council now; Henry signs and seals everything they put in front of him."

"Can't you prevail upon him? After all, you are his closest relative."

"No, I can't. He turns more and more to those Beauforts. I'm sorry you've been relieved of your command ...I voted against it ... but on the other hand, I'm glad you're home. We need you in the King's Council."

"I'm afraid you overestimate my influence, but I shall do my best."

"Good, good!" exclaimed Humphrey. "Together we may counterbalance Beaufort and the Queen's party."

"With a few more, we might even overweigh it," ventured York. "My brother Salisbury has written me that the Queen served him a bad turn. I daresay he may add his voice to ours."

In summer, the dissension between the rival factions grew worse. York and Gloucester charged Somerset and Suffolk with gross mismanagement of the French holdings and accused them of being self-centered, even traitorous.

One afternoon, during a heated argument in the Temple Garden with York, Salisbury and Gloucester on one side, ranged against Beaufort, Somerset, Suffolk and Northumberland on the other, York reached out and broke a white rose from a bush, saying, "This will be my device. Let those who side with me, wear a white rose."

Somerset reached out for a red rose and countered, "Let those who maintain the party of the truth, pick a red rose with me."

Their quarrel would turn into bitter civil war between the red rose of Lancaster and the white rose of York.

CHAPTER SEVEN

February 1447

Suffolk stood with his back to the fire in one of the private rooms at Windsor, deep in conversation with Somerset, returned from France, who leaned back, his booted feet propped on the fender.

"We cannot put off much longer this French business; King Charles is becoming more importunate weekly. Rumors about Maine are spread by every merchant and traveler who arrives from France," said Suffolk.

"I wish my uncle Beaufort was here," said Somerset.

"He weakens daily and we fear he will not rise from his bed again."

Suffolk crossed himself. "Truly, I sorrow to hear it ... for our sakes as well as his. We have much need of his wise counsel now. However, I have a plan."

"It had better be a good one."

"Only time will tell that, but listen well and tell me what you think. At the next parliament ... which will be sometime soon."

Somerset broke in, "Great heavens, man, didn't you have enough trouble with the last Parliament with Gloucester and his charges of bribery and betrayal?"

"Be patient and hear me out. My idea is that this time *we* will bring charges against Gloucester."

"Of what?"

"For a start, the malpractice of his Protectorate. There's always his first marriage with its alienation of Burgundy which we can justly point out is one of the major causes of our weakened position in France."

"Never work."

"Why not? Humphrey of Gloucester has ever been headstrong and selfish ... and careless enough -- so that we can gather plenty of evidence against him. If we handle this right, we can fulfill our pledge to deliver Maine, reinforce our peace with France, and put the blame on Gloucester."

Somerset rubbed his chin and shook his head. "If you try to start anything against Gloucester you'll have half of London rioting in the streets. You know the people love him."

"Not London, then -- what would you say to Bury St. Edmunds?"

"Call a Parliament at Bury?"

"Why not?" Suffolk shifted and turned his left side to the warming fire. "My Lord Humphrey's not nearly so popular there."

Somerset laughed. "In the heart of your holdings? I'll warrant not. But how much *evidence* have you against him?"

"Enough to remove him from all influence, if not from this world."

"Really? Reliable evidence?"

"Yes; much of it gathered by your uncle, the Cardinal."

Somerset stood up. "It might work; it just might."

"I'll sound out the King and we'll speak more of it later," said Suffolk and left to seek out Henry in his chamber.

"Your Grace," he addressed the King. "It is time that you call a Parliament to raise funds for your meeting with your cousin, the King of France."

Instead of his usual vacillation, Henry agreed immediately. "Ah, yes, the Queen has been urging that we implement our treaty. I shall summon the Lords and Commons. February, do you think?"

"Yes, that will give time for the call to go out and to be answered. I'll go now and relay your orders, if it please you." He moved to the doorway and then stopped. "By the way, what do you think of holding the Parliament at Bury St. Edmunds? It would give those who share your cares of government an opportunity to visit the shrine of holy St. Edmund."

"Why Suffolk, a most commendable idea. I like it. Send out the word -- St. Edmunds -- in February."

The King arrived there on February 10, in freezing weather, accompanied by an over large body of armed men who wore his cousin Somerset's livery. Henry had protested the size of the escort but Suffolk insisted that as chief councilor his first duty was to protect his sovereign.

Henry scoffed. "Against whom or what would you *protect* me, dear Suffolk?

"I scarce can say it, your Grace ..."

"Am I so frightful that you fear to speak anything to me?"

"Nay, my Lord." Suffolk was grave. "It is what I have to say that is so frightful."

"Come, come, man. I daresay anything you have to tell me I can hear."

"Well, then ... Humphrey of Gloucester has been plotting against you for many months."

Henry stared at him. "I do not believe you," he said flatly.

"Your Grace," Somerset declared, "We scarcely would believe it ourselves had we not been faced with insurmountable evidence."

"You, yourself know," put in Suffolk, "that your uncle opposed your marriage to the Queen."

"But he came around."

"I fear not. What has been his attitude toward the French treaty?"

"He has been against it ... but that does not mean he has been against Margaret or me," cried Henry.

"My Liege, he has so courted the Londoners and so inveighed against any peace with France that he believes he can arouse them to revolt against you when they learn you have given up Maine," argued Suffolk.

"He wishes to be Protector again ... or... King," added Somerset ominously.

"I still do not, *cannot* believe it."

"Remember how Gloucester's wife, the Lady Eleanor, plotted against your life?" they asked.

Henry crossed himself hastily and considered. ... It was true, he admitted silently, that he had often of late felt the devil wrestling for his mind ... Could it be Gloucester's work? Perhaps there was some basis for these accusations. ... "You say you have evidence?"

"When the Lord Humphrey is arraigned before Parliament it will all be presented, completely and legally," said Suffolk.

"I can hardly believe it ... well, we shall see. I shall reserve my judgment."

"Of course. Meanwhile, for safety will you accept my escort, Sire?" pressed Somerset.

Henry nodded. "Your men can expect no pay from me, though. I would not so squander my people's money for I have no fear of Gloucester."

Somerset assured Henry, "Naturally, as a loyal relative of close kinship and love to your Grace, I am only too glad to pledge my own purse to my Sovereign's aid."

"You are good to say so, and I am touched by your devotion, but I hope you are mistaken about our uncle. However, if there should be any truth in this claim, I would be remiss if I did not try to save him from the consequences of any rash act. Now, let us find the Abbot."

The great Abbey was one of the holy places Henry liked most to visit. It had been built to contain the shrine of St. Edmund, a King of East Anglia. The saint, who had also been a boy King, was slain at the age of 21 by Danish invaders when he refused to abjure his faith.

On a cold, biting morning, a week after the session opened, Gloucester arrived in Bury St. Edmunds with a large company of followers wearing his badge and livery. If his purpose had been to awe Henry, he was badly mistaken. The King, now keyed up with revulsion at the constant tales of Humphrey's intended treason, sent messengers to inform him curtly that he was relieved from attendance on the King. He was ordered to repair to his own lodgings. Puzzled and cross, Gloucester turned his horse, and hoofs ringing sharply on the frozen cobblestones, rode through Dead Lane to his rooms at St. Salvator's beyond the town's north gate. People remembered later that as Gloucester went through the narrow lane, his horse stumbled and the Duke almost fell.

He was not through dinner when Dorset and Buckingham and others of the Beaufort faction burst in upon him and placed him under arrest. Scarce able to speak for anger, he had no choice but to go with them.

Preparations for a trial were begun. Henry was distraught, seeking solace in the Abbey. He said he wanted to show Christian mercy and forgive his uncle but Suffolk overrode him, persuading him that Humphrey must be tried in order to scotch treason once and for all. Henry, in tears, agreed.

He felt sick and overwhelmed. He needed counsel; he needed comfort. He sent a messenger to Margaret, begging her to join him. "You must come," he wrote. "Only you can give me the strength I need."

When she received his message, she and an escort of squires left Windsor with its thick walls and its roaring fires to jog and slip over rutted, icy roads to go to comfort her husband. The wind shrieked and the blinding sleet which stung her face almost hid the road. Her breath froze on the lining of her hood, and despite heavy woolen robes and a fur lined cloak, her Provencal bones were chilled and aching from the English winter.

At the Abbey, she shed her sodden cloak and rushed to Henry who gathered her in his arms. "My dear, my dear, you're so cold. I never should have brought you out in such weather. Let me warm you." He sent for a hot drink for her and chafed her hands to get the blood going. "I know I shouldn't have ... but I am so worried ... all I could think of was how much I needed you."

With dry slippers, a flagon of mulled wine and a seat by the roaring fire, Margaret thawed out. Henry told her of his anguish over his uncle. "What if Humphrey is guilty as Somerset claims? What can I do? He is my uncle - my father's brother - nearest me to the throne...but," he faltered, "If he intends to sin, he must be stopped ... it is my duty as King."

Margaret did her best to comfort him. "Perhaps Somerset exaggerates or is mistaken. It may all be a misunderstanding.

"Look, it's late and I am tired and still cold. Let's go to bed where you can warm me. I'm sure it will all seem better tomorrow."

But it didn't. In the morning, in their quarters next to the Abbey, the King's squire brought the shattering news that Good Duke Humphrey had been found dead.

Henry sank to his knees with a prayer on his lips for his uncle. "To die unshriven ... the poor man ... and under a cloud. Mayhap he shall obtain some measure of mercy for his presence in such a holy place. Margaret, we must make a gift to the Abbey for Masses for my uncle."

Margaret was less worried for Humphrey's soul than for what would be made of his death. While Henry rose and hastened to find the Abbot, she questioned the servants. No one knew the cause of the Duke's death. He was fifty-six, a goodly age. He had been in a fit of chagrin at his arrest. No doubt he had suffered a stroke but no man knew for sure. Last night he had been alive. This morning he was dead.

Jesu! -- And I arrived last night. What a chance for my enemies!

Margaret had reason to worry. Before the day was out, in every corner of the town there were murmurs.

"The Queen and her meinies have slain our Good Duke." In the streets, taverns, homes, even in the churches, the whispers spread.

"Margaret and Suffolk connived at his destruction."

"The Frenchwoman came and our English Duke died."

Angry mutterings increased and Henry's retainers grew restive. Suffolk and Somerset began to fear for their lives.

Margaret questioned them sharply about their complicity in any murder. "Answer me straightforwardly, did you slay Duke Humphrey?"

"No, my Lady," said Suffolk, shaking his head solemnly.

"No, Madame," joined in Somerset. "We never lifted a hand against him, and he was never alone, as many men can testify."

"In God's name, my lords, this is no time for dissembling. Did either of you *cause* his death?"

Again they protested their innocence but Margaret was not content. "I could understand it if you had done something ...not condone, but at least understand. But I must know what happened so I can know what to say about it...and the rumors that are abroad."

"We have done nothing, I swear, absolutely nothing to Gloucester," repeated Suffolk. "He has died as a result of his own temper ... of an excess of choler which evidently flew to his brain."

"The man was no longer young, and no doubt his body was weakened by a surfeit of much feasting and drinking over the years," argued Somerset.

"We are not so uncautious or so much the fools as to be a party to such a murder," put in the older man.

"But you planned the Parliament meeting here and you had him arrested."

"Certes, and is not that alone further proof of our innocence?" Suffolk ran his hand across his forehead. "Had we not painstakingly gathered evidence, piece by piece, of Gloucester's actions, evidence that would have proven him guilty of treason and broken him forever? Evidence that might even have sent him to the headsman? Do you think we would have thrown that advantage away.?"

"No, but there are many who will not be convinced."

"Aye. In death he has succeeded in doing to us what he could not do alive." Somerset was bitter. "Had he lived but a short while longer he would have been discredited. Now he will be used by our enemies as a martyr, a rallying point for the disaffected."

Margaret struck her palm with her fist again and again. At seventeen, she was distressed, needed counsel. "If only I knew what to do. How sorely I miss Uncle Beaufort."

"What do you hear of him?"

"He lies gravely ill at Winchester --sick unto death. The word is he neither speaks nor seems to hear. God grant him peace." She crossed herself and wiped a tear from her cheek. The two men murmured, "Amen."

"Now, my Lords," she said, calmer now. "We must do what we can by ourselves. Perhaps the situation will turn out less grave than we fear."

Somerset muttered, "Perhaps."

"Well, we can but try. First, my Lord the King must order that Duke Humphrey's body be displayed naked before Parliament and the people so that all men may see that he died naturally. Next, Gloucester's obsequies will be carried out with royal ceremony so that no one can fault us for slighting his honor. Oh, that he had not died in this place and at this time!"

Although the Duke's body was duly laid out, this did little good. Truly, people could see for themselves that there was no mark on him, but still the rumors flew.

"Poison, a woman's weapon. It would leave no mark."

"Perhaps he was smothered between two featherbeds - that's what happened to Thomas of Gloucester in Richard the Second's time -- I heard my parents speak of it."

"Remember what happened to Edward the Second? A burning spit was thrust up through his bowels, and that never showed, neither. The woman who prepared him for burial said there was nothing left of his insides."

They savored the horror of it and slowly, through much repeating and embellishing the story, attributed the deed to Margaret. The conjecture spread throughout the kingdom and greatly injured her cause. Year after year, the rumors flourished, never to be proven false, and many who had no love for the Good Duke ended by mourning his death.

But there was one in the kingdom who did not mourn. Richard, Duke of York, Earl of March and Ulster, Lord of Wigmore, Clare, Trim and Connaught, was now, without lifting his hand, the second man in the kingdom.

CHAPTER EIGHT

1447 - 1449

To Margaret's and Henry's sorrow, Cardinal Beaufort died just six weeks after Humphrey of Gloucester.

"I miss him already," said Margaret. "He was so kind to me."

"I, too; God assoil him. He was more like a father to me than an uncle. I have no close relatives now -- only cousins -- Somerset and York." Henry stared at the embers in the fireplace. He caught himself and gave a half-hearted laugh. "No, I'm wrong there. I almost forgot my two half-brothers, Owen and Jasper, but I don't really know them. They're off in Wales. But father, mother, uncles -- English ones, anyway, all have gone to join our Savior." His voice faltered.

"Dear, dearest, I am here."

"Oh, yes. The best thing Uncle Beaufort ever did for me was to suggest our marriage."

York determined to take advantage of the deaths of the older men to enhance his own position in the Council. He was a wealthy, experienced warrior of proven administrative ability -- with a lineal claim to the throne better than Henry's.

Margaret feared York might prove dangerous so she did her best to balk every move he made to assume more authority. She liked him personally and was fond of Cecily and her increasing family, but it was because of this very family that a tiny flicker of distrust began to grow in her breast. The flicker was fanned by warnings from Suffolk and his wife Alice.

Somerset told her about the scene in the Temple Garden with the two parties ranged against each other. If she had to take sides she would support the men who had been so good to her -- and Henry, she added.

During one unpleasant Council meeting about their claim in

France, Margaret questioned York's advice. Later, Henry, who had put in a rare appearance, reproved her. "Really, I see no reason why York shouldn't be consulted on this troublesome French treaty. After all, he was our lieutenant there all those years. Besides, the people trust him. I think he might just possibly know more about this French situation than Suffolk does. Anyway, it anything should happen to me ..." He crossed himself. "Since the blessed Lord has not seen fit to give us a child --"

Margaret, angered, broke in, her voice rising, "Oh, Henry, stop it. Why don't you come out and say what you mean ... that you made a bad bargain, that I am the one who is at fault for the *troublesome French treaty.*"

"You're twisting my words." He was alarmed by the unaccustomed bitter shrillness of her tone. He tried to placate her. "You are the cause of no trouble."

"Yes I am. And it is trouble. All because I am a barren wife."

"It is too soon to tell," he said softly.

"Too soon? Too soon? Do I not hear whispers, jests? Soon we shall have been married two years. When York's wife was married two years she carried her second child. No wonder you seem to prefer them to me and my friends, for you are ashamed to have given two counties for a barren wife." She buried her face in her hands and wept.

"Hush, Dear. It is not so. I do not know why you are so upset. I am sure that with our Savior's help it will all work out. I shall pray for it. We shall have peace with our Uncle France, and children, too. Cease, now, your crying. This is not like you." He was pleading, for her anger and tears troubled him deeply.

She heard the worry in his voice and was contrite. It was too easy to upset him; she should have known better. But she was tired of bearing the burdens -- she was tired of worrying. She wished she could relax and lean on him. She didn't want to have to always be strong. It made her more miserable than ever, but she raised her face and smiled bleakly at Henry...*Poor soul, perhaps things are not as he wishes, either.* "I am sorry; it is just that I had thought that I might be ... I had hoped that this time ...

it was late ... but today my flux came upon me. It was a great disappointment."

"Perhaps you have been too active."

"No, no ... I was especially careful. It must be that I am barren." The tears began again.

"It is still early. We may yet have many children --"

"The people do not think so. I well know that the prime duty of a Queen is to breed."

"True," admitted Henry. "They would like to have the line secured; but failing that, there is always York, and he is a popular man."

Indeed so ... popular. Perhaps too popular. She started to weep again, despite herself, savoring the luxury of acting like any simple, emotional wife. "York, York and Cecily. When they ride through London with their children it is a constant reminder to the people that she is fruitful while I am barren. How I wish they were somewhere far from here so that I would not constantly be shamed by them."

"Shh, now, do not worry. We have each other." He pulled her to him and held her close while she quieted.

"Yes," she echoed, her voice muffled, for her face was pressed against his chest. "We have each other." Dully, she added, "God grant that you never have cause to rue it."

Henry tipped her face up. "I had planned a surprise for you ..."

She smiled weakly. "A surprise?"

"Yes, and a happy one. I had not intended to tell you yet but mayhap it will cheer you ... on the other hand ..." His eyes twinkled with unaccustomed pleasure.

Her own smile became surer; she knew her husband rarely teased; he was enjoying himself so it must be something special. "Tell me, Henry. Tell me. You know I cannot abide suspense."

"Well, it's a gift -- of sorts. Try to guess."

Her smile faded. Just a gift -- how strange he should be so elated about it when he cared so little for worldly things. But whatever it was, he had planned it to please her. What should she guess? She didn't want to spoil his pleasure... "A dress?"

"No -- better."

"A jewel?"

No -- better."

"Land?"

"No; I think perhaps even more pleasing to you than that."

"I am out of guesses. You'll just have to tell me."

"In a minute." He sat down and drew her onto his lap. "Margaret, as you said, we have been married almost two years. There have been troubles and sorrows, I know; but still they have been the happiest two years of my life. I wish you were as happy as I; I love my Daisy very much."

"I'm sorry, my Lord. Really, I am happy ... it was just this disappointment ... I miss Uncle Beaufort, too... but honestly, I am happy." A lie but a white one.

He jumped to his feet, almost upsetting her, and said in mock severity, "But not happy enough. I am the King and I command you to be happy. Would it make you so to have your old friend, Katherine, with you?"

"You know it would ... is? ... *could?*" Her face brightened but she was afraid to be too hopeful. Perhaps she did not understand what her husband meant.

"Yes -- Katherine. I know how you have missed your family and friends ... even with our love --"

"Henry, I have never --"

"Shh. I know you haven't complained but I also know the old saying, *old friends are best* and I want you to have the best. I wasn't going to tell you till she arrived, but your Katherine is on the way. She'll be your lady-in-waiting. Now, does that cheer you?

Margaret was speechless. She threw herself into Henry's arms, tears streaming down her face.

"By Saint John," he exclaimed, his eyes bright, "Here I thought to make you happy and I've made you cry all the harder. I guess I just don't understand women."

Margaret was indeed much happier with Katherine as one of her ladies. Much as she loved Alice, the Marchioness Suffolk, and her other attendants, Katherine was a lifelong friend from home. She caught up with all of the news of her parents and France; they sang the old songs, and laughed over reminiscences. In her new pleasure, Margaret ignored for a while the affairs of state and the court intrigues.

But these continued. Suffolk grew increasingly restive as York fought for more influence in the Council. He approached Margaret on this.

"We never should have brought York home from France," he admitted.

"Could we re-appoint him?"

"Not without offending Somerset who holds the position now and is planning to sail any day."

"Then that won't do. Is there anyplace else we could send him? What about a Crusade to the Holy Land? Henry would like that."

"If there's anything we don't need it's another war. Right now the pay for all our French garrisons is in arrears, as well as for our men along the coast. I fear it will get worse, too, before it gets any better, and they are growing impatient."

"There must be some way to get rid of our troublesome cousin."

"I have it!" Suffolk struck the table with his fist. "Ireland!"

"Ireland? Will he go?"

"If we handle it right. If Henry points out that York did so well in France that England has need of him in Ireland, a parlous and worrisome country."

York was not fooled by Henry's enthusiastic appointment of him as Lieutenant of Ireland. He made as many excuses as he could to delay departure. Patriotism and his enemies on the Council forced him finally to go, but, "Before I take up my duties," he said, "I must see to my holdings in the north." He stretched his business two years before he arrived among the wild kerns. Margaret and Suffolk congratulated each other that he was out of London, his hand removed indefinitely from the Council.

York used his time well to cement northern alliances. When

he finally went to Ireland he left behind him many firm friends among the nobles, men who were willing to look out for his interests and advance them whenever possible, especially if it would help their own. Two of the mightiest of these were Cecily's brother, the Earl of Salisbury and the Earl's twenty-one year old son, Richard, recently created Earl of Warwick, now the premier Earl in England. Cecily, as usual, accompanied her husband; and still another son, the third living one, George of Clarence, was born in Dublin Castle.

While York was making friends, Margaret and Suffolk were losing theirs. In February, 1448, three years after the marriage contract, Henry gave up Maine and Anjou to the French. Margaret foolishly chose this time to urge the advancement of Suffolk whom the people blamed for the loss of those counties.

"I don't care what the people think," Margaret said, "Suffolk has helped us and loyalty should be rewarded. Henry, you should make him a Duke to show you support him. That will serve his enemies right." She did not mention that it would also *serve* her own enemies, of which she feared there were many.

The announcement of Suffolk's dukedom was accompanied by discontented mutterings among the Commons. Margaret's move to have her friend elevated was the worst thing she could have done for him and herself.

At the next Council meeting, Salisbury made a great show of referring to Lord Suffolk as *Duke* William. "I have news from the north, bad news, but then, *Duke* William, you probably already know."

"Know what?' asked Suffolk.

"Know of the slaughter."

"What slaughter?"

"The Scots. Our men."

"No, I don't know. What about the Scots and our men?"

"Well, at least you must know about the unrest from one end of England to the other. People can hardly believe we've turned over Maine and Anjou to the Queen's uncle. They're angry."

"Stirred up by some envious nobles, I warrant. They'll soon simmer down."

"So you think," countered Salisbury. "But word has come that the Scots have taken advantage of the discord and raided our border."

"That's hardly news. Anyway, Northumberland should be able to handle a few Scots."

"Yes, your friend Percy of Northumberland should have been able to *handle* them. He led an army over the western March but there were more than *a few* who fought like the demons they are. The couriers say six hundred Scots perished --"

"Good."

Salisbury drew it out as if enjoying his tale. "I was saying -- six hundred Scots, but three thousand of proud Percy's men were also killed -- fighting or -- those who fled, drowned in Solway Firth."

"Jesu! You're sure?"

"Oh, yes, quite sure. I fear this may hurt the Queen for Northumberland has ever been her friend, eager to do her bidding."

Suffolk narrowed his eyes in anger. "Do you imply --?"

"No, no, my Lord *Duke*. I imply nothing. I merely state that Northumberland's friends are probably not very popular right now."

The disaster brought bereavement and sorrow into almost every dwelling in the north. Daily, discontent and restlessness grew. Ordinary lives were hard, with little joy. To this had been added grievous loss and a sense of hopelessness. Their lives were not going to get any better.

When Henry learned of the catastrophe he was sorely troubled. "My poor people. We must pray for the Lord to help them bear their sorrows."

The Dukes of Buckingham and Exeter, members of the Privy Council, thought something more concrete than prayer was called for.

"Your Grace, would this not be a good time to comfort your

people by showing your concern in person?"

"I do show concern. I have ordered Masses for the slain and their families."

"More than that -- go on a progress through the north."

Margaret questioned this. "If the people are as upset as we hear, wouldn't the King be in danger? Is this wise? Would he be safe? Wouldn't --"

Henry interrupted. "My dear, how could I be in danger from my own subjects?"

Exeter hurried to agree. "The people love their Sovereign. We wouldn't suggest it otherwise. Trust us -- King Henry's presence will bind the country together."

So in one county after another, there was holiday, with the colorful pageantry of pennants flying, armor flashing, the riders slowly and majestically picking their way behind mayors and aldermen in full regalia. There was free food and wine.

"Look, Nell. Run Doll, run. There is our King! Long live King Henry!"

"May the King live forever!"

"See, Mak. Look, Wat, the Queen ... a proper looking young woman. Long live the Queen!"

The royal couple sympathized with widows, bereaved mothers, shy orphans. A regal blessing was balm for hurt souls. Saddened hearts were lifted by the Queen's tender regard.

Margaret watched her husband and was pleased to see that he was enjoying their progress. His blue eyes sparkled and his serious mien was replaced with a broad smile. He was touched by the affection of his people. These honest yeomen and farmers were men he could feel close to ...*how happy must be the well-ordered life of a simple shepherd ...*

Their way was sometimes hampered by the press of people, beggars pleading for alms; sick men darting out of the crowd to touch the King's hand in hopes of a miraculous cure. Henry would not let his attendants beat back the crowd. Margaret shuddered to see diseased hands reaching out but Henry seemed to welcome their contact. In return, the poor unfortunates blessed him.

Often the way was rough going. Country roads, which in Norman times had been built wide enough for two carriages to pass or for sixteen knights to ride abreast, had, in many places been allowed to deteriorate. There were boggy holes and rickety bridges. In some places, the woods encroached on the roadway so much that the riders had to go in double or even single file and the way had to be cleared by axe and rope before the carriages and wains with the royal supplies could pass.

Henry noted all this and determined to have his marshals see to the repair of the King's Highway. Towns would have to be taxed for this or the royal exchequer raided.

The main streets of the towns had been cleaned in prospect of the rulers' arrival. Though rakers had carted away the usual filth, by the time the procession reached the city, the citizens, in order to clean their own dwellings, had thrown into the street their discarded rushes and kitchen refuse. Chamber pots were emptied out of doors and windows. It was against the law, but men excused themselves by saying *everyone does it.*

In the shambles, rotting animal heads and entrails were thrown into the streets. Fishmongers and poulterers also used the streets for their offal.

Margaret and her attendants all carried musk balls which they held to their noses when the stench grew too great.

Withal, the company had a merry time. They visited guild halls and markets and attended plays put on especially for their visit. Once, as their train moved slowly through a town, a wild-eyed man broke away from the watching crowd and threw himself in front of Henry's horse. The King had to pull up sharply and two soldiers rushed to hurry the man away.

"Mercy, Sire, mercy!" cried the anguished man.

"Hold," Henry signaled to the soldiers who halted, the man held roughly between them. "Who are you and why cry you for mercy?"

"Sire, I am Tom o' the Beck, and I am villein to Sir Ranulf. My daughter Margery has run away and married off the manor and now I must give up my lone ox to Sir Ranulf ... without it I'll not be able to plow."

"That is the law, is it not?" asked Henry.

"Yes, Sire, but it is an unjust law. Mercy, Sire. I have a poor, sick wife and no goods but my ox and a few chickens."

"Does this man speak true?" asked Henry, looking around.

Some of the men and women in the crowd nodded. Others looked at the ground. A large, well dressed man pushed his way through the crowd. He bent his knee to Henry and said, "I am Sir Ranulf, your Grace. He speaks but part of the truth. His daughter has married off the manor but I think she ran away only with her father's connivance ... to avoid the fine. It is I who should cry you mercy, my Lord. I would rather that the girl would marry on my estates so that I would not lose the children she will bear. We grow more and more shorthanded. I do not want his scrawny ox except that it is the law. Besides, he has urged others to flee, too."

Margaret, who had been listening, joined in the conversation. "Would the girl ... Margery ... come back?"

"Never," said her father.

"Did she in sooth *run away?*"

"Yes, Lady ... from Sir Ranulf. But I admit I knew of it."

"He encouraged her," complained the landowner, his voice thick with anger. "He's a trouble maker ...it's not the first time he's told people to break the laws --"

"Unfair laws," put in Tom o' the Beck.

Henry looked on the man with pity and said, "But it is the law since time out of mind ... the villein's labor and the labor of all born on the manor belong to the owner. It is a King's duty to uphold the law --"

Margaret broke in. "But a Queen ... and a King ... can give a wedding gift -- especially to a maid named Margery. Here, Tom," she handed him a heavy velvet purse. "This will redeem your ox and perhaps provide one for the first babe."

Tom bowed low while the crowd cheered and waved until the royal train disappeared down the road.

The progress was a success. In their excitement and pride, the people laid aside their sullen discontent and doubts. The sharp ache for their dead in the border war dulled a mite. Henry and Margaret told each other how glad they were they had come. There was real affection here. See how their subjects held their children up to see; how hands reached out to touch the hem of a royal garment; how lustily they cheered. The couple heard the shouts of approval all along their way, shouts which clearly belied the old rumors of hostile murmurings. They were a well-loved King; a golden Queen. Surely all would go well now.

Meanwhile in France, nothing went well for the English. King Charles had won not the two years he required as a minimum, but four. He had put down petty factions and united his country; he had built up a disciplined army; he had plenished his treasury. Using English forays into Brittany as an excuse, Charles had declared that the Anglo-French treaty had been breached. The truce was at an end ... all the fault of the English. From their positions in the newly ceded Maine, the French sent out four armies to lay siege to the towns the English held in Normandy. These, one after the other, like ripe fruit, dropped into waiting French hands. Somerset, with his troops, retreated to Rouen to await reinforcements from home. None came. Supplies nearly gone, he was forced to parley with Charles.

The word finally reached Margaret and Henry that Somerset had capitulated, relinquished Rouen, Harfleur and four other cities, besides giving a pledge for payment of 50,000 pounds.

CHAPTER NINE

1450

The news that they had lost Normandy was a thunderbolt. Everywhere, men asked each other, "What happened?"

"Why?" "Who's to blame?" Or said, "If only great King Harry were alive."

The people were bitter. For a hundred years they had struggled to win France, had spent men and money -- to no avail. Families were bereaved; trade slackened; taxes rose; returning, unemployed soldiers turned to riot and crime. Men needed someone to blame. Were not the miserable conditions, now crowned by defeat, the fault of the government? Who in the high seats was responsible? Why, the King's chief minister, Suffolk. He was the cause of their misfortunes. They would tear him down, this false advisor, this friend of the Frenchwoman, this new-made Duke.

In February, the Lords and Commons met together in the Great Hall at Westminster. The walls and ceiling echoed with charges and counter charges against Suffolk. Arguments went on for two months, and after interminable wrangling, Parliament finally settled on twenty six articles of impeachment, among them the accusation of high treason. He was, they said, responsible for the giving up of Maine and Anjou and for the loss of Rouen. Not in the indictments, but there were also charges that he had been guilty of the death of Humphrey of Gloucester.

When the list of Suffolk's supposed crimes were read aloud to the King in Council, with the demand that he imprison or banish the Duke, Henry stalled for time. He said he would think about it, wanted to reserve his judgment, to pray over it. "A few days only -- no longer," his Councilors said.

The Painted Chamber, Margaret's favorite room with the brilliant frescoes, failed to lift her spirits. She didn't see the bright battle and biblical scenes that usually enchanted her, so deep were her worries when Henry brought her the list of accusations against her first and dearest English friend.

"So many charges. So many charges. Margaret, what do you make of this?"

"I make of it that these men must hate Suffolk very much to make up such lies."

"But why should they hate him so?"

"That I do not know." She looked out the window, down at a small boat crossing the broad river. "Jealousy, perhaps. Revenge -- there must be some he has injured. Greed, even -- if he is attainted there are those who would hope his lands would fall into their own hands. But belike it is more through hate of me."

"Margaret!"

She turned away from the window. "Oh, yes, my Lord. I hear the whispers about the court as I come into a room or go down a hall ...In the streets I hear the shouts after I have passed. I am *the Frenchwoman.* I am the reason you gave up Maine and have now lost Normandy. They hate me and all my friends."

Henry reached out and gently opened the fingers which she had clenched into a tight fist. "You must not say that. It is not true."

"Do you think they love me?" she asked, her voice bitter.

He did not answer for a while and then said simply, "They do not hate you, I am sure."

"Why, then, are they doing all this? And why did they kill Adam Moleyns?" Kindly, stout Adam Moleyns, Bishop of Chichester and Lord Privy Seal, who had been one of the first Englishmen Margaret had met, who had been one of the embassy that came with Henry's marriage offer, was recently dead, slain by a rabble of soldiers in Portsmouth when he went there to pay the troops. It made no sense.

With Adam's death, the members of the King's Council grew frightened, pensive or cautious, according to their different natures. Henry ordered special Masses sung throughout the kingdom for the repose of Moleyn's soul. Margaret swore vengeance.

Suffolk was forced to appear before Parliament and King to answer the articles of impeachment. Against the charge that he had plotted to sign away Maine and Anjou he said, "Here are the letters patent which his Grace gave me before I went to France. See, they authorized me to do anything needful to procure the alliance and treaty. I am no traitor."

Henry affirmed, "That is the very letter I gave Lord Suffolk. The Council concurred in it, too."

The Duke knelt before the throne. "Long have my family and I labored for our King and country. At nineteen, I fought at Hafleur with King Henry the Fifth and there my father gave his life ... I, myself, have fought for the King thirty-four years ... I am an honest man, a simple soldier, a knight. Never, never have I in all my fifty-four years, yielded to bribery or betrayed my sovereign. These charges are too horrible to speak more of, utterly false and untrue, and in manner impossible. God knoweth I am, and shall be, and never was other but true to you, Sovereign Lord, and to your land."

Henry tried to defend Suffolk, while the Duke's enemies insisted the was guilty of at least some of the charges and even demanded his head. Henry did his best. When he adjourned the hearing, nothing had been decided; no one was pleased.

In the royal apartment, Margaret was waiting. She insisted, "You are the King. Just tell them that you trust milord Suffolk and that is that."

"But it isn't that easy."

"I don't understand."

"Margaret, there are powerful lords who hate the Duke -- no, no, not you, the Duke."

"All right, they hate him -- that is obvious. But what can they do?"

Henry stared at a bloody battle scene and fingered the cross he wore about his neck. "They can withdraw their support from the crown."

"But what good is their *support* if you can't do what you want?"

"Please, please ... I don't want to talk about it any more."

"I know you don't want to. I don't want to, either, but we

have to do something. You're not just going to turn Suffolk over to his -- our -- enemies, are you?"

"Of course not." He added, "Though he must be punished in some wise ..." He shook his head. "I don't know what to do. I just don't know what I *can* do."

He looks so worried; this is making him ill. Somehow the pressure on Henry must be lifted while we protect our friend. If only Uncle Beaufort were alive -- he would know what to do. How can I make all the hard decisions alone? Uncle gone, and now my enemies are trying to remove Suffolk -- they won't be happy until he is gone from my side ...

She had an idea. "They want him out of the way -- well, why not send Suffolk to the Tower for a while?"

"The Tower? What good will that do?"

"It will give us time for your fractious barons to find something else to wrangle about."

"Do you think they will be satisfied with such a light penalty?"

"Henry, I repeat, you are the King. Why should they not be satisfied with your judgment? Besides, I'll warrant that with Suffolk away from court, these trumped up charges will soon be forgotten."

The Duke's enemies grumbled when they heard that he had been moved into one of the royal apartments in the Tower.

"I tell you, he'll be back in favor before we know it."

"Not so. We'll wait and see -- and if he's out, we'll know it."

"I, for one, am content to have him away from court. In the Tower he won't be so close to Henry's ear."

"The Queen will have him out and at her side in no time."

"We'll see; we'll see."

Margaret missed Suffolk's support in the Council meetings.

A month had passed with no further trouble or even mention of the Duke. Her idea had worked and she thought he could safely return to court. She decided it was time to release him from his confinement.

Suffolk was eager to leave the Tower. He was a brave

soldier, a man full of years, but the place made him nervous. He confided to Margaret that an astrologer once told him that if he might escape the danger of the Tower he should be safe.

"I had not thought you superstitious," Margaret remarked.

"I do not think myself superstitious, either, but I do believe that some men and women have a kind of second sight to discern events that most of us cannot perceive."

"My dear friend, as long as I have anything to do with it, the Tower shall pose no danger for you."

The minute Suffolk re-appeared at court, restored to full favor, waiting enemies moved. Accusations were repeated, more charges were added to old indictments. In both the Commons and the Lords, Suffolk was denounced as traitor, responsible for the loss of Normandy. Margaret and Henry were shaken to learn that their subjects were calling Suffolk's release a show of contempt. The Council was split, with most, even his former friends, turning away from him.

As crowds gathered in angry knots, cursing the Duke and his part in Margaret's betrothal and England's lost lands. Suffolk realized that his friendship could only endanger his King and Queen. When Henry was again pressed to banish his councilor, Suffolk himself agreed it was necessary.

"You can't mean it. It isn't fair," cried Margaret. "The Lords know you are not guilty."

"Not guilty, but unpopular, and unpopularity feeds upon itself. They hope to remove all blame for themselves by placing it on me," he replied.

"And on me." There were tears in Margaret's eyes.

"No, no!" Henry broke out. "There is no blame for you, Margaret."

Suffolk disagreed. "Seriously, I fear it may be so."

"Henry, don't do this," pleaded Margaret.

Suffolk motioned for her to be quiet. He turned to Henry. "You must, my Lord. If not, I am afraid that since the Queen has shown me favor, they may insist you send her home to France."

Henry was incredulous. "They wouldn't! They couldn't, could they? There's no reason."

Margaret's eyes widened with apprehension. "Oh, there's

reason enough if they wished. They could use the pretext of my childlessness."

"Your Grace, you must not underestimate the temper of an aroused people. They might ..." he groped for words ... "Well, remember Richard the Second ... and Edward ..."

It was true, Henry knew. Kings had been unseated in England before. After all, he was on the throne only because his grandfather had wrested it from Richard, the rightful King. Richard had lost the support of his people because he was an ineffectual ruler. Henry shared some of Richard's weak traits, yet his people loved him for his sweetness, kindliness, and generosity - still. How long could he sit secure if the people mistrusted his closest advisor?

Henry had no question in his mind and heart about his right to be King. He was God's anointed, but evil men conspired to overrule him, to drive away his friends, perhaps even his wife ... he could think of no way out. He could not bear to lose Margaret. Solemnly he laid his hand on Suffolk's shoulder and in a voice almost too soft to be heard, said, "If it must be."

Suffolk relaxed a little as his ship pulled away from the shore and set its course for Calais where he had friends. Trouble was behind him. Tomorrow would be better.

However, in the Dover Roads, just as it seemed he would make Calais, his ship was waylaid by sailors from Kent. When the lead vessel hove into sight, Suffolk read her name and blenched. She was the *Nicholas of the Tower*. The astrologer's words roared in his ears. Then, a mood of quiet acceptance came over him. As the Kentishmen swarmed over his ship, he asked that his friends not be molested; and at the command of the Nicholas's master, he quietly let himself be transferred to that ship. As he boarded her, he was met by a great shout of "Welcome, traitor." Despite himself he flinched, but except for that he seemed almost unconcerned as his eyes traveled from face to face before him. His dignified and calm assurance merely further enraged the sailors who clamored for his life. They edged near.

The ship's captain drew his sword and forced the men back. "Not so fast," he yelled. "Milord Duke never had no proper trial by the people."

They shouted with malicious glee, "Let's give him one now."

With the butt of his sword, the captain roughly pushed the man who had been his King's chief councilor down onto a bench. The trial was soon over, for the sailors lost some of their taste for the sport when Suffolk refused to be moved by their charges, answering only a simple, straightforward, "I am not guilty," and that only when he was prodded by the ship's master. Sentence of death was swiftly passed and he was allowed to go below with his confessor who had insisted on boarding the ship with him and who had vainly pleaded with the sailors.

"Shrive him well, Sir Priest," said the captain, "for I am sure he has many sins."

"Aye, that I have," murmured Suffolk, "but not those which you charge."

Through the night, the Duke confessed himself to the priest, asking absolution for his earthly sins, and prayed to God for forgiveness for his spiritual ones. At times, the old priest dozed, but ever when he wakened, he saw Suffolk in a calm attitude of prayer, or else ready to give as much consolation as he received.

In the morning, the Duke was stripped of his velvet doublet and his russet gown. Clad only in hose and singlet, he was let down into a small boat waiting beside the Nicholas. Here, furnished with a wooden block and a rusty sword, was the toothless ruffian who had won the draw to be Suffolk's executioner. When they pulled away from the larger ship, the Duke knelt, crossed himself, and placed his head upon the block.

The sailor said, "Let's see how a famous knight dies," and swung the rusty sword. He was more eager than skilled, however, for he had to hack at the Duke five times before he severed his head.

The men took his body and flung it upon the sands near Dover, and impaled his head on a pole nearby. Jesting, they laughed that this was truly a fitting end for William de la Pole of Suffolk.

The Duke's grieving friends who had waited helplessly on their own ship through the long night, now landed and kept careful guard by his body while they sent messengers to Henry for orders respecting his burial.

CHAPTER TEN

1450

The obsequies were over; Suffolk was at rest where he wished. In a premonition of death he had written his will, directed that "my wretched body ...be buried in my Charter-House at Hull, where I will my image and stone be made, and the image of my best-beloved wife by me...if she lust; and my said sepulture be made at her discretion ...desiring it may be to lie so as the Masses, that I have perpetually founded there ...may daily be sung over me."

Henry, alternately weeping and praying for his councilor's soul, led the procession from the building. Suffolk's friends followed and then Margaret, holding the seven-year old new Duke by the hand. The widowed Alice remained behind, kneeling alone at the crypt in a last private farewell. As the procession silently wound its way down the path, the sound of solemn chanting from the monastery hung on the soft May air, heavy with the sweet scent of lilacs and apple blossoms. *This beautiful, beautiful land,* thought Margaret. *How it belies its true, cruel nature.*

The murders of Moleyns and Suffolk were but two visible signs of an underlying unrest and disquiet. For a hundred years, English lives and treasure had been spent in France and what was there to show for it? English pride had been humiliated. *Surely we couldn't have lost ... not after the glories of Crecy and Agincourt...someone must have betrayed England. The King's councilors, the Queen's party, must have been forsworn.* There were troubles piled on troubles, too. Now, at French urging, Burgundy had prohibited the import of English cloth into Flanders. Gone was their best customer, and English clothiers sought in vain for work. Spinning wheels and looms stood idle; meager savings were exhausted. Helpless, angry men heard their children whimper with hunger.

In the southeast, there was a steady stream of soldiers

returning from the lost French provinces to seek work -- work that wasn't there. They had to turn to beggary or crime to get a few pieces of rough, brown bread and a cup of ale. While they slept in barns or under bridges, others were rich and slept in soft beds, paraded vainly, wore fine clothes and ate light bread.

In their frustration, men turned against local officials such as Crowmer, the Sheriff of Kent, who collected high taxes and turned them over to Lord Say, his father-in-law, the King's Treasurer. The people said these two stuffed their purses, that the King never saw the taxes.

Painstakingly copied broadsides were passed from town to town by travelers: minstrels, pedlars, jugglers, or disaffected clerics: anyone who moved about. In many a market place and tavern, knots of townspeople gathered to hear these. In a village outside of Dover, near where Suffolk's body had been recovered, a crowd listened while an apprentice scrivener read aloud:

> Truth and poor men been oppressed,
> And mischief is nothing redressed.

"Aye, that's true," shouted a baker. The scrivener shrugged his mantle closer about his shoulders and continued,

> So poor a King was never seen
> Nor richer Lords have ever been.
> Lord Say holds the Commons down
> He keeps the taxes from the crown.

He stopped.

"Go on. Is there more about Lord Say?" He held the paper up again. There's more if you want it."

"More, more!

> Be ware, King Henry, what you do.
> Those traitors never will be true.
> Let them drink as they brew.

"That's good, that's good."

"Yes, if the King knew, he'd do somat about things," shouted a farmer.

"Oh, I dunno - what about Suffolk? The King must have known about him -- right there he was with him," put in a fuller.

"No, the Queen hid it from him," insisted the farmer.

"Maybe, maybe not," said an ex-soldier. "Anyway, someone knew about the Duke and someone saw he didn't get away."

"And I say," declared a red faced man, "Let the King beware."

The man next to him cautioned, "'Ware yourself. Who knows how long their ears are?"

"I'm not afraid."

"Well, maybe some of us are -- and have cause to be." He lowered his voice. "I hear the Queen is so wroth she has sworn to raze the whole county in revenge for Suffolk."

"Just let her try; just let her try," grumbled the red faced man, but he turned and walked off and the crowd broke up, some of them glancing over their shoulders fearfully. The reader took his paper and moved on to the next town.

Incidents like this were repeated all over the shire. Suddenly the welling discontent had a leader. From somewhere, no one except a few Yorkists, knew where, an Irishman named Jack Cade, a veteran of the French wars, appeared, to give purpose and direction to the rebellious people of Kent.

Whether it was his own idea or whether the Yorkists suggested it, no one ever learned, Cade assumed the time-honored name of Mortimer. Perhaps he hoped the name would be a rallying cry; perhaps his sponsors believed it would remind men that there were those who had better titles to the throne than did Henry, for Richard of York claimed his descent through Philippa Mortimer, daughter of the second son of Edward the Third, while Henry could claim descent only from the fourth son.

During Whitsuntide week of 1450, Cade raised a considerable force of Kentishmen. He told his army of yeomen, husbandmen, and many an honest laborer and guildsman, that the King was bound by law to set right the injustices they had suffered. From every corner of Kent they came: Thomases,

Henrys, Johns and Williams, Richards, Roberts, and Edmunds: a host of honest English commons mixed with a dangerous, explosive leaven of rogues and knaves.

Soon London was in an uproar bordering on panic at the threat of 20,000 men camped outside its gates. Merchants shuttered their shops. Guildsmen and apprentices armed themselves. Wives and daughters trembled behind locked doors. The rich buried or otherwise hid their goods. The poor prayed.

Henry and Margaret were at Leicester where Parliament was in session. When they learned of the ominous gathering, Henry dissolved Parliament and they hurried to London. But once there, he made no move to force the rebels to disband. He was reluctant to attack his subjects.

Among the legions who had come up to the capital with their grievances, there was deep disappointment ... and grumbling.

"Ain't he even goin' to hear us?" said one.

"We might as well've stayed home," his fellow added.

"What are we going to do?" asked a young boy.

"Well," put in an old soldier who had a scar won in the French war, running the length of his face. "If he won't come to us, why maybe we'll have to go to him..."

"Aye, and not with no scraping and bowing, either," threatened another.

The boy looked frightened. "I wouldn't want to do nothing wrong ... but you'd think he would hear us."

"He'll hear us, all right," laughed the soldier. "He'll hear us."

The restless army had been encamped for over two weeks before the Council met to examine their petition of grievances. Some advised treating with Cade; others said, "Call the royal troops." Divided, they turned the problem back to the King.

Henry was shocked by the petition which contained fifteen items, among them that it was openly rumored that Kent should be destroyed and made a wild forest in revenge for the death of Suffolk, and that the King gave crown lands to favorites so that he was reduced to taxing the Commons to obtain revenue.

Margaret read the petition with growing anger and frustration. It was filled with the old complaints, the old lies.

"Henry, this petition, this rebellion -- it's a plot."

"Why do you say that? -- I'm not disputing you, I am just trying to find out -- so often other people seem to see things I don't."

"That's because you are kind and good, not evil as are the men behind this." Margaret thrust the documents at her husband. "Here, read these two items." She pointed to two that were especially galling to her. "They charge that the King's lands in France have been alienated, and they demand that the responsible parties be punished. You know who they consider *the responsible parties*. Why should the *King's lands in France* be of concern to the men of Kent? It is the old plot to discredit me and my friends." She looked at Henry with tears in her eyes. She was trembling and fighting to keep her composure. She had brought troubles down on her husband when she wanted only to help.

Why do the people blame me for problems that began before I was even born? Why, when I want love, do I receive only hate? This wasn't the way I dreamed things would be ...this isn't the way they should be ... something is wrong.

She took up the petition again. "Here, look at this ...*offices have been given to persons of low birth while Lords of the royal blood were put out of the King's presence. Persons of low birth* ...They speak of our friends, yours and mine. How dare they? How dare they?" She shook the paper. "*Lords of the royal blood ... out of the King's presence.* That, Henry, can only refer to York -- unless they mean worse -- to bring up that old lie about Humphrey's death!"

Henry was disturbed by his wife's growing distress. "Do you think maybe we *should* call York back? In such a short time we have lost the counsel of my uncle, the Cardinal, and Suffolk, God assoil them. I feel the need of someone of experience."

--No, not York, who had opposed my friends; who, with his brood, was so popular, who so easily stole the love of the people. No, not York. Henry doesn't realize the danger his cousin poses. I have worked too hard to save Henry from York's influence to

allow his return now. Oh, God, I need help ... but will have to rely on my own common sense ... there is no one to help Henry but me.

"My Lord, I am but a woman, but I would reject this false petition and bid the rebels disband. They are only troublemakers who will disperse at the first show of force. Who are they to send *you* demands? Show them that you are King and demand *they* keep the King's peace. A few troops, a few broken heads if necessary, and you'll see that unruly rabble melt away."

The next day, Henry and the Duke of Buckingham went to Blackheath with the royal troops, determined to defy the insurgents. As Henry rode, his armor catching the sun, the plume on the crest of his helmet waving jauntily, his soldiers close behind him, the people of London cheered him mightily and took heart that their King was now acting like the true son of his father. He, surrounded by loving, shouting subjects, also took heart and for a while, encouraged by the lusty cheers reverberating in his ears, believed that he might prove a powerful prince and warrior, after all. How proud his Margaret would be of him!

At Blackheath they found Cade's band was gone, silently decamped in the night, evidently at last on their way home. Henry sent a small part of his men under the two Stafford cousins of Buckingham to pursue them while he returned to London, if not triumphant, at least relieved he had not had to shed his subjects' blood.

"You were right," he said to Margaret as she helped unbuckle his armor. "A little show of force and they dispersed. This has been a good day. The King's name still has strength in England."

By nightfall, the dreams of the morning and afternoon were shattered. Henry and Margaret looked out of the palace windows on another mob, this time their own troops. By the light of scores of torches and flickering cressets, they could see the upturned sullen faces of their own soldiers, mouthing words they could not make out. Occasionally they heard a shouted curse. Captains rode up and down before the riotous soldiers with oaths and threats, finally forcing them back to their encampment.

While they watched the scene below with bewilderment and growing alarm, Buckingham rushed in, pushing his way past the guards at the door. He was in tears. "Ill news, my Lord!"

"By Saint John, *more?* What now?"

"My cousins, the Staffords, they are slain...most of their company with them."

"But those soldiers out there? What is going on?" asked Margaret.

"My kinsmen pursued the rebels they thought were fleeing. But Cade stopped at Sevenoaks. My cousins were ambushed. Only a handful of their men escaped back to London, and so hotly have they complained of the poor planning that led to their defeat that they have unsettled all the rest. Those men out there are mutinous! We tried to muster them against the rebels ... to avenge the ambush ... but they say they won't be led against their countrymen ... they will not fight them."

Margaret looked out at the royal troops, now in a straggly line, slowly marching away. Would they return? "Mutinous? Is the King in any danger?"

"I don't think so. The people hold him in affectionate loyalty."

"What do they want, then?"

"They say they want the false councilors ..."

"And that means--?"

"Madame, I would not say. But I do know they are crying out especially against Treasurer Say and Sheriff Crowmer."

"Then speedily commit those two to the Tower," Henry ordered. "That may mollify the crowd and keep the men safe. What else do you advise we do?"

"I'm afraid we can only wait and watch. Your soldiers won't move against the Kentish rabble now, but I think if the mob were to pose a threat to you, they would protect you." He hesitated, then added, "Meanwhile, it might help to call York to your Council. They trust the Duke."

Margaret broke in, "His Grace has decided against that, especially since this upstart rising casts doubt upon York's loyalty."

Buckingham looked levelly at her. "My own life speaks my

loyalty to the House of Lancaster, and I would pledge that life and honor on the loyalty of York."

"You speak from love ... your wife and his are sisters."

"Yes, I speak from love ... love of my King and country. I urge you to summon York."

Unafraid for his own life, Henry visited his troops to gauge their temper. He heard muttered threats against his friends and advisors, against his beloved wife. He no longer dreamed of a noble victory; he knew now that he was not -- never would be -- a warrior King like his famous father. He was what God in His infinite wisdom intended, he told himself. He could easily accept it. But Margaret ... till now he had never really believed that his people hated his wife and court. The flatterers and opportunists who surrounded him had kept from him --*protecting the King, they called it* --any criticism of their actions. Now he saw for himself that men on every hand actually reviled Margaret and her adherents. He was profoundly shaken by the revelation. He blamed himself for the Staffords' deaths and he was in a panic lest Margaret, too, be harmed.

Henry's nights were troubled and his dreams filled with bloody apparitions of the slain Adam Moleyns, headless Suffolk, and the murdered Staffords. He feared to go to sleep and prayed long hours until exhaustion overcame him and he fell into a fretful doze, but soon he would wake and call for Margaret. Finally, he determined to retire to Kenilworth Castle in Warwickshire although the Londoners petitioned him to stay in the capital, saying the King's presence protected them.

"I am so worried I scarce know what to do, Margaret told Katherine. "If we go to Kenilworth, Cade and his men will think we are fleeing. I fear it is only the King's name that keeps any semblance of order."

"Then why not stay here?"

"Because of my greater fear that the King is near the breaking point. He hasn't slept the night through for the last fortnight. I am afraid the worries that beset him will undermine his health.

Unspoken by both women was the memory of the mad French King whose blood ran in Henry's veins.

"Weighing both sides," Margaret went on, "I think we ought to go. You have not been to Kenilworth yet; it is a most pleasant seat. Henry lives there almost like a country squire. If anything can help restore his peace of mind and calm his spirit it should be a visit there."

They left their worries behind in London. As soon as Henry was freed of the dreaded decisions he was being called upon to make, he unwound, began to sleep untroubled by nightmares. Lines that were forming on his forehead eased; he seemed to stand straighter and he joked, though rather stiffly, with his attendants. He interested himself in every aspect of the castle. He discussed accounts, talked with tradesmen, chatted with laborers who tended his fields and flocks.

Margaret was pleased to see her husband relax. *..I knew Kenilworth would help him. Might it solve another, greater ...* the greatest problem? She had ripened into mature womanhood. At twenty, she fulfilled the promise of the child bride. She had little trouble beguiling Henry to spend long afternoons riding out with her, followed by sweet evenings of song and tenderness. *...Surely, here, now, in the peace and quiet of Kenilworth we will get an heir.*

The peace and quiet of Midland Warwickshire were not mirrored elsewhere. Insurrection and rebellion were spreading over the country. On the 29th of June, Ayscough, Henry's old confessor, the man who had married them five years before, was dragged from the high altar by his own parishioners, taken to a nearby hill and unshriven, cruelly put to death.

On the very day that Bishop Ayscough was murdered, men of East Anglia and Sussex joined those of Kent and returned to Blackheath with the rebel leader Cade, who was flaunting the armor of the dead Lord Stafford.

On Wednesday, July first, Cade, still calling himself *Mortimer,* advanced to Southwark across the river from London. He threatened to fire London Bridge if he was not admitted to the city. Someone gave him the keys to the gate and Cade and his men thundered over the bridge. When he reached London

Stone he struck it with his sword and proclaimed, "Now is Mortimer lord of this city!"

The rebels demanded the apprehension of Say and Crowmer whom Henry had left in the Tower in ward. Say was dragged before the Mayor and Aldermen to stand trial at the Guildhall. When he demanded a trial by his peers, Cade's men seized him and beheaded him with no more ado. Crowmer, who had slipped away, was cornered at Mile End by a howling mob. His fate was the same as Say's. The two heads were placed on poles and paraded about the city. As the poles were thrust up and down, the grisly heads bobbed. The rebels forced the heads to *kiss each other* while the Londoners shouted curses. Someone in the crowd recalled how they had turned out to greet their new Queen five years before. He reminded them of the festivities and pageants of peace and justice kissing.

"Here's what peace and justice we got, and here's what we'll do to that kind of peace and justice, too." The dead bobbed and kissed once more as the crowd roared with laughter.

CHAPTER ELEVEN

1450 - 1451

Within the month, Henry and Margaret rode back into the city across London Bridge. Henry shuddered and turned his face away from the sight of Jack Cade's head impaled on the bridge, a grisly reminder of the uprising. Margaret also shuddered but she forced herself to look at the blackening features. Traitors must be punished. Let others see and take heed.

Most of the rebels had been more fortunate than Cade. Days of looting had ended with a night of desperate fighting back and forth on the bridge, which the King's men won. The Kentishmen had been granted a general pardon and a promise that Henry would hear their grievances if they would only disperse. And so, shouldering their packs, they trudged home. Nothing had been amended; nothing had been changed, except their bitterness which was intensified.

Cade was attainted and a thousand marks placed on his head. A friendless fugitive, he was taken in a few days by the new Sheriff of Kent.

When word of the insurrection reached York in Ireland, he left his command, and in August landed in Wales. Margaret and her friends in a panic for fear of a new uprising, sent forces to intercept the Duke. He slipped past them and marched toward London with a growing band of followers.

Margaret tried to get Henry to take steps to meet the threat York posed but Henry would take no action. Since his return from Kenilworth he was turning further inward, at times almost divorced from reality. When Margaret urged her husband to use his influence to stop York, he said, "It is with the Lord, my dear."

"But you, my Lord, are the Lord's representative here on earth. You are the one consecrated and anointed in holy Church to lead your people, to command."

"Oh, Margaret, I cannot do it." He raised his hands to his

temples. "I do not know what to do. Whatever I do seems wrong. No, I cannot act against my cousin York for he has committed no offense."

"You will not be acting against him. You will be keeping him from dire sin."

"Sin? What sin?"

"Treason."

"That cannot be. York has always been loyal to us," he said stubbornly.

"But he is coming toward London with a host of armed men."

Henry shook his head. "I should be unworthy of our blessed Jesu's blood if I thought ill of our kinsman York."

She persisted. "What of our friends who are dead -- murdered?"

Henry signed the cross and closed his eyes. "We have no cause to believe he was in any way bound up in that."

"And what of me? It is noised about that York and his party speak against me ... that they intend to have me put by ... for my barrenness and other causes ... to send me back to France."

"Margaret, Margaret." His eyes were wide with apprehension. He pulled her to him and took her in his arms. "That cannot be true, either. No one could be that wicked. You are my wife. You would not leave me, would you? You *could* not." She felt his body tremble as he held her.

She answered solemnly, "Never, if I could help it."

"Swear it," he begged, holding out the cross he wore on a golden chain about his neck. "Swear you will not leave me."

"Nay, nay. Do not fret, my dear." She tried to comfort him and calm his sudden fear. She drew herself gently out of his arms and put hers about him and pulled his head down upon her breast. "I swear it; I shall not leave you."

"On the cross."

She placed her hand on the cross and said, "I swear I shall not leave you, ever, of my own free will."

"She did ..." he faltered.

"She?"

"My mother."

."Oh ..."

What troubles him? How can I make him realize the seriousness of York's threat without increasing his fears? Henry must act to protect his power, yet how can I convince him without disturbing his balance? He needs peace of mind, not pressure. Well, I will do what I can to protect him ... and myself.

To soothe her husband, she assured him once more, "I will never leave you; I swear it."

Later, alone in her own apartment, she pondered their talk, trying to understand his sudden outburst. His mother's departure from court when he was little must have wounded him more than anyone had realized, she decided. Perhaps brooding over it these many years explained some of his moods.

Margaret could not know the plight of the sensitive six-year-old lad, son of a dead hero-father whom he could never hope to equal, abandoned by his widowed mother's withdrawal from court in order to pursue her own life with a new marriage and a new family.

The most famous and powerful knights in the kingdom had charge of the young ruler's upbringing and education. There had been rough discipline and sterile ceremony, but little love and affection. Few knew or cared that the lonely, orphaned boy cried himself to sleep night after night. His mentors were bound up in their own interests, busy seeking power for themselves.

In time, Henry learned to simulate bravery and to hide his tears. His teachers drilled these things into him, but devotion and affection he had miraculously learned from his own heart. Some, starved of love, become incapable of offering it; Henry, starved of love, needing it so much, was incapable of offering anything else.

When Margaret realized that Henry would not take action against York's advance, she begged him at least to call Somerset home from Calais.

"We need his advice; he will help protect us," she urged.

The recall of Somerset showed how little the Queen understood the mood of the people, for to them Somerset represented all that was wrong with the government. Suffolk they blamed for the loss of Maine and Anjou; Normandy's recent loss they blamed on Somerset. Margaret, they coupled with both.

When York arrived in London with his followers, Henry granted him an audience. With a flourish of trumpets, the Duke entered the great chamber with its hangings of cloth-of-gold and rich tapestries, accompanied by his brother-in-law Salisbury, and Salisbury's twenty-two-year old son, Warwick. Henry was seated in the state chair under the royal canopy with Margaret beside him. They were attended by Edmund Beaufort, Duke of Somerset, recently arrived from the French disaster, as well as by Exeter, Kemp, Wayneflete, and many other firm friends.

York, instead of reporting on Ireland, began with a complaint that the King's officers had tried to prevent his return. Henry realized it probably was Margaret's doing. He meekly apologized and said there must have been some mistake. Margaret colored and addressed the Duke.

"Ah, Cousin, we greatly regret any hindrance that was put in your way, but how were we to know it was you who approached the port in the dead of night? We thought you were still in Ireland, carrying out your King's commands. You must have heard that we have been sorely vexed by rebels of late ... some of them even using your name. So, when word reached us that the mighty York was coming, and unannounced, we naturally feared that it was some usurper. Can you blame us?"

"Most gracious Queen, if indeed you thought it was not I, then of course no man would think you to blame."

"Good. We are most happy to see that you have arrived safely in spite of all, though it would have been much less trouble for you had you notified us beforehand."

York bowed deeply. "I thank you, my Lady."

Henry gestured to dismiss the company but York put out his hand and continued, "Now that I am here, your Grace, it is meet for me to take up with you the business of the kingdom. It grieves me, Cousin, to be the bearer of heavy news. There is fresh unrest in the north and west of England, as well as in those counties which gave you so much trouble this summer."

"Un ... unrest? New unrest?" Henry slumped lower in the state chair and began twisting his signet ring.

"In town after town, and throughout the countryside we heard of gatherings of disgruntled commons, and men spoke everywhere against your officers."

"Stirred up, mayhap, by jealous barons?" interjected Somerset from his place beside Margaret.

"Stirred up by their own grievances." York addressed Henry and disdained to look at Somerset.

Salisbury broke in impatiently, "Not the least of which is their complaint that Richard of York has been too long kept away from his rightful place in the King's Council. The people are tired of the country being mismanaged by ... by..." he sputtered and broke off, indicating with an encompassing wave of his hand Somerset and the others standing near Henry and Margaret.

She glanced with growing uneasiness from one baron to another and saw that many agreed with Salisbury. Warwick stared with unveiled hostility at Somerset, and even some of her friends nodded their heads in agreement. Salisbury sounded so reasonable ...*If only I could make them see that York and his party are at the root of the country's troubles. If York had his way he would soon be the true ruler in England, in deed if not in name. As York would rise, Henry would fall. It is unthinkable. Henry is the King; how can I make him act like a King?*

York took a parchment from a squire. "I have here a list of complaints which we pray your Majesty amend."

He was about to read them off when Margaret stopped him. "You have them written out -- fine." She reached for the document and when she had it in her hands she leaned over and spoke urgently and softly in her husband's ear. He listened, his eyebrows raised, and then he nodded and spoke to the assembly.

"As my dear Queen has pointed out, it would be unwise for us to decide anything right now -- in the heat of the moment." He inclined his head toward Salisbury. "We know that you, my Lord, would not wish us to take the advice of but one man, so we shall appoint a Council ... a full Council, to study these complaints and to take steps to remedy them."

Margaret drew a breath of relief and leaned back in her chair. Henry had accepted her suggestion. But suddenly she heard him add, "Besides this, we shall summon a Parliament to convene at Westminster on November sixth next."

It was not at all a good idea to call a Parliament so soon.

"All the Lords shall give their voices in this matter. Let no one say that anyone ever came before Henry of Lancaster with a just request and went away bootless." He stood, satisfied with his plan, smiling benignly as though no one had ever impugned his judgment or justice. "Now, my Lords, you may retire. With God's sweet Grace, we shall meet in November to consider this weighty matter."

"Do you suppose he really believes it ... that no one ever went away bootless?" young Warwick asked his uncle later.

"Maybe; I don't know how his mind works, but I do know the Council idea wasn't his."

"They put him up to it, the Queen and her Somerset," said Salisbury.

"You must admit it was adroit. I've been complaining he's taking too narrow advice so they counter he can't take my advice alone. Wasn't much I could say after that," said York.

"Let him have a *fair* Council, a full one, as he put it, and no one will complain," put in Warwick, "But the council is packed with the Queen's friends right now."

"At least we got him to call a Parliament," said York. "I could tell that it came as a blow to the Queen. If she'd known what he had in mind, she'd never have let him do it for the Commons are with us and she knows it."

All was not unpleasant politics and business. Somerset's return brought a new air of gaiety to the court. So that he might be near Henry to give him ready counsel he moved into the palace with his wife Eleanor, now one of Margaret's ladies-in-waiting, and their children. They, so recently under siege in Normandy, expanded in the free English air. The boys would race shouting through the halls and chambers. Their mother made a half-hearted attempt to calm them but Margaret would smile and say, "Let them be; they remind me of my brothers. I like to hear them laugh. Just so they do not disturb his Highness. I would not advise they take their hounds into the chapel with them again, though. My Lord was wroth."

Henry really enjoyed the boys. Sometimes he would go to the stables with them and they would all go for a quick canter from which he returned refreshed....*Ah, if I just had some sons of my own, I would like them to be like the Beauforts...*

Although Edmund Beaufort, an attractive, likable man in his forties was popular with the Court party, he bore the blame, however unfairly, for the loss of Normandy. Probably not even Henry the Fifth could have held it under the same circumstances. The cheese-paring Parliament had refused to garrison the fortresses adequately. The fortresses themselves had been allowed to fall into disrepair. The crowning blow was the new weaponry. England's famous bowmen were no match for French cannons.

The defeat rankled Somerset no less than his countrymen.

Once, while Margaret was deep in conference with him, they overheard the younger Edmund boasting that had he been given a chance he would have beaten any fifty Frenchmen and made them rue the day they sought to drive the English out. His father, who *had* been given just such a chance and failed it, was embarrassed by his son's boasting.

"A busy tongue bespeaks an idle brain," he snapped.

The fifteen-year-old scowled and moved off with Katherine, Margaret's chief lady, while Margaret said, "Be not too harsh with the lad. Methinks he speaks but to impress Lady Katherine."

"Katherine? Is the wind in that quarter?"

"Do not worry. Her heart lies elsewhere."

"I hope so, for he's at an impressionable age. I know the maiden to be gently raised and winsome, yet he should seek higher. His great, great grandfather wore the crown of England."

"A heavy weight, Edmund Beaufort. A heavy weight." Then in a lighter tone she repeated, "Do not worry about him. He is at an age where he must love someone and she recognizes his affection as puppy love. And although she is young herself, she is wise and good ... she will not hurt him. But as for ambition ... you, my Lord, have a more forward whelp ... one who does seek higher."

"What do you mean?" He was puzzled.

Margaret laughed. "Your young Henry ... he thinks he is in love with England's Queen."

The Duke started in wide-eyed wonder and sputtered ... "But, but ..." Then he leaned back and roared with laughter. "Well, at least he shows good taste. Not only the highest woman in the kingdom ... but ..." Abruptly his tone changed, suddenly grew serious ... "the loveliest."

Margaret lowered her head and then looked up at him. "You are kind to say it. Methinks you and your boys have learned our soft ways of chivalry during your stay in France."

"Nay, Madame. I speak but plain English truth."

Margaret reached out and put her hand on his arm. "I thank you for your friendship. I ... we, Henry and I ... have much need of it these days."

"Madame ... Margaret?..." He took both of her hands in his. "I am a soldier, not schooled in words. Dare I be brave and say what I feel is more than friendship? May I call it ...*love?*"

She smiled tenderly, "You may, dear friend, for I have need of that, too ... from you ... and from your sons ... and from Eleanor, your wife." She pulled gently away from him and quickly left the room.

As soon as Margaret was alone, she put her hands to her cheeks. *They must be blazing.* She had hurried away so that Somerset would not see how shaken she was by his words. She had recently felt a growing tenderness toward him ... more than her words indicated. She was sure that the least encouragement on her part would bring a further declaration of love from him. She wanted to hear it, yet she dared not. She was Henry's wife and would be true to him alone. Anything else was sin.

She was no light coquette to flirt with court gallants. She

was the Queen. During the days she busied herself with her own duties as well as sharing many of Henry's, but at night she had time to dwell on unwelcome thoughts.

What if she was not barren? What if the fault lay with Henry? She blushed to think of it but sometimes her passion was not returned. Henry was deeply loving and considerate but she found herself wishing that he would show more ardor and desire for her. She longed to hear ...what? She did not know. To feel...? She did not know that, either. There must be more to love than she had experienced, but what? She had a vast emptiness that longed to be filled.

What would happen if she took a lover? No ... no... she would not. Might she then bear a child? No, no ... no matter ... she would not. She would keep her wedded vows. She whispered her old motto as a talisman ..."Constancy binds me..." It bound her irrevocably to her husband. She prayed to God to sustain her against temptation. And the child? The desperately wanted child? If she bore one would it save her and Henry? *No, no, the child she bore must be royal ... the King's ... the King to be. She would learn patience from Henry. It would rest with God.*

Other problems were more quickly solved. Soon Somerset had proof that Katherine was indeed no threat to his plans for his son, for the Lady was wed in a splendid ceremony to Lord William Vaux, one of Henry's captains. But the normal joys, loves, flirtations, the petty jealousies and give and take of every day life had to give way. The time for the Parliament session drew near and Margaret and Somerset knew it was deadly serious business. Somerset had taken Suffolk's place in the government. *Pray God he not take it on the block.*

York's adherents raised the question of the succession. There was no sign that Margaret and Henry would have issue, yet no successor had been formally proclaimed. In May, Thomas Yonge, a law apprentice, drew up a petition to be presented to Parliament that York should, because of his noble lineage and direct descent from Edward the Third, be declared Henry's heir apparent.

"Here it is, my Lord," stormed Margaret, shaking a copy of the new petition in Henry's face. "Here it is -- now will you believe that York has his mind set on treason? Why else should he care who is named heir? You are a young man with many years ahead of you."

"God grant it may be so," said Henry, crossing himself as his wife continued, her voice shrill, "Yes, God grant it, but I fear York may look too high. If he wishes you no harm, why, why, I repeat, would he care to be named heir? York is fully ten years older than you. Why then? I'll tell you what I think. Kings have before now been unseated by overweening subjects, that's why!"

Henry drew back from her ferocity. "Yes, yes," he whispered as though to himself. "My own grandfather, whom God rest, supplanted Richard the Second... perhaps we are now reaping the harvest of that sin." He spoke louder, "Oh, that I could withdraw from this evil world. I do not know what to do."

"I can only tell you," said Margaret more gently, "What I think you should do. I am but a woman but I have given this much thought."

"Yes, pray give me your thoughts for you know I have ever found them useful and wise."

"Block this petition, then."

"If only we were to have a child ..." Henry was wistful.

"That is another thing," said Margaret, her eyes flashing. "By bringing up the question of the succession, York ever emphasizes the fact that I am barren. It is a direct affront. I had not thought he could be so hateful."

Nay, my sweet, I am sure that was not his wish."

"Well it seems to be. Henry, for my sake will you deny this petition?" She implored him, "It is so hard to have this ... this shortcoming ... thrown in my face."

He patted her shoulder. "For your sake, I would do anything. Are you sure that is what you truly wish?"

"Truly, my Lord."

Henry was unable to prevent Yonge's petition from being presented to Parliament where it found favor with the Commons, but the Lords sided with Henry and Margaret and denied it. Then, at Somerset's urging, Henry dissolved the session and

Master Yonge, as a warning, was, for his boldness, sent to the Tower.

For six long months, York had worked in every legal way to advance his cause and he was scarcely a whit further than when he had set sail from Ireland. Now he believed that force alone would remedy matters.

CHAPTER TWELVE

1452

In sullen discontent, York retired to his castle at Ludlow while the country seethed with discord. Sporadic outbursts of trouble and fighting broke out across the land.

The Council, remembering how the royal progresses had calmed rebellious hearts in Warwickshire the previous summer, urged the King and Queen to make another progress. So, Henry and Margaret, attended by a train of over two hundred lords and ladies with their servants, set out from the palace at Greenwich to visit the unquiet counties. The spurs of the knights and their ladies jingled gaily while a steady hum arose from the long line as it moved along the road. Men and women called to each other while here and there came a snatch of song from one or another courtier mixed with the shouts of sumpter men to their mules. Near Henry was the drone of his clerics and chaplains who prayed constantly for the well-being of the King and the success of his mission.

As his chief minister, Somerset accompanied Henry. So, too, did James Butler, the Earl of Wiltshire and Ormonde, who had been appointed the King's Treasurer. An Irishman, he had taken an intense dislike to York who had so often sided with his enemies. Butler was a cheerful, prepossessing rapscallion with a nimble tongue and flashing, deep blue eyes that looked with favor upon all the ladies. He rode beside them, one at a time, giving each in turn his full attention, from the oldest dowager to the fourteen-year-old Elizabeth Woodville. They were all half in love with him with his curly, black hair, strongly cleft chin, and outrageously flattering manner. He was reputed to be the handsomest man in the kingdom. The woman with whom he spent the least amount of time was his wife, Elizabeth, but she ignored his wandering for he always went back to her. A few of the women pitied her but more of them envied her. Jamie of

Wiltshire always returned to the warmth of her arms and it was she who bore his heirs. For this, she would put up with much.

On the long, wearing progress, Butler spent many hours regaling Margaret with hilarious tales of his wild Irish countrymen. His brogue grew thicker and thicker and his stories more and more improbable. The Lord of Wiltshire was, Somerset warned her, a professional Irishman and the truth was not in him. But he and Margaret whiled away many an otherwise dull hour. She never dreamed that some in her train might gossip about the time they spent riding beside each other.

The itinerary was planned to take the company into the heart of England to show the King and Queen to their subjects. Henry and all his attendants enjoyed the hospitality of the chief barons of each region who received the entourage with mixed feelings. Paramount was pride that the King had chosen their castle to honor with the royal presence, and hope that a generous ruler would bestow upon the host some worthwhile gift or land to add to his demesne. But in return for this honor was the burden of feeding two hundred men and women with their attendants and mounts, and providing space for each to bed down at night. Great halls and small halls, solars, lofts and corridors: each nook and cranny was filled with chattering lords, ladies, clerics, all of whom brought their own bedding and whose servants vied with each other for the best accommodations for their masters and mistresses. Stables, yards, and surrounding fields were filled with champing horses and mules while stable boys and grooms ran hither and yon with armloads of hay and great wooden or leathern buckets of water. The slopping water and pawing of hundreds of hooves turned the courtyards into seas of mud.

Only the newest castles and manors had anything better than the most primitive facilities, and even these were overtaxed by the tremendous influx of guests. At times, the stench that arose from the wastes of well over two hundred people and their animals was overpowering. When it got too bad they would all move on ... or when the food ran low.

Extra trestles with great planks for tables were set up in dining halls and lords and ladies jostled each other for places near Henry and Margaret at the raised table in the place of honor where they were served by their host and his lady. The less fortunate diners were served at rough tables set up outside under pavilions or canopies. Oxen, sheep, pigs, chickens: enough meat for a month was eaten at each meal, and a year's supply of wine might be poured at a single dinner. Still, the lord was proud to entertain his sovereign, and the less he could afford it, the prouder he might be. Besides, he was sometimes well rewarded by the grateful Henry. And if the crown lands and the King's Treasury began to suffer again, no one was yet complaining. Not even the commons, for did they not share in the glory of the royal progress? The smallest merchant of the town, along with his apprentices and servants, the lowest vassal of a lord, the simple husbandman: all got to see their King just as if they lived in far off London. It was a week, a day, or even only a few moments, but never to be forgotten.

"We saw the King and Queen."

It did not, could not last; next day, next week, or next month, the heavy lives of the common people were seen again for what they were. The King's officers and the county sheriffs still imposed oppressive taxes; party still influenced elections; factions still meted out unequal justice. The rosy glow had been ephemeral; the dark clouds were permanent. Men were, if anything, because of their letdown, unhappier than ever. They had seen the King but nothing had changed. Their murmurings grew louder.

For their part, the nobles were no more satisfied. Bonville still quarreled with Devon; Percies rode once more against Nevilles. Each sought, sometimes with arms, for his own advantage, and Henry was too weak to hold any of them within bounds. The country was being torn asunder.

In Westminster Palace, after the progress, life was much as usual. One afternoon when Margaret and Katherine were sitting alone in the solar, the other ladies having gone into the courtyard to see a traveling mummer's show, Jamie Butler, the Earl of Wiltshire entered with a message for Katherine.

"Lord William bids you come at once to your apartment," he said.

"Did he say why?"

"No, but he said it was important."

"Oh, dear." She rose hastily, clasping to her breast the sewing she had been doing. "Madame?"

"I am sure it is all right," reassured Margaret, "but hurry along."

As soon as Katherine left, the Earl walked over to Margaret's chair.

"I hope nothing is wrong," she said, "nothing serious."

He stood behind her chair and said, "I assure you, there is nothing wrong, but on the other hand, there is something most serious."

She looked over her shoulder at him. "You speak in riddles. I do not understand."

"It is meet I speak in riddles, for love is a riddle."

Margaret was uneasy. She wanted to change the subject. "Pray, sing for me, Jamie, for I have been strangely sad of late and a gay song would cheer me. Use that lute over there."

"Only if I may sit at your feet," he said, bringing over the instrument. He tuned it quickly, plucked softly at the strings, and sang in a low voice:

> Lully, lully, lully, lullay,
> The falcon hath borne my mate away.
>
> He bare him up, he bare him down
> He bare him into an orchard brown.
>
> In that orchard there was an hall
> That was hanged with purple and pall.
>
> And in that hall there was a bed
> It was hanged with gold so red.
>
> And in that bed there lieth a knight
> His woundes bleeding by day and night.

> By that bed's side there kneeleth a maid,
> And she weepeth both night and day.
>
> And by that bedside there standeth a stone:
> Corpus Christi written thereon.

As the last sad note of the lament hung on the air, Margaret asked, "Jamie, do you call that a song to cheer a person?"

"Not really, but my own heart grieves. Do you prefer this?"

> My love is not to be found
> Alas, why is she so?
> And I am so sore bound
> I may not come her to.
> She hath my heart in hold
> Wherever she ride or go --
> With true love a thousand fold.

"Not so sad but not cheerful, either.

"However, it speaks my mind."

Margaret laughed. "All knights claim to be in love with the ladies."

He laid the lute aside. "But I am not *all knights* nor are you the ordinary *ladies.*"

She did not like his tone. "No, I am not and you had best remember -- I am the *Queen.*"

"*Remember?* I cannot forget. I have a constant reminder. I see you and your loveliness day after day. It breaks my heart to see you so close and yet untouchable -- by me." He reached toward her and she backed away.

"Be ware, sirrah, lest you overreach yourself."

"Would you think I overreach myself if I say what is in my heart? That I am a man and you are a woman?"

"A married man and a married woman .. and more ... an honorable knight and a Queen."

He knelt in front of her. "A Queen, yes ... the Queen of my heart who makes my knighthood of naught to me when it comes to love."

"Jamie Butler, were I not familiar with your eternal flattery, I would warn you that you come close to treason against your King."

"The only treason would be if I betrayed the growing love I have for you. I did think you returned it, that I read it in your eyes. Did I mistake you? I thought you showed some affection for me when we rode side by side so many miles together."

"If you thought I had more affection for you than any other of my friends then you did mistake me."

Margaret was flustered. Had she unwittingly given him cause to think she regarded him as anything more than a friend? And what if he truly loved her? She looked at him -- so handsome, so bold and forceful ... if only Henry had some of Butler's qualities ...it would be so easy to melt into this man's strong arms ...

She was upset that her body was betraying her. She defended herself, "If you thought you saw anything more than friendship in my eyes you were mistaken."

He rose and pulled her to him, his lips upon her golden hair. "Oh, Margaret, I'm talking life -- the life you owe yourself. I've seen some of the light go from your eyes. I've seen worry replace your laughter. I want to re-awaken that love of life you had when you came to England. Margaret, you need to live!"

For a moment, she stood trembling within his arms, her body hungry. *No, no, no. This was not what she wanted. She was the Queen; she could not be weak.* She whispered, "It cannot be." Then, in a firmer voice, "Henry is my wedded lord."

"A fine husband for a passionate woman!"

At his scornful tone, Margaret pulled away, "Be that as it may, he is my dear lord and I am his alone. I swore it. And were it not for the love I bear your wife, you would rue this day. For her sake, I shall put your rash words from my mind."

He made a mock bow and smiled. "Pray, do not do that. Rather let the memory of my love keep you company when the King forsakes your bed for his chapel."

Margaret was about to make a sharp rejoinder when she caught sight of two of her ladies standing in the doorway. How long had they been there she wondered as she abruptly dismissed the Earl who went off whistling.

CHAPTER THIRTEEN

1452

During the summer, while Margaret and Henry were gathering golden opinions among the commoners and nobles of Southeastern England and the Midlands, York sent out letters to the discontented, asking for support.

By January 1452 he had gathered a small army. He sent another letter, this time to the King, blaming Somerset for the loss of Guienne as well as for the unrest in England. Then he set out for London.

"How will you answer this boldness?" asked Margaret.

"I am not sure. It depends upon York. I think I must hear him."

"But those are all lies."

"Mayhap not lies ... York is an honorable man ... it may just be a misunderstanding."

"No, Henry. Not mere misunderstanding, but lies."

"I will still hear him. I owe him that."

"Messengers say he comes with an army. Somerset wants to protect us. He can lead your forces."

"No. If York comes armed I will meet him myself with my men and I will hear him."

Henry, with his forces, moved to Coventry to intercept York. The King sent messages to York, ordering the Duke to meet him there but the Duke turned south, straight for London.

York had miscalculated. The gates of London were closed against him. Next, he moved toward Kent where he hoped to gather the men who had followed Jack Cade. There, too, he was unlucky for the people were tired and the time was not yet ripe for another rebellion.

Henry and his troops waited at Blackheath, blocking York's way back to the Welsh marches. York prepared to fight his way out of the trap while his friends, Salisbury and Warwick, along with the Bishops of Ely and Winchester, argued for a compromise.

"Brother, we've had enough of foreign wars," said Salisbury. "We don't need to start a war here at home. It would destroy England."

"No one wants to start a war. If Henry would only get rid of Somerset. He is the one who is destroying England with his greed and self-serving advice. Let Henry get rid of this upstart Beaufort and I'll be glad to send my troops home."

Warwick spoke, "The King knows how you feel about the Duke."

"How could he not? I've sent him enough messages."

Warwick continued, "The King will not banish his counselor on unproven charges --"

"Unproven? His guilt is as plain as --"

Warwick broke in again. "Unproven as yet -- but the King promises to put Somerset into ward to answer such articles as you lay unto his charge."

"Meaning?"

"As we see it, this means that Somerset will be arrested and tried for his part in the loss of Normandy. Nothing can -- *or should be* -- done without a trial."

"Would you be satisfied with that?" asked Salisbury. "Also, you must pledge that you mean no harm to Henry."

"God, He knows that I am faithful to my Lord the King. It is only Som... Satisfied? With the King's word I must be satisfied."

With that, the Duke of York reluctantly sent his army home and readied himself to meet his royal cousin in peace.

York sent a message to Henry at Blackheath, informing his liege lord that he was willing to repledge his faith to his King in acceptance of Henry's pledge in turn that Somerset would be held until he answered the many charges against him.

To show his good faith, York dismissed all but his squires of the body. He went, unarmored and unarmed. He dismounted and walked the final yards, slogging through the mire and fighting the bitter March wind, to the tent marked by the royal standard.

Escorted into the King's tent, York made his obeisance.

Henry's greeting was cold. "We cannot understand why you have come in arms against us. Long ago you swore fealty to us and we have ever tried to be a good lord to you. It ill becomes you to disturb our peace." Though Henry's words were stern, when he sat back in his chair he seemed to be more nervous than ever, twisting his ring and glancing over his shoulder.

"I am sorry to trouble you, my liege," said York. "But my complaints -- valid complaints -- seem always to fall on deaf ears. Somerset is a traitor which you will discover when he is examined. He sacrifices your interests and England's in order to raise himself up --"

He was startled when Somerset stepped out from where he had been waiting behind a hanging.

"Foul, foul!" exploded York who had been betrayed. Henry would not look at him but stared at the ground.

"Foul or not, you are under arrest for disturbing the King's peace," said Somerset.

York had no choice but to ride to London as a prisoner before a victorious but troubled Henry.

When Margaret heard how York had been tricked, she said to Katherine, "I don't understand. It's not like Henry. Perhaps he never really gave his word ... if he did it was only to keep from fighting York. This constant unrest troubles Henry so ... I do not know how to help him. And Somerset is as much at fault as York.

Were the two Dukes jealous of each other, never saying it aloud, but each of them, however unlikely, eyeing the crown? Both were descended from Edward the Third, both were cousins of the King. True, Somerset was descended from the Beaufort bastard line, but they had been legitimated. The two men were ever at each other's throat.

"I am sick of their eternal quarrel. Sometimes I think we -- and the country -- would be better off if Henry just let York have his way. But then I think how Somerset has always been my friend, and I dearly love his wife. I have so few friends in

England." She burst into tears. "I wanted people to love me ... but they don't. Nothing is the way I thought it would be."

Katherine drew Margaret into her arms to comfort her. "Madame, you have many friends -- the people who know you, love you -- and his Majesty adores you."

Margaret blew her nose and wiped away her tears. "I'm sorry to be so silly. I'm all right now. It's just that I am so tired."

A captive York was a greater problem than a York outside the gates of London. Henry, Somerset, Buckingham, Exeter, and the Bishop of Ely, with Margaret, met in Council to decide what to do about the Duke.

Somerset appealed to Henry. "Now that York has shown his hand by coming against you and bringing his army to the gates of London, will you finally agree that he has treason in his heart?"

Margaret watched her husband's reaction. Whenever she had broached this subject he had refused to listen, dismissing it with "Oh, Margaret, that can't be."

This time he took up York's excuse. "He says his only quarrel was ... is... with Somerset. He insists he is loyal to me in every way."

Margaret thought she detected a note of doubt in Henry's voice.

Somerset started to object but she silenced him with a gesture. "A strange way to show loyalty," she said. "If York was loyal why did he try to raise the men of Kent again?"

"Yes, remember their *Mortimer*," put in Somerset who couldn't keep quiet.

The Bishop leaped to York's defense. "The Duke had nothing to do with that."

"Perhaps," muttered Somerset.

"Besides, he was in Ireland," continued the Bishop.

"And where did Cade come from?"

"We're not getting anywhere this way," observed Buckingham. "We have Duke Richard in ward. He maintains that Somerset should be arrested for the loss of Normandy -- and for other matters."

For other matters? What other matters? Katherine told me that there are rumors that Somerset is too friendly, whatever that means. They rumored the same about Suffolk. Is my friendship to prove deadly?

Somerset's voice broke into her thoughts. "And I maintain that York should be made to confess his treason. He aims not only for my life but for Henry's as well. Let us take care of him once and for all."

"No!" Henry was adamant. "I was already forsworn in the matter of my promise to imprison you. That I shall not do but neither will I punish York."

"I agree," said Exeter. "There is no evidence that he intended to unseat the King. Besides, York is popular with the people. To be practical, we dare not stir them up. They very properly barred his entry into the city but to be plain, I don't think they'd stand for his murder."

"It isn't murder when you punish a traitor," retorted Somerset.

Buckingham spoke again. "May I suggest a course of action? We cannot mediate what looks to be a personal quarrel between York and Somerset -- yes, Edmund, there's too much personality in this -- but we can put up a block between York and any ambitions he *may* have."

"That course is ...?"

"To -- as he may think -- save his life, give him the option to take a public oath never again to appear in arms against his sovereign, but to be his faithful and obedient servant through life."

"Good, good." Henry was pleased with the course which would avoid spilling any subject's blood. "If he takes such an oath it will prove his loyalty."

"And if he doesn't keep it?"

"York has ever been an upright citizen and loyal subject. I have every faith in any oath he may give."

York duly took his oath in St. Paul's Cathedral in the presence of the King, the Bishop of Winchester, and most of the nobility. Afterwards he was released, free to return to his castle at Ludlow, leaving his sworn enemy in high favor at court.

CHAPTER FOURTEEN

1453

Katherine held a basin while Margaret retched. "I feel awful."

"Here, let me bathe your forehead. Try a sip of water."

"Oh, no. Last time I tried to drink a little it came right back up." She sat back and drew a deep breath. "I'm sure I'll feel better later on. Remember -- I felt so bad yesterday that I didn't go to Mass and Henry was cross. He thought I should have gone anyway. He was very unlike himself and scolded me. He said I didn't *look* sick - I'd stopped throwing up by then - and now, here I am, sick again. I wonder what's the matter with me?"

"I can venture to guess."

"Maybe I ate something bad." The meats were highly spiced to cover the taste of spoilage and stomach upsets were not unusual. However, Margaret's constitution was strong. Henry was the one to feel queasy after meals.

Katherine shook her head. "I don't think it was the food. No one else is sick."

"You say you can guess. What is it, then, Madame Doctor?" She stopped suddenly, a look of fear in her eyes. "Do you suppose someone is poisoning me?"

"Of course not. If I am right, it won't take a doctor to see what's wrong." She smiled. "How long since you have bled?"

"I haven't --" Margaret broke off. "Do you suppose? Could I?"

"Why not? Isn't that what you want? What you have prayed for?"

"Oh yes, yes, yes!" She burst into tears. She took the cloth from Katherine and wiped the tears away. "I hardly ever cry; why do I cry now?"

"For joy," answered Katherine, a tear on her own cheek.

Margaret figured. "It's February. I think I have missed only one month. I've quit paying attention because after eight years I thought I must be barren." She laughed and cried together. Then she sobered. "I must be practical. Something could happen. If I tell Henry and I'm wrong, it would be too cruel. Let us keep this secret another month."

Before another month passed, Margaret was sure. She had stopped being sick. Her waist was as slender as ever but her breasts were fuller and also tender.

Katherine agreed, "There is no doubt you are with child. Can you not just be happy now instead of sad as you have been these past weeks?"

Margaret had received word of her mother's death on the heels of her pregnancy. "How I wish I could have shared the news with Mother. It's just not fair. Her letters always sounded cheerful - and hopeful - but I know she must have been disappointed that I had no children. Every woman wants grandchildren."

"Your sister and your brothers have children."

Margaret began to cry again. "But I didn't. I failed her."

"You failed no one. You are going to have a child and your Lady Mother knows it now." Katherine crossed herself.

"Yes, but somehow it doesn't seem enough. It's not fair."

When she said that she seemed to see her mother and remembered her words, *No one ever promised you that life would be fair.*

To take her friend's mind off her sorrow, sensible, practical Katherine asked, "When are you going to tell the King your good news? I think several of your ladies suspect something. You do not want him to be the last to know."

When Margaret went to Henry's chamber, his page said that the King was at prayer.

"Don't disturb him. I'll wait until he is through." Henry was usually happy to see Margaret and indeed was glad enough to put by government business but recently he had been short with her if she interrupted him at prayer. He explained that his wife had precedence over court and council matters, but no one and nothing came before God.

Now that she had decided to tell Henry of her pregnancy she was impatient to share the news she had kept from him until she was sure. In truth, she was not just puzzled by what she thought of as her husband's excessive piety, she was jealous of it. She knew she was attractive. The young knights - and even some of the older ones - followed her with approving eyes. She had but to suggest she wanted something and several gentlemen were ready to spring to her aid. Had she wished, she could have had any number of lovers who would be far more attentive than Henry.

She was, at twenty-three, a mature, desirable woman, yet she had to coax her husband to visit her bed. He would rather be in his chapel.

She had come from a court where warm, affectionate banter was *de rigueur*, where every knight had his lady love. She had had to reconcile herself to the cold, English manners. She never flirted for she sensed that that way lay danger. But why was her husband so reserved, even with her? Lately, too, she felt he was drawing further apart, further inward. *Perhaps my news will change it all.*

Henry rose from his knees and came out to greet her. "Yes, my dear?"

"Remember when you gave me a surprise gift?"

"A gift? Is there something you want? You have only to say."

"No, no. I have a gift for you. A surprise."

Margaret had thought to tease Henry, to draw out her pleasure in her news but his lack of interest in receiving gifts made teasing impossible. Instead, she curtsied deeply before him.

"My Lord, I am going to give you an heir."

"I don't understand. Is there some new claimant?"

"No, Henry. I am going to have a child. *We* are going to have a child."

"A child? We are going to have a child?" he repeated, unable to take it in.

"Yes, my lord husband. I am pregnant!"

"After eight years?"

"Aren't you glad?" She faltered. *What is the matter?*

Henry shook his head as if to clear away a spider web. Then he reached out and pulled Margaret to her feet. "Oh, my love, of course I am glad. It is the answer to so many of my prayers. It is a miracle."

He drew her to him and then held her away, looking into her eyes. "Are you sure? Have you consulted Master Francis?"

"Yes, I am sure and no, I have not talked to Master Francis."

"Are you all right? Shouldn't you sit down?"

She laughed. "Yes, I am all right and no, I needn't sit down." It was clear that Henry's knowledge about pregnant women was as limited as the rest of his knowledge of women. She was afraid he was going to treat her like a fragile goblet. However, she was glad to have his protection and loving concern. Perhaps this would be the making of him.

"When is the babe to be born?"

"Not until October if I have reckoned right. We will have months to prepare for the Prince."

"The Prince? You can tell?"

"No, dear, but I am sure I am carrying a Prince, the answer to my own prayers." She had thought about this ever since she learned she was pregnant. *I will have a boy, an heir, and York can stay in his castle. And if I should have a girl it will at least show I am not barren and next time it will be a boy.*

Her happiness was short-lived. When she entered a room conversations stopped. She became aware that some of the lords and ladies whom she thought of as her friends looked askance at her even while they mouthed congratulations at her good news.

"What's going on?" she asked Katherine. "Am I imagining it or are some of the household turning away from me?"

"I don't think it's your imagination. They don't talk to me the way they used to -- although they've always been a little distant, envious probably, because of our friendship - and because I'm French.

"No one tells me this directly, and I don't like to tell you at all, but I have heard that there is gossip that the King is not the father -- or even that you are not pregnant, at all."

"Those rumors always start when a Queen is expecting. There is something more here; some of the women are too bold. What can they have heard that makes them so?"

Margaret went to Anne, Duchess of Buckingham, a kind,

motherly woman whom she trusted. The Duke had always been a friend to the King and Queen. The Duchess was sister to Cecily Neville, as was the Duchess of Northumberland. *Those girls certainly married well*, thought Margaret. "Please speak frankly. I am going to have great need of friends when my child - my son - is born. Indeed, I have need now..." She searched for words. "I sense something is wrong."

"Wrong?"

"I thought everyone - at least my friends -would be joyful at our news but I see them - maybe not exactly turn away from me, but they avoid me. Why? Do you know?"

The Duchess frowned and looked off into the distance as she, too, sought for words.

"Well, your Grace," she began and then faltered. She took a deep breath and went on. There was no help for it. She owed it to this young woman to tell her what she had heard and what others said they had heard. She squared her shoulders and continued, "The Duke congratulated his Highness on hearing the news and then the King said, "The Queen's pregnancy must be due to the Holy Ghost."

Margaret gasped. "My Lord disavowed the babe?" The blood drained from her face and she swayed until the Duchess steadied her.

"I don't think he meant to. Perhaps he was just confused."

"That explains it. Jesu, what can I do? She shook her head. "It's not true. I have been faithful." The tears rolled down her face and the salt they carried to her lips was mixed with bitterness and fear.

An adulterous Queen could be put to death or mewed up in a prison or convent. The child could be taken from her.

When she regained her composure, she sought her husband.

He was, as so often, at prayer. This time she did not wait but pulled him from his knees and held him at arm's length. He looked at her, alarmed at her red rimmed eyes and tear streaked face.

"What is it? What has happened?"

Margaret began to cry again, so hard he could scarcely understand her.

"The babe -- you --"

He grasped her shoulders. "Is something the matter with the babe?"

"No, no, but they say you said -- *mon Dieu* -- they say -- you --. The say you said you aren't his father!"

"What are you talking about? Who says?" In unaccustomed anger, he repeated, "Who says? I'll have their heads!"

Reassured by Henry's reaction, Margaret calmed down a little. "Didn't you say the Holy Ghost must have been the father?"

"The Holy Ghost, the father?" Puzzled, he pondered. The words were familiar. "I may have said your pregnancy was due to the Holy Ghost."

"See -- you did say it!" She wept.

Henry drew her to him. "My dear -- my Daisy -- all I meant was that my prayers to the Holy Ghost had been answered." It was his turn to shake his head. "To think that a grateful thanks to God and his miracles should be so misconstrued by wicked people! You see how silly you were ... I hope this upset won't hurt the child --*our* child. Now you must go and rest. I'll send your ladies to you."

Margaret's smile at her husband was wan as she withdrew. She was safe -- and so was her child -- but she feared that Henry's innocent remark had not only been misconstrued by her but by others as well. It would be spread by her enemies. How they would revel in it.

And so it was. For those who wondered who stood in for the Holy Ghost there was Somerset; too bad Suffolk was long dead; Jamie Butler; or any other of Margaret's admirers. The harm was done.

CHAPTER FIFTEEN

1453

Westminster had become hateful to Margaret. Her pregnancy, which should have been a time of happiness, brought only rumor and scandal. As she moved through the palace, she heard whispers which stopped when she entered a room. She heard muffled laughter when she left.

If Katherine had not heard these too, Margaret would have thought she was imagining slights. She hesitated to tell Henry because he was troubled enough by the loss of more French territory, as well as more wrangling in the north.

He was also upset by word that Constantinople had fallen to the Turks. That old, old dream of rescuing the Holy Land from the infidels was just that -- a dream. Neither his father nor his grandfather before him had lived long enough to go on a Crusade and now he realized he wouldn't either. Margaret told him it didn't matter, that he did other good deeds. But it was a disappointment, one more thing in the world gone wrong.

In summer, Margaret begged Henry to move to the royal hunting lodge at Clarendon. They would live a simple life there -- something Henry always preferred - and they would have a limited staff, leaving behind the men and women Margaret believed had become spies.

Life at Clarendon was pleasant and peaceful away from London and Westminster with its calls for business and onerous formality. Though he was still troubled, the King enjoyed hunting and Margaret, no longer riding, enjoyed long walks and picnics with her few ladies.

The peace of one such picnic -- her last -- was shattered when the head forester rode up with the appalling news that the King had fallen ill and had been taken back to the lodge.

"What happened? Has the King had an accident? Is he all right?"

"No accident, your Grace. We were riding along -- his

Majesty was saying we should cut some trees -- and then he sort of sagged. He looked ... I don't know ... as if he had a fright ... but I didn't see anything it could have been. I asked his Worship what was the matter but he didn't answer. He would have fallen off his mount if I hadn't caught him ... but he wouldn't talk to me ... or anyone. He's in the lodge now and his squire said I should get you."

When Margaret reached the lodge she met Master John Faceby, Henry's physician, outside the King's chamber. He was nervously plucking at the front of his gown. Margaret brushed past him to go to her husband. He lay on the bed, unmoving, unwitting.

"Henry, Henry, what ails you? Speak to me -- what is it, what is the matter. Henry, look at me."

He neither answered or even turned his gaze on her but lay motionless, his eyes empty.

The King's attendants stood in a frightened huddle. Margaret was stunned. What was the matter? What should she do? She must think ... but she couldn't. The shock was too great. She'd think of something ... later. For now, she said, "Take off the King's shoes, loosen his clothes. No, take them off and put his night clothes on ...or, bathe him first ...make him comfortable ... give him a sip of wine..." She turned to the doctor who had followed her into the room. What is the matter with the King? What can we do for him?"

"Your Grace, I believe the humors have gone to his head. The rush of them has overwhelmed his wit." Faceby stopped his twisting, grasped the edges of his cloak in each hand and assumed a solemn look. "I have certain skills. With my care I am sure he will soon mend."

It was not to be. Despite potions, pills, embrocations, cupping, baths, poultices, and fomentation's, Henry remained in a semi-catatonic state.

Margaret knew that if Henry did not recover soon a Grand Council would have to be called. They would be sure to appoint a regent and York was the logical choice. She held a slim hope that she might be appointed but she realized that was unlikely. At any rate, for the present she was determined to keep the state of his health as private as possible.

She prayed he would recover before she was brought to bed.

Of course the King's condition could not be kept secret. Clarendon was not that far from London. She decided that she and Henry would be better off at Westminster, especially after the birth of their child. Early in October, Henry was carefully and slowly moved back to the palace. Master Faceby, whose treatment of Henry was as useless as ever, accompanied his royal patient. The doctor's only professional help for the Queen was to procure a midwife for her approaching confinement.

Margaret had six weeks since Henry fell ill to worry about her situation. She would be helpless during the birth and for some time afterwards. Worse -- her child would be even more helpless. What if some enemy of Lancaster (she would not name the one she had come to fear the most) injured the child or stole him?

Whom could she trust? What might someone not do for a reward -- or for power?

Katherine tried to calm Margaret's fears. "Your Grace, your ladies love you. You have no cause to fear any of them." Margaret was adamant. "My Lord cannot help me now. I must rely only on you and a very few, very closest friends. I would rather not even have the midwife but I suppose I must."

She had no choice but to have witnesses at her lying-in. Not just friends, but women of impeccable character, women of noble birth who could verify that her child was her child, out of her body and not an impostor. These ladies, though, she said, must not be allowed to touch her newborn. They could gossip all they wished, say she was unbalanced; perhaps that she feared in her pains she might blurt out things better kept hidden -- the true father, perhaps--. Be that as it may, she would not have them close enough to endanger her child, her son she was about to bear.

When Margaret's labor began, the midwife was aroused from her sleep in a nearby chamber, and Eleanor, the Duchess of Somerset was summoned. The midwife, a cheerful, apple-cheeked, round little woman, bustled about the room, making a great show of untying any knots she could find. Despite the freezing December weather, she threw open the windows. "Nothing closed," she insisted.

As Margaret's ladies answered her summons and gathered at the end of the room, the midwife cautioned them, "No knots ... untie any sashes ... no knots." She gathered several ewers of water and of wine, and unrolled a large bolt of soft cloth and laid by some cording. "I have scissors in the hall, but nothing sharp in here ...not now."

She spoke to Margaret, "Mother Nan is here now so don't you worry about a thing. I've brought over a hundred babies into the world. Master Faceby -- he knows me and he knows me work. He says to me, 'Mother Nan, you're the best.' My ladies, they know me well, the ones I've delivered -- some five and six times. You can ask any of them."

Margaret merely nodded as a griping pain hit her. When it passed, she said, "Nan, yes, you're here because Master Faceby said you know your work and your mothers like you. I want to like you, too, but I warn you, if anything happens to my babe and I live to know it, you can look to your head."

Poor Mother Nan blenched. Many of her ladies had cried out strange things and uttered oaths ... who would have thought they knew such words? Some even cursed their husbands ... but none had ever threatened her...

I've heard tales about you but I thought that was all they were -- tales. Now I'm not so sure. I did think this birthing would set me up -- 'tisn't everyone called in to deliver a Queen. Master Faceby will hear from me!

The midwife continued her work, supporting Margaret on one side with the Duchess of Somerset or Katherine on the other, walking her up and down the room and lowering her into the birthing chair from time to time. She wiped sweat from her patient's face and when she saw the pains were closer together and so bad that Margaret cried out despite herself, Nan forgot her fear and said, "There, there, sweeting,, it's Eve's curse but God in His mercy has given us help." She pulled a small vial from a pocket in her kirtle. "I'll just put a few drops of henbane on your tongue and you'll almost forget the pain."

Margaret pulled herself up from the chair and knocked the vial from the midwife's hand. "No, no," she raged. "I must be aware. I must protect my son. I tell you, I would bear ten times this pain to have this child."

Margaret, at twenty-four, was in good health and luckily for her and for Mother Nan, the birth was uncomplicated.

The midwife, who received a fat bag of gold coins, was happy to hurry from the palace while her exhausted patient finally rested peacefully with a healthy son.

Margaret named him Edward for he had been born on Saint Edward the Confessor's Day. She also wanted to call the country's attention to the fact that he was in the direct line of descent from Edward the Third who had ruled England for fifty years. She was determined that her son be acknowledged rightful heir to the throne.

William Wayneflete, the Bishop of Winchester, and a friend of Henry's, christened little Edward in Westminster Abbey with great solemnity but little cheer. The Prince's godparents were Kemp, Archbishop of Canterbury; Somerset; and the Duchess of Buckingham. The font was arrayed in cloth of gold. After the squalling baby's immersion, he was received in a king's mantle of velvet, richly embroidered with pearls and precious stones, and lined with fine white linen to keep the brocade and gems from rubbing against his delicate skin.

Henry was still ill; Margaret did her best to emphasize her position as Queen and mother of the heir. For her churching a writ of summons under the Privy Seal commanded the attendance of the ladies of highest rank in the nation to attend at the Palace of Westminster. Ten duchesses, eight countesses, one viscountess, and sixteen baronesses witnessed the event. Margaret's churching robe was adorned with five hundred and forty brown sable backs.

With gathering strength, she moved Henry and three-month old Edward to Windsor where they had more privacy than at Westminster. She hoped the quiet there would hasten the King's recovery.

In January, Buckingham made an extra effort to get Henry to recognize his son. The Duke took Edward in his arms and beseeched the King to bless the baby. When Henry would not even look up, Buckingham shook his head and admitted, "It's no use." This had been a last ditch effort before they would have to call a meeting of the Grand Council. The country could not go on without a leader.

"Let me try," said Margaret, taking Edward in her arms. He was crying at being passed from his nurse to the Duke and then to his mother. She pleaded, "My Lord, my dear, this is Edward, your Prince. Look at him -- how fair he is -- your son, whose birth we awaited so long. Please, please, look at him and give him your blessing." Henry remained immobile. Margaret, Buckingham, and even some of the attendants were in tears.

Margaret handed Edward back to his nurse and knelt at her husband's feet. She raised her tear-streaked face. "Henry, my love, speak to me. I need you ... your son needs you. It's Margaret ... it's your Daisy." Henry raised his eyes, glanced over at Edward and then lowered his head again, silent as ever.

Buckingham led Margaret from the room.

There was no help for it but to call a Council. Their first action, as she had feared, was to summon York who was quickly named Protector.

Within a month, Somerset was arrested and his position as Governor of Calais given to Warwick. Exeter, chief Lancastrian in the southwest, was also arrested.

What Margaret had feared had come to pass.

CHAPTER SIXTEEN

1454 - 1455

Margaret paced back and forth in the Queen's chamber, trying to decide what to do next.

"Katherine, it is easy to see what York means to do. I know it was he who put Norfolk up to demanding the impeachment of Somerset."

"But why try to impeach him now for the loss that happened so long ago?"

"Because Henry is disabled and Somerset is now my chief prop. But if York thinks so easily to undercut me, he underestimates me. Where he lops off one supporter, ten more will spring up. I shall gather such an array of nobles about the Prince that no one will again dare impugn my honor nor his descent."

"Oh, Madame --"

Margaret whirled. "Oh, Katherine," she mimicked bitterly. "Do not try to make light of it with easy words. I know what they are saying. Were it but idle, thoughtless chatter, I would gloss over it, too, but I know there is a deadly, vicious plan behind this evil gossip. My lord lies ill ...useless. If the people can be convinced that Edward is not the true Prince, then the way is paved for Richard of York. But while I live, he never shall replace my son." She resumed her pacing.

"Do you think York intends use of arms?" asked Katherine, wondering if her William would be going to war.

"If he does, he will find I am well prepared. There are men aplenty loyal to Henry's house; men who owe him much. Buckingham has ordered two thousand of his device, the Stafford knot, to be made up ready for distribution to his followers. The Lords Clifford, Poynings, and Beaumont are arming their retainers to defend the King. Jamie Butler calls out his Irish kerns. Even sick old Kemp is so alarmed by this move against Somerset that he has commanded his servants to ready themselves for trouble. York and his kinsmen, the high Nevilles, may find more than they bargained for - they have stirred up Northumberland and his wild brood. And the Duke of Exeter comes here today to tell me of his plans."

Only Somerset, sitting in the Tower where his friends on the Council sent him to avoid impeachment, was rallying no men. There he bided his time, waiting for a turn of Fortune's wheel. He had no intention of proving another Suffolk. But while he sat in the Tower, his sons were determined to do all they could to aid their lady, Margaret.

When Exeter arrived, Margaret greeted him warmly. A page took his cloak. Another brought him a flagon of hot mulled wine.

"Thank you," he said to the Queen. "It is beastly cold outside."

"As usual. If I could change but one thing about England, it would be the weather ... but to more serious matters ..."

As Exeter settled himself and sipped his drink, Margaret appraised him. She had long been on friendly terms with the Duke who had been Admiral of England for eight years, almost as long as she had been Queen. She had always felt a slight reserve toward him which he had made no effort to dispel. Many gentlemen of the court used flattery or favors to ingratiate themselves with her. She had watched this one carefully. He seemed aloof from party. He viewed them all with an impartial eye and kept his judgments to himself. *If once he gives his friendship,* she thought, *he will be steadfast, a rock.*

She had need of men like Exeter. She would sound him out.

"Lord Admiral, I am glad you came. I have heard good report of you from Northumberland's son, Egremont."

"I must thank him for that."

"He says that you will uphold King Henry's cause ... and Prince Edward's."

"I will, as I am a loyal knight. I have sworn fealty to his Grace."

"There are many who swear who are later forsworn."

"Not I."

She looked searchingly at him. "Would you uphold the King's family ... even against York?"

His grey eyes were steady. The skin crinkled at the corners and he smiled a thin, lopsided smile. "Especially against York."

"But he is your father-in-law!"

His smile was sardonic. "You know my wife?"

"Not really. She comes seldom to court."

"No, for she is still but fifteen. Our fathers betrothed us twelve years ago. Whatever was in my lord of York's mind then, he looks not with favor upon me now."

"A strange marriage," ventured Margaret.

"It has ever seemed so to me, your Grace. I recently spent some months with my young wife, and she has borne my child. But now I am forbidden her presence. I believe it was Saint Paul who said it is better to marry than burn. I am in the dubious predicament of doing both. I think perhaps my mighty father-in-law begins to think me not good enough for the Lady Anne; yet is my blood as high as his. My great grandam, Joan Plantagenet, was granddaughter to Edward the First."

"Oh, yes, I know about her. I've heard she was supposed to be the most beautiful woman in England."

"The Fair Maid of Kent --"

"Who married Edward, the Black Prince," said Margaret. She looked puzzled, "But their son was Richard ...?"

He laughed. "You've learned your history well, but you forget, she first married Thomas Holland, my grandsire. Had she met the Black Prince first, I might have been a King."

She thought about it seriously. "No ... for then you wouldn't be you."

"That might be all right, too."

Margaret smiled. "I think I like you as you are --"

He made a mock bow. "Simply simple Henry Holland, Duke of Exeter, here to serve my King."

"And Queen, too, I hope; and the royal Prince."

"You may count on me. When I placed my hands within the King's and pledged him fealty for my title and my lands I did it with a whole heart."

"Then let me speak bluntly. I believe I have enough votes in the Council to be decreed Regent until my lord recovers. Will I have your vote, too?"

"With all my heart. But is a vote wise? There are many who will be against it -- some will prefer York and some will not want a woman ... it's not been done in the memory of man."

"Both my mother and grandmother acted as regents when their husbands were away at war."

"Oh, I don't doubt you could do it ... you are capable ... but this is England ..."

"Verily. But it is the only way I can hit on to protect Prince Edward's position." She smiled at him again. "After all, you wouldn't want him to have to say someday, 'I might have been a King.'"

When Exeter left, he had agreed to help. She watched after him a long time, musing ...*a strange man ... I like him.*

Christmas 1454 was kept at Windsor with little festivity for Henry had been ill for over a year and the fourteen-month-old Prince Edward was too young to understand the religious ceremonies. Even so, there was a quiet mood of expectancy in the air, an atmosphere of tension. Henry's physicians, his body servants, and Margaret -- all believed that he was getting better. He still recognized no one and seemed not to know who he, himself, was, but he had begun to feed himself, to answer simple questions, and to pay attention to people as they moved about in his room.

Margaret, who had sat by his bed and chair for so many months, was now advised to leave the King's chamber. The doctors were afraid that her presence might disturb his humors and throw him back deep into his brain fever. The physicians wanted him completely well before they risked upsetting his precarious balance. So Margaret again paced back and forth in the ante-chamber, or played half-heartedly with Edward, hoping, yet scarce daring to hope, that her husband really was mending.

On Monday, the 30th of December, with all the doctors standing near, Margaret led the toddling Edward into his father's room. She had been warned to create no excitement, that Henry was *as a man who wakes after a long dream.* The edges of his mind were still fuzzed by that sleep. He moved slowly, deliberately. Occasionally he passed his hand in front of his face as though to brush away an annoying cobweb. As he repeated the gesture, his sleeve fell back and Margaret was heartsore to see how thin and gaunt his wrist was. But his eyes cleared as he caught sight of her and his son. He smiled and the chamber's wintry gloom lightened.

Half rising, Henry spoke, his voice, so long unused, faltered. He cleared his throat and said, "My dear, they ..." he gestured toward the doctors who stood watching, carefully, clinically. "They tell me I have been ill. They tell me that while I was ill you were safely delivered of a fair boy ... this is ...he?"

Margaret gently pushed Edward forward and sank to the floor on her knees. "Yes, my Lord, this is he, your son, the Prince of Wales."

Edward went closer to his father and looked up at him shyly. Then he ran back to his mother and tugged at her sleeve until she rose. Henry was pleased that the little lad had approached him bravely before running back to Margaret. Truly, he was a valiant boy.

"What have you named him?"

"Edward, my Lord."

Henry raised his hands. "Now thanks be to God. Why just yesterday I sent my almoner with a gift to the shrine of St. Edward. Surely this is a fortunate omen. Edward ... Edward ...a holy name."

"And a kingly one, too," said Margaret. At a nod from the doctors, she ventured closer to her husband, for he was taking all in good part and showed no agitation. "Henry," she asked, "do you remember aught that happened while you were ill?"

"No whit, I fear. I never knew till a day or so ago what was said to me, nor did I know where I was ... I remember we were at Clarendon, though --" He broke off, suddenly anxious, and he bit his lip and passed and repassed his hand over his forehead. Margaret looked desperately at the gaggle of doctors, and Master Faceby, sensing there was something about Clarendon that deeply disturbed Henry, quickly moved forward to say, "Edward, for Saint Edward, for the child was born on Saint Edward's Day ... as you say, your Grace, a glorious omen." A terrible moment when Henry's sanity lay in an unsteady balance was safely passed. Some hideous thing, real, or dreamed, and therefore to the King in his recent state, more real than daily life, was glossed over. In a perilous instant he was snatched back from renewed madness by a doctor unskilled in science, but filled with earnest love.

After the interruption, Henry continued, "Who are the lad's godparents?"

"Cardinal Kemp, my lady Buckingham, and my lord of Somerset," said Margaret.

"I am well pleased. Surely you have wisely chosen those who will help in the spiritual upbringing of our child. We must summon them and bestow upon them some gift to show our appreciation."

"I grieve to tell you, my dear, but the Cardinal has been in his grave these nine months," said Margaret gently.

Henry shook his head in bewilderment and crossed himself. "God assoil the good old man. One of the wisest lords in my country died and I did not know it. How much, how much has happened."

"Yes, we had much need of you. But now everything will be all right -- you are back with us," said Margaret.

"As from a long trip ..." Henry shook his head once more.

"And," she added, "the Duke of Somerset is in the Tower."

Master Faceby moved forward swiftly for Henry showed signs of agitation again. "Forgive us, your Grace, but perhaps his Majesty should rest now. There is so much necessary business, I know, and news of so much import, but for today ... perhaps... enough." He rubbed his hands. "Such good news ... Prince Edward ... his Majesty is healed now ... but tired."

Margaret wanted to say more about Somerset, about York. She had a hundred worries to pour out but Henry was tiring so she merely said, "A small misunderstanding which you will easily clear up. There will be plenty of time for that later, but now it is time for our Prince's nap, and I must take him to his chamber." She laughed. "I have become a regular goodwife and the nurses complain I usurp their duties." She bent down, lifted the little boy and carried him from the room.

As the days went by, the doctors let Margaret spend more and more time with Henry. Although his madness was a thing of the past, she could not help but be saddened at how greatly he had changed. His eyes had taken on a worried, almost frightened look, and his full lips had narrowed, with tiny lines at the corners.

His auburn hair was dull and she could see grey in it although he was only thirty-three. His old, occasional mannerism of twisting his rings or fingering the cross he wore about his neck had increased into an almost constant habit.

Bit by bit, Margaret filled him in on all that had happened while he lay ill. She told him how York had reorganized the government after the Council had made him Protector against her wishes. The Duke had made his brother-in-law Salisbury Chancellor; had put young Warwick on the Council --*no, I won't tell Henry of Warwick's wicked slander of me* --. Slowly, she brought out how York had intervened in the quarrel between the Percies and the Nevilles on the side of his Neville kinsmen; imprisoned Somerset; dismissed Henry Holland, Duke of Exeter, from his post as Admiral and sent him to bloody Pomfret. It was not to be borne -- York was acting as if he were King.

She was careful not to burden Henry with too much at one time for fear he might relapse. She was faced with a dilemma. If Henry was caught up too violently in the struggle between her friends and York it might make him ill again. But because he might become ill, it was imperative that her position be strengthened so that she might control the government if need be to save the crown for Edward.

Except for this worry, the days of Henry's convalescence were happy ones. The royal couple spent long hours together, reading aloud, playing backgammon in which Henry delighted; Margaret singing or best of all, both of them playing with Prince Edward. He was not a shy child and quickly made friends with his father. Henry was supremely happy. He would ride the little boy on his knee or toss him in the air till Edward shrieked with laughter and feigned fright and Margaret would scold that "the child will be too excited to sleep."

During the long months of Henry's madness, he had been

fed in his room. Now, Margaret arranged that most of his meals still be taken there. Except for the visits of his councilors when they dined in state at the high table, Henry and Margaret were served in the King's chamber with few in attendance. It was a peaceful time, and slowly, under his wife's careful guidance, Henry grew stronger and more sure of himself. He learned, equally slowly and carefully, what Margaret thought should be done about the changes York had made.

The Duke had resigned the Protectorship as soon as Henry recovered. Exeter was released from Pomfret with the King's blessing. Somerset was set free from the Tower and the accusation against him of treason quashed when Henry declared that Somerset was a true liegeman to him. In addition, he was given back the title of Captain of Calais which was taken away from Warwick. Fortune's wheel had turned. Somerset was now up, York down.

The three Richards, York, Salisbury, and Warwick, who were systematically excluded from the Council, went home to their northern estates. By the spring of '55, most of York's work as Protector was undone. In May, Margaret was strong enough to call for a Council to "provide for the safety of the King's person against his enemies." When this news reached York at Sandal Castle, he sent out several letters. One went to Salisbury and one to Warwick, bidding them join him for conference. And one went to the Pope, begging him to absolve York of his oath taken at St. Paul's.

CHAPTER SEVENTEEN

May - October 1455

The morning sun was pale as Margaret watched Henry's army march out of London along Watling Street, the old Roman Road. It was a small but glorious force for at its head rode Henry, King of England, accompanied by one quarter of the greatest lords of the land. Peaceful Henry might be, but he was determined to uphold the honor of his house. He didn't care a great deal about his claims in France, but here in England he was King, and determined to brook no traitorous uprising.

When the three Richards marched toward London with a "request" that Henry "deliver such as we will accuse ... and we will not cease for no promise till we have them which have deserved death, or else to die therefore," the usually mild King declared, "I , King Harry, charge and command that no manner of person, of what degree, or state, or condition that ever he be, abide not, but void the field and not be so hardy to make any resistance against me in mine own realm; for I shall know what traitor dare be so bold to raise a people in mine own land. And by the faith that I owe to St. Edward and to the Crown of England, I shall destroy them every mother's son...and for a conclusion, rather than they shall have any Lord here with me at this time, I shall this day, for their sake and in this quarrel myself live or die."

Margaret's heart swelled with pride. *This is the way I dreamed of him!*

No one could compare Henry to his illustrious father but he was no coward. What he saw as his duty, he would do. If that duty required him to meet York's army which outnumbered the royal forces, so be it.

Margaret watched the bright banners which fluttered slightly as the men moved along. First, the royal standard, borne by Sir Philip Wentworth, then the portcullis, ensign of Somerset. These were followed by the Stafford Knot of Buckingham and his son.

149

There was the great Percy of Northumberland; there the handsome Irishman, Jamie Butler, Earl of Wiltshire and Royal Treasurer; there was the wyvern of brave Lord Clifford, hero of many a French battle; Courtenay of Devon, new won to the Lancastrian cause; Sir John Wenlock and Lord Roos, both of whom had been with Suffolk at her betrothal ten years before. There was Sir William Vaux, Katherine's husband, and a score of others of Henry's household.

Margaret's throat tightened and she felt a stir of pride as she watched the long line move on, colorful, bright pennons streaming out behind. The men were the highest in the land - and they were her friends.

Here and there a young, untried knight had trouble curbing a mettlesome horse, and he pranced momentarily out of line while his lady watching him glanced covertly about to see if the others were properly admiring him who would no doubt prove to be the bravest. In contrast, the older, experienced soldiers sat their horses stolidly for they knew that many a weary joint would be galled and fretted from the heavy armor and jouncing before camp was made for the night. As the line passed along, a light drizzle suddenly blew in from the river, making the gay banners wilt and hang limp, and chilling Margaret and her ladies. They went in, chattering, hearts still light, spirits undampened. They would see their gallant men before too long and the tales they would have to tell of brave exploits would make up for the intervening empty nights.

In less than a week, however, Margaret saw a much shaken Henry return to London in defeat. Gone were the arms of Somerset, of Percy, the Stafford knot, the wyvern of the Cliffords. The pennons now bore the white rose and falcon of York and the bear and ragged staff of Nevilles. The King no longer led his army. Instead, he rode with York on his right hand and Salisbury on his left. In front, was young Warwick, bearing the great sword of state.

The Yorkists had clashed with Henry's Lancastrians at St. Albans and smashed them, due, some said, to the military prowess of Earl Warwick.

Dead were Percy of Northumberland and mighty Clifford. Stafford, Buckingham's son, had been shot through the hand with an arrow and was to die in agony from the infection of it. Henry, wounded slightly in the neck by an arrow, had stood in front of the royal tent and stared in horror at the grisly, hacked face of his friend and kinsman, Somerset, who lay dead, sprawled grotesquely, across the street under the gently swinging sign of the Castle Inn. In time, the story was told that the *Witch of Eyre had said, "'ware the Castle."* Had she? or did the teller of the tale believe that the future can be foretold? Royal castle or tavern sign - was Somerset doomed by God? By fate?

Buckingham, an arrow in his face, took refuge in the nearby Abbey. Somerset's son Henry had been so badly wounded that he had been carried from the town in a cart.

"Mon Dieu," Margaret whispered in disbelief when she heard of Somerset's death. "Gone -- all my friends --gone." Suffolk, Uncle Beaufort, old Kemp, and now Somerset. She wept.

Not all the King's men had fought so valiantly. Jamie Butler had fled the battle when it turned against the Lancastrians. When Margaret heard of his flight, she laughed bitterly and exclaimed, "And that is the dastard some dared say shared my bed. God knows he was never lover of mine but at least I had thought better of him than that."

As soon as the rebels reached London with their captive King, York took the title of Constable of England. He made his sister Isabella's husband Treasurer; made Salisbury Chancellor of the Duchy of Lancaster. Warwick took Somerset's old position as Captain of Calais. The grievously wounded young Henry Beaufort, now the Third Duke of Somerset, mended slowly and was committed to the care of Warwick, his father's deadliest enemy.

Henry, who had ridden through the streets of London as a

veritable prisoner, broke down when he was alone with his wife at Westminster.

"Margaret, Margaret, I do not know what happened ... how it could have happened... So much blood ... so much death ... I thought to punish those proud men, but ..."

"Shhh. It's all right --"

"No, not all right; all wrong. I meant to be your *chevalier* ... I failed you. I failed my people ... so many dead ...I failed ... how could it happen...?"

She did her best to comfort him. "You did not fail. You are still King and my *gentil chevalier*. There will be another -- better -- day. The people love you, you know that. But now we must get you well from that wound. Your neck must hurt. Fortune has turned against us for a while but I thank *le Bon Dieu* that York did not slay you along with our friends."

"No. I do not think he meant that ... meant me ... if he did, then ..."

"Hush, now. Everything will be all right. Just get well."

Henry calmed down while Margaret hid her own worries. What had York intended? What next?

Now all could see that Henry was only a figurehead. Though he held the title of King, York held the power. Henry watched with a heavy heart and Margaret with apprehension and growing anger while old friends of Lancaster were won over to the White Rose. What Duke Richard had not won by arms, he gained by policy. He forgave his enemies and allowed all the peers to take seats in the Parliament. Even Buckingham, despite his dead son, in the interests of harmony inclined toward York. Jamie Butler once more disgraced himself in Margaret's eyes; this time by making peace with her enemies.

Wenlock, one of the old marriage embassy, saw which way the wind was blowing and deserted his friends in favor of the Duke. His reward was the speakership of the new Parliament which confirmed all of the appointments made by York and absolved his party from any guilt for St. Albans. Official blame for the battle was placed upon dead Somerset, and Parliament declared that "nothing done there never after this time was to be spoken of." Henry was forced to reaffirm publicly his trust in the loyalty of the three Richards.

Margaret was powerless. Kept from any influence in the affairs of state, she had no place to turn her attention except to her husband. What she saw there was ominous. In July, she took the King and Prince Edward, now almost two years old, to Hertford because her watchful and loving eye saw that the tumultuous and tragic events of the past two months weighed so heavily upon Henry's spirit that he boded fair to have another breakdown.

She could not even share her deep grief over the loss of Somerset, one of her first friends, her loyal, loving knight. Henry was too upset already. She would not add to his distress. Despite all her care, he suffered a second attack in October. It was a good deal less serious than the first one, but once again York was named Protector of the Realm.

York was now up; Lancaster down.

CHAPTER EIGHTEEN

November 1455 - March 1456

Margaret, in the royal castle at Hertford, fretted. Uneasy, she woke early. She rose and dressed quietly, loath to disturb the women who slept in her chamber. Now, despite the cold and damp that rose from the River Lea, she paced the stone flags of the courtyard. The few guards, stable boys, and scullions who saw her marveled that the Queen was up so early, but none dared greet her, not even the churchmen hurrying to chapel, for they could see that she was deep in thought and would probably meet any interruptions with impatience. Her temper and irritability had grown with each succeeding day until even Katherine went in fear of her increasing snappishness.

She who had once been deemed to bring the bright touch of sunny Anjou summer to court was now the embodiment of the chill English fall. Her light laughter had been replaced by a mocking, derisive tone. Her open gaze was shadowed now with suspicion. Her generous mouth, once so ready to smile, was narrowed by pain and disillusionment. Her heart ... how had it not been wounded? She had come to England prepared to love all. In place of affection and loyalty she had found hatred and treachery. York, Cecily, the Nevilles, Wenlock, and even the common people: all whom she had hoped to make friends, were enemies. And those who had dared to give her love? Beaufort, Suffolk, Somerset, Clifford, the Staffords ... dead ... for her sake and for Henry's sake. While she walked about the courtyard, the wind changed and the mist, which had been hovering over the river, rolled over the castle walls and swirled about her like ghosts. Her furred woolen cape did little to keep the chill from her marrow. Still she paced, thinking, thinking --*what of Henry?*

"*P*oor soul," she murmured. Her heart ached for him. He was so good and kind and of such a gentle nature that no one could help but love him. She had loved him more than ten years and would go on doing so as long as they lived. She felt toward him as she did toward their son. He was to be cared for, to be protected. It was not, she thought ruefully, what she had expected. It was not even fair. She smiled her new, thin smile as she remembered her dead mother's words of so long ago, *No one ever promised you that life would be fair* and *What cannot be helped must be endured.* Isabelle had had much wisdom. What would her mother have done in her place? *"Oh, Mother, Mother,"* she prayed, *"What shall I do?"*

Time lay in York's favor. As Protector he held the reins of government. He had the very power of the crown now. If Henry should die, the Duke would never relinquish his hold; Edward would never mount the throne of England.

While Henry lived, he would flicker in and out of sanity as had his French grandfather. Margaret was tied to him by the indissoluble ties of the church and the more demanding ones of affection, but the deep, passionate and unquestioning love which dwelt in her heart and which she so gladly would have lavished on her husband, was now turned toward little Edward, her son and her hope. She vowed ...he *will* be King.

The peace and quiet of Hertford had not saved Henry from a new attack. All that the move had accomplished was to get them out of York's way -- out of public sight. There was little that Margaret could do here; she must be closer to London. As she walked, pondering, the bells sounded for Lauds; and Henry, led by two attendants, shuffled along the path toward the chapel. He smiled as he saw his wife and exclaimed, "You are up betimes. Do come along with us to prayers."

It was one of his "good days" and she determined to take advantage of it. "My Lord, nothing would give me greater pleasure. Afterwards, when we break our fast, I need to speak with you."

Later that day, Henry ordered his chief steward to pack up immediately and move the whole household to the royal palace at Greenwich which lay but a short gallop from London. The unhappy steward, under instructions to keep the royal family at Hertford, under surveillance, had no choice but to obey the King who seemed to be in complete possession of his wits. The beds, the linens, the clothes, tableware, royal furniture, hangings: all were packed and laden onto the horses and mules, and in a few days the household was established at Greenwich.

That winter, half the lords of England, in London for the new Parliament, visited Margaret at Greenwich. In January, she called a meeting of the new young Lancastrian peers. Present was twenty-one-year-old Henry Beaufort, now since his father's death, Third Duke of Somerset. He had only recently been released from the custody of Warwick and bore him great malice. Also there were twenty-year-old John Clifford, and the newly forgiven Jamie Butler, whose wife Elizabeth, one of the Queen's favorites, had pleaded his cause so persuasively that Margaret held her hands, kissed her cheek tenderly and said, "Bess, my dear, you shall have him back. And none shall speak to him of St. Albans."

So, James Butler was back. The King and Queen truly forgave his flight from the battle and his later brief friendship with the Yorkists but his acceptance at court rankled in the heart of many another, especially Clifford and Beaufort whose fathers had been slain at St. Albans. Also summoned to Margaret's meeting were the two Percies, Henry, the new Duke of Northumberland, and Egremont, his younger, more hot-headed brother, both enemies of the Nevilles.

They all met in the audience chamber from which the chill was scarce taken despite a roaring fire in the giant fireplace. Margaret, dressed in a gown of velvet of Lancastrian blue, sat at the head of an oaken table. She opened the discussion. "We must get his Grace away from York's influence, for men say it is the Duke who reigns, that the King is but a puppet."

"Did the Duke not go so heavily guarded, I myself would put him out of all influence," said Clifford, slapping at the hilt of his golden dagger with his open hand.

Young Somerset snorted. "Good for you, then, as well as for him that he does go guarded for the people of London bear him so much love that they would tear you to bits should you harm him."

"By the body of my father, it would be worth it," muttered Clifford.

"In that case," drawled Jamie Butler negligently, "Why don't you go ahead and try it?"

Clifford leaped to his feet while the two Percies hauled him back down. Somerset turned on Butler, "Had you the cause that we have --" he began, but Margaret cut in, "Peace, my lords. Brawling will do us little good. It is not daggers and force that we need -- not now, not yet. It is cool heads and sensible ideas."

The meeting accomplished nothing except to deepen her dejection. She had little faith in the young lords ... they were too brash, too untried. Would they be able to overcome the experienced Yorkist leaders? Would they be able to put by their own special interests and cooperate with each other? Somerset, the Percies, and Clifford ... she feared she could not rely on any of them to put England's interests ahead of their own. Clifford, especially, troubled her. There was a streak of cruelty in him. He was not now, nor ever would be, a *parfit gentil knight*. But those days were gone, if they had ever truly existed. Perhaps war demanded cruelty.

She much preferred Henry's peacefulness but it could not hold the crown. She had no choice but to depend on the young lords if she wished to secure her son's succession.

One of Margaret's other visitors was Henry Holland, Duke of Exeter, who once more sat on the King's Council and again held the title of Admiral of the Sea though there was little love between him and his father-in-law, York. A comfort to Margaret in these gloomy days, he more and more often found his way to Greenwich. Late one afternoon, after a visit with the ailing King, Exeter stopped to talk to Margaret as had become his wont.

"His Grace was right cheerful today," he said.

"I am sure your visit helped. He is always glad to see you. Sometimes he does not comprehend all that goes on about him, but he does respond to love and loyalty ... and I appreciate it... more than you can know. I wish there was some way I could repay you."

"Madame, I seek no repayment ... except equal love."

"That you have -- from both your King and Queen."

Margaret went on. "I know we owe you much ... even the meager funds we receive from the Parliament would not have been allowed us if you had not petitioned them."

"I wish I could do more. If Somerset had only been able to join up with me at Leicester ... or if I could have reached St. Albans ..."

"What's done is done. And by the way, never speak of St. Albans in Henry's hearing. I think it is that, more than anything else that had unhinged his mind this time. We must look to the future now."

They fell silent, each wondering what the future held. The sun had moved from the window and shadows gathered about them. The servants had not yet lit the candles and the only light came from the glowing fireplace. In the distance, the chapel bells rang for vespers.

Exeter reached out his hand and laid it over Margaret's. She looked up but did not move.

"Your Grace..."

"Yes?"

"I want you to know you have my love and sympathy."

"You are kind to say so."

"Nay, not kind --" He broke off and rose abruptly. He turned and faced the dark windows so that she could scarcely hear his words. "I am not used to this sort of thing."

Margaret rose, too, and moved beside him. "What sort of thing?"

"I am a man of honor; I love my King. And yet -- I also love my Queen."

She gave a brittle laugh. "I would that all our subjects loved their Queen."

"Madame, do not toy with me. I think you know what I mean."

She dropped her eyes. "I think I do, but you must not."

"Why not?" he cried. "Why not? You know my marriage is no marriage and you ... I see you, a woman of beauty, love and fire ... yoked to a madman ... Why should I not say what tears at my heart ... that I love you?"

"Hush." She softly touched her fingers to Exeter's lips. "The words, the thoughts, you speak are sinful."

"Are we not taught that we are sinners all?"

When she did not answer, he went on, "And does Christ not love us -- withal we sin?"

Margaret smiled slightly at this. "A clerkly argument. Perhaps you should match wits with my husband when he is well. It is the sort of logic that most interests him."

"That's not fair!"

"My lord, you are not fair to me."

"How not?"

"I am a married woman ..."

"By God, I know that all too well. Tell me," he pressed, "How *not fair?* Be honest."

She trembled, bit her lower lip and said, "Because ..." She could not go on.

"Because you love me?" he insisted.

She nodded her head almost imperceptibly. It was so dark that Exeter could not see the tears that wet her cheeks. "Please go now," she whispered. "We will speak again later."

Sometimes in the lonely nights Margaret pictured Exeter's features with the crinkles at the corners of his eyes, from years at sea, she supposed, and his lopsided smile. Sinful though they might be, his words of love warmed her, made her feel alive, a woman. Surely, she rationalized, as long as she remained faithful to Henry, she did no grave wrong ... but she breathed not a word of her feeling for Exeter, not even to her confessor.

As much as she could, she put thoughts of this impossible love from her. She did not let it intrude on the happy hours she spent with little Edward who was learning to talk and who often sent his mother and her ladies into gales of laughter with his chattering. She spent endless hours, too, with Henry. She and his doctors had the King back on his feet by February and able to appear in person before Parliament to show them that he was well again. They had no choice but to dismiss York from the Protectorship one more. The Duke relinquished his office, but this time he retained his other titles and almost all of the power he had assumed during Henry's last spell of madness.

CHAPTER NINETEEN

May 1456 - March 1458

Especially galling to Margaret was Warwick's growing popularity. Now she had two enemies.

"His overweening pride is insupportable," she complained to Katherine. "I hear that ever and anon he brags of his feats at St. Albans, expressly against orders."

"Can't the King stop him?"

"Henry doesn't know of it and he is so newly recovered I fear to trouble him."

"What good does it do Warwick to boast? Don't you think most people recognize it for what it is -- empty words?"

"If it were only bragging and empty words I wouldn't worry, but he puts false ideas into men's heads. I think he tries to undermine the King -- to advance his Uncle York. If I had proof, Earl Warwick would lose his head, but I have no proof, only reports."

What rankled Margaret most was Warwick's audacious slander of her and her son. She would never forgive him for that. She pondered how to make him pay. If she had her way, she would have his insolent tongue torn from his lying mouth. In the meantime, she had a plan to discomfit the Earl.

Warwick, on his part, to strengthen his position as Captain of Calais, made a tactical visit to Canterbury, Dover, and Sandwich, where he enhanced his popularity with the rough English seamen. He thanked them whole-heartedly for their support in supplying his Calais garrison with provisions, and promised to do his best to make the Channel safe for English shipping. In more than one tavern in Sandwich and Dover, men raised their tankards to the name of Richard of Warwick.

"He's a good un, he is."

"Thanked us, 'e did, just like a regular Kentishman."

"You wouldn't hardly think he was a Lord; you know why? He cares about us, that's why."

"Aye, not like our high and mighty Admiral."

"Admiral --ptah!" the man spat. "Our Admiral Exeter don't hardly see the deck of a ship from one month to the next anymore."

"Up in Lunnon mostly -- with the Queen and her other minions."

"What do they know of the cares of a simple sailor?"

"But Warwick -- high as any man in the kingdom, yet he comes here, right down on the docks, afoot, to talk to us. He's a good un, a real good un."

It was the early fall of 1457. Margaret and Henry were staying at Coventry, in the heart of the royalist midlands. York had been reappointed Lord Lieutenant of Ireland but he had refused to go. He would not be shunted aside again. Margaret was pondering this troubling development when Henry of Somerset galloped into Coventry on a horse cruelly winded. The young Duke had pushed on day and night to bring the news. When he came into the Queen's presence, his doublet was begrimed and his face was streaked where great drops of sweat had rolled down across a coating of dust. When he took off his cap his damp hair clung to his head. After a hurried bow he said, "I came as quickly as I could when I heard the news. Privateers have attacked and looted Sandwich."

"Rest yourself a few moments, Duke Henry," said Margaret. She told a page to bring some wine for the exhausted man and called for another to bring a ewer and basin so that he might wash. "Naturally I am interested, but I do not quite see what is so urgent that you come in such haste -- and like this."

"They were French privateers," he explained.

"Well?"

"Under the leadership of your old friend, Pierre deBreze."

"DeBreze?" she asked incredulously. "Sandwich?"

"Yes. Breze. And Sandwich ... not Calais."

"Hush," she cautioned. "I must hear more of this, but first wash and slake your thirst."

He did so while the Queen dismissed the servants. She and

Somerset moved to an oriel where her ladies could not overhear their low voices.

"I cannot understand what happened," she said. "It was not at all what --" she broke off.

"No, but as far as we can tell from the scattered reports we've received, Breze, with a fleet, tried to catch up with Warwick at Calais but somehow missed him. Then the Frenchman decided that he might damage Warwick by hitting at his supply lines, so they landed at Sandwich."

"Are you sure it was Breze? Do the men of Kent know that it was?"

"Yes, Madame. The Seneschal of Anjou and Normandy is well enough known so there is no doubt. And the Kentishmen know that he has long been a friend of yours. Wenlock has been spreading the word that Breze was instrumental in arranging your marriage. They are saying that the raid is our fault, that you ... we ... are hand in glove with Breze and his master, the French King."

"Fools!" she exclaimed hotly, beating her clenched fists against her sides.

"Who? The French or the Kentishmen?"

"We," replied Margaret. "Never, never did I dream if Pierre could not close with Warwick that he would attack an English port. How could he have thought that this would help me in any way? I had thought him a better friend to me than that."

"Perhaps his men got out of hand. They probably were all keyed up for plunder. There is a report, too, that some of his ships broke away and raided Fowey in Cornwall on their way home."

"Oh, no!" she cried in disbelief. "Not Cornwall ... it has always been friendly to us. Prince Edward bears the title of Duke of Cornwall. Where was the Lord Admiral when these raids were made?"

"No one knows. I rather imagine that Exeter thought it might be a good idea to know nothing of any French attack on Warwick or Calais. I daresay that he, too, never dreamed our own coast would be in any danger."

As a result of the forays, the Council appointed Warwick Keeper of the Seas. Margaret wept with frustration at the miscarriage of her plans. She had further alienated Henry's people and she had been the cause of a heavy blow to Exeter. Only her enemies had been strengthened by her act.

Of all the people saddened by the hate and rancor eating at the very fabric of England, none was more affected than her King. He prayed constantly for an end to the faction and strife. In January, 1458, at the beginning of the New Year, still imbued with the love and hope of the Christmas season, without consulting his wife or anyone else, with his own hand Henry wrote a message to each of his great lords summoning him to a Grand Council at London which would be held to create a lasting peace among all parties.

First to appear in London to answer the royal summons was Salisbury who came with five hundred horsemen. Next was York who brought with him four hundred followers wearing his colors of blue and murrey. They stayed at Baynard's Castle, one of Gloucester's old residences. At the end of January, Somerset and Exeter came with three hundred men. The Yorkists were already quartered in the city so a nervous Godfrey Boleyn, Lord Mayor of London, insisted these Lancastrians abide outside the town to prevent strife. Their ranks were soon swelled by Northumberland and Clifford who rode in with fifteen hundred men. Warwick came at the end of February and brought with him six hundred followers wearing scarlet tunics embroidered with his ragged staff.

Each day there were meetings to settle old quarrels arising out of St. Albans. Henry poured his heart and energy into the proceedings until an accord was finally reached. Warwick agreed to pay Lord Clifford one thousand marks indemnity for the death of his father. York was to pay the widowed Duchess of Somerset and her sons five thousand marks. The Percies, because of recent raids, were to pay the Nevilles eleven thousand marks. York, Salisbury, and Warwick pledged forty-five pounds yearly for a chantry at St. Albans for the souls of those killed there. All who had fought at St. Albans, both the slain and the survivors, were declared faithful subjects of the crown. In addition, Henry agreed that the three Richards should once more take their rightful places on his Council. When these articles were ratified under the Great Seal of England, the happy King proclaimed a day of public thanksgiving.

Margaret, wearing a dress of cloth of gold and a jeweled coronet, moved forward to take her place in the procession bound for St. Paul's Cathedral to offer up a thanksgiving Mass.

"Wait, my dear," said Henry, who wore his crown and state robes. "Please, I want to arrange this."

She was puzzled but she bowed low and stepped back. Henry smiled. "I thought it all out last night. Since this is Lady Day I particularly want to dedicate our work to our dear Lord's Mother and have it be especially memorable. Here, Henry, come this way," he said to the young Somerset who detached himself from the milling group of nobles. "You, too, my Lord Richard," he said to Salisbury. "I want you two to stand here and clasp hands. You'll start out."

The two men glared at each other but moved to the head of the line as Henry indicated.

"Now, Exeter, you and Warwick next, our two seamen. No, you needn't hold hands now but I want you to do so when you walk."

They moved stiffly into place, Exeter scowling at the new Keeper of the Seas.

"I'll come next ... by myself. And now, my Lady Queen, you're to follow on the arm of our gallant cousin York. And then ..... well, the rest of you just fall in line and follow two by two." Henry beamed on them all as he took his place in line. "Ah, just see what Christian charity and mercy can accomplish. Jesu be praised, we shall now have a land of love and peace!"

York smiled and raised his strong, sinewy right arm. Margaret placed her fair left hand on his bronzed one and returned a smile for all to see. And so, on that Lady Day, they held a love-day procession to the church, the bitterest enemies, hand in hand, while the censors swung, the bells pealed, and the Londoners shouted themselves hoarse for joy.

CHAPTER TWENTY

April 1458 - September 1459

It was April, a month after Henry's optimistic love-day. A last, few light clouds scudded away. Lingering rain drops caught on pink and white apple and plum blossoms sparkled in the sun. Pages threw open windows, letting in the warm breeze which bore with it the sweet, light scent of the buds. From a nearby branch came the tentative song of a bird to mingle with the soft music of a courtier's lute. It was a day, said Henry, "to fill all hearts with peace."

As the King left the solar, Margaret and her ladies rose from their deep curtsies and took up their sewing once more. They were mending vestments for Henry's chaplain and an altar cloth.

"For Henry's sake," commented the outspoken Jacquetta Woodville, "I could wish others in the kingdom had half as much peace in their hearts as he ... or he a little less."

"Aye," agreed Margaret. "I fear the King is much too good-hearted to understand the evil in man's hearts."

Elizabeth, Jacquetta's daughter, bit a thread and looked up. "Speaking of evil, did you hear that three men were hurt in the crush that formed when Warwick and his scarlet coated ruffians left for Calais?" she asked.

"I don't see what that has to do with evil," put in a young woman who admired the Earl. It's hardly his fault if a lot of giddy apprentices flock after him."

"Hardly his fault?" retorted Elizabeth. "Why, he encourages these people to run after him. I've heard that it takes six oxen daily just to break the fast of those who hang about his London palace. He maintains fully thirty thousand men on his estates. I'll wager he could raise an army as quickly as could the King. He is overbearingly ambitious."

"I imagine you would know," said the other spitefully, for Elizabeth's recent marriage to Sir John Grey, a great match for a penniless girl, had aroused envy among the others.

Margaret broke in to keep peace between them. "Have you

heard that my lord Bishop says that the Prince is learning his Latin at a great rate?"

They paid scant attention to her.

"There must be something fine in a man who is held in such honor ... not only in London, but also in Calais, Kent, and Yorkshire!"

"Kent?" scoffed Lady Grey, "That is where your great Lord Warwick spread his lies about the French raids. And everyone knows that is where the silly folk go about repeating his story that our Lord Prince is but a bastard."

The words were scarcely out when the unthinking speaker gasped and clapped her hand to her mouth. She looked at the Queen with widening, frightened eyes. The rest of the women fell silent, their needles moving with unaccustomed speed.

Margaret disdained to show that the last remark affected her, though her heart wrenched. *Will that evil slander never be put down? If it lies in my power, some day I will call Warwick to an accounting.* She rose and said quietly, "I see that it is dry outside now. Let us go into the garden for we have been too long inside and have been given too much to idle gossip. I pray Godspeed to my Lord Warwick and hope that he will long keep our city of Calais in loyal hands."

It was the feast of St. Anne. Henry was preparing to leave the high table after his simple meal when Margaret laid her hand on his arm. "One moment, dear. I want you to hear what Exeter is saying." She turned to the Duke who sat at her right. "Go on. I want the King to hear this."

Exeter leaned forward. "I was telling her Grace that you will no doubt soon be receiving an angry delegation from the Hanse towns."

"Whatever for? We've had no trouble with them."

"Not till last week, that is."

Henry motioned to a page to remove the ewer and basin, for he was finished washing. "What happened last week?"

"Warwick attacked a number of German ships ... I have not heard how many ... but he captured five of them, I understand,

and has taken them to Calais as plunder." Exeter sat back, watching the King's reaction.

Henry was stunned. "But England has a treaty with the Hanse towns ... we trade with them. Are you sure of what you say?"

"I am. I'm surprised you haven't had repercussions from it yet. I've had it from messengers both from Sandwich and Dover. It's all people are talking about up and down the coast."

"This is serious news. If what you say is true, it is piracy, pure and simple ... and against our friends."

"It's true, all right."

"What are you going to do?" asked Margaret.

"Oh, dear ...yes, I guess I must do something..." Henry began to twist his ring. "First, we'll send an apology to the Hanseatic League ...we'll have to see they get their ships back."

"They'll demand Warwick be punished, you know."

"I don't really see how I can do that. We certainly don't want to stir up any more ill will now that the old trouble of St. Albans has been smoothed over."

"But my Lord, you can't let him go scot free; he'll just do something else," Margaret pointed out.

"I was keeper of the Seas ten years without anything like this happening," said Exeter.

"True. You're probably both right, but there may be more to this than we know. Maybe he had some cause ...I don't want to condemn him out of hand." Henry struck the table. "I know -- I'll appoint a commission to investigate the whole matter."

"But --" Exeter started to object.

Margaret touched his knee in warning and broke in, "An excellent idea. And since this deals with nautical matters, I suggest Exeter here head the commission."

"No," said Henry. "I don't think that's a good idea." He smiled at the Duke. "I know you would do as good a job as possible, but I don't think you could be completely impartial. And Warwick would not exactly welcome any adverse decision you might give. No, my dear," he turned to Margaret and patted her hand. "Let us give no one cause to doubt our justice."

"You are right, my Lord, I did not think of that. We'll have to choose someone else."

Within a few days, Sir Richard Woodville, Jacquetta's husband, was appointed to head the commission to examine Warwick's recent actions. Although Woodville was a fast friend of Margaret's and did his best to condemn Warwick, others on the commission who favored the Earl blocked all efforts to call him to an accounting for a full six months.

It was a jaunty Warwick, just turned thirty, who arrived at Westminster Hall in November to be questioned by the commission. He went into the upper Council chamber laughing, assuring his friends that he had no fear of any *investigation* conducted by a mere *squire*.

The proceedings were midway along when Warwick heard great shouts from the hall below. From a melee of cries and curses and clashing swords he made out loud voices calling his name. With a mighty oath, he drew his sword, pushed open the heavy door, and bolted down the steps, taking them two and three at a time. There, in the hall, his adherents were fighting with men wearing the liveries of Somerset and Wiltshire. Shouting his own name as a battle cry, Warwick plunged into the thick of the fight. Other Council members were hard behind, some drawing weapons to join the quarrel, when suddenly the palace kitchen workers poured into the hall. Brandishing wicked pokers, knives, clubs and cleavers, they made straight for Earl Richard. Seeing himself so outnumbered by this black guard, he could but try to retreat in good order. His doublet torn by a sword thrust, Warwick cut and slashed his way to the water stairs to the outside of the building where he and most of his men escaped by boat down the Thames.

Three of his followers lay dead, with many wounded. An equal number had been slain on the Queen's side. The Earl wasted no time in sending word to his friends that he had been ambushed.

In Westminster Hall, a white and shaking Margaret confronted young Somerset and Wiltshire. "How did this brawl start? And why?"

Jamie Butler, Wiltshire, shrugged his shoulders. "We do not know."

"'How?' or 'Why?'"

"Neither, your Grace. Some say that one of the Earl's men drew a knife ..."

"Well, the Earl claims that it was one of your men ... or Somerset's ... who started it."

"You see," drawled Butler, "We'll probably never know."

"The King will be upset. He'll say, and with good cause, that this is what comes of these large bands of retainers lounging about without enough to do," said Margaret. "I think that it would be politic to withdraw to your estates for a while, at least."

"Do you think that wise? With Warwick still in London?"

"Wise? God's blood, Henry!" exploded Margaret. "I think it wiser than to attack Earl Richard and then let him get away. Now ride from here post haste ... before the Earl brings charges against you. I fear it was an ill deed that someone did, but I will try to turn it to advantage. If no one can say how the affray began, belike it was indeed caused by Richard's men. I am sure that the King will want to see justice meted out so that such brawling will not continue in his kingdom."

"...And so, my Lord, said Margaret, "you see how it is that when great men stubbornly put themselves ahead of the law, it encourages these incidents. Six Christian souls have been sent to death because of Warwick's jangling followers."

"Yes, yes," Henry agreed. "A terrible thing. Those poor men, God save them." He signed the cross. "But I don't think it was Warwick's doing. I understand he was with the Council when the quarrel began."

"He may not have been there in body, but the fault was his. In his pride he boasts that he maintains a larger retinue than you. Surely pride was the source of the trouble ... and a great sin."

"Yes, pride is the greatest sin."

"Then perhaps the Tower?"

"The *Tower?*" exclaimed Henry in disbelief.

"Oh, Henry!" She stamped her foot in exasperation. "Here you have seen how Warwick has caused the death of your subjects by overweening pride and balk at a short stay in the Tower for him. You are too lenient ... and kind ...my Lord, for the good of your own subjects. This proud man needs a lesson. I know it would be good for his soul, too."

"Mayhap you are right ... you usually are. Somehow you see things more clearly than I ... Very well, then, I'll sign an order committing Earl Richard to the Tower ... but just for a short while."

She smiled and patted his shoulder. "Good, my dear. You'll see, he'll soon amend."

Warwick heard of the intended order and fearing that should he come to the Tower he would never again see life outside it, he galloped off to tell his father and uncle in Yorkshire of the most recent plot against him. From there he sailed back to Calais.

In the spring of 1459, Margaret left London, and accompanied by young Edward, traveled once more about the Midlands. It was not the usual, peaceful progress of former years, though. In Warwickshire, in Staffordshire, and in Cheshire, the Queen gathered her friends, spoke of loyalty, hinted of coming strife, rallied her forces. Henry set up his standard at Coventry while Margaret had the five-year-old boy distribute collars embroidered with his emblem, the white swan of the Bohuns. From a thousand Midland throats came the solemn promise that this lad would be their next King.

York was uneasy. Henry by himself was no threat, but with Margaret swaying him to do her bidding, there was no telling what might happen. As the French woman enhanced her power, danger loomed for those who wanted to curb her.

He sent word to Salisbury to join him at Ludlow Castle. Salisbury, still smarting at the Lancastrian attempt on his son's life, set out for Ludlow with 3,000 of his Yorkshire tenants. At the same time, he sent messengers to Warwick in Calais, bidding him hurry back to England to help them overthrow the Queen.

CHAPTER TWENTY-ONE

October 1459

Men from every shire of England moved toward Ludlow for a showdown between the Yorkists and Lancastrians. Warwick, heeding his father's call for help, landed in Sandwich with six hundred troops from the Calais garrison, and marched up through London and on to Ludlow to join his father and uncle who had brought up his vassals from the Welsh march. They pitched camp beside the River Teme, not far from York's home, Ludlow Castle.

Margaret and her forces joined Henry at Coventry. She was overjoyed that the King was in one of his good spells and willing, even eager, to ride at the head of his army of 50,000 against the rebels.

There was discontent in the Yorkist camp. Men who had been pressed into service against Margaret, not Henry, grumbled.

One said, "Nobody told me it was going to be the King I was supposed to fight."

"What if we killed him?" asked another.

"Not me," said a boy no more than fourteen. "I wouldn't kill the King!"

"Ha! Much you know," scoffed a grizzled veteran. "You get in the middle of a fight and someone comes at you, you ain't going to stop and ask, 'Pardon, my Lord, be you the King?' before you bash his head in. If the King comes against you, you're going to try to kill him just like you would anybody."

The boy threw down the bill he was sharpening. "Then I won't fight at all. I won't kill the King."

"He's right," said another. "It's one thing to fight for your rights but something clean different to raise your hand against your own anointed King."

Another soldier objected, "If the King's so good, how come he don't pay more heed to us, his people?"

"It's the Frenchwoman and her advisors -- they keep everything from him. He doesn't know about us."

"Well," said a farmer, scratching his head, "I dunno, mayhap what you say is true, but I still don't like going against the King. I might just decide to take myself off from here. My old woman was right cross to have me marchin' off."

"You wouldn't desert?"

"Why not?" asked another, speaking boldly for the night was closing in and faces were hard to make out in the dark. "I mind I still haven't gathered our winter's wood and the days be getting colder, besides, I already paid my woodpenny"

Warwick's men complained the loudest. Before they set sail from Calais, his captains, Blount and Trollope, old veterans, had exacted from the Earl a promise that they would not have to fight Henry. Now the soldiers feared Warwick was forsworn. To forestall a mutiny, the three Richards took precious time to ride to Worcester where, in the Cathedral, they took their solemn oaths that they meant no harm to the realm nor toward the King's person. They avowed they were in arms only in self defense against the plottings of the court party.

Henry was resting in his tent, a few days' march from Ludlow, when word was brought him of the rebels' oaths. A herald had come with a request that Henry meet with York.

"Thanks be to the blessed Lord!" exclaimed Henry. "My cousin and his kinsmen are not traitors, after all, and we can parley peacefully and return to our homes."

Margaret and the captains who had gathered there looked at each other in consternation.

"Surely your Grace does not believe these varlets?" burst out Exeter.

"Yes, my Lord, I do," retorted Henry. "And it ill becomes you to speak of these men, my kinsmen, in such wise. They took their vows in holy Church."

Margaret frowned at Exeter. She laid a gentle hand on her husband's arm. "I am sure it is but excess of choler that caused Exeter to speak so; it is a common failing with him. But it irritates him, as well as the rest of your friends, to have these cozening ...cousins...forever try your good will with false vows."

"False vows?"

"Yes. Lies on the Blessed Sacrament." She crossed herself. "When York first rose in arms against you, didn't he swear a like oath in St. Paul's? And the second time, he swore in the abbey of St. Albans. And what of his promise on Lady Day?"

Henry considered. "You may be right," he admitted slowly.

"And you are right, too, to see so clearly, however painful, the falsity of these empty words ..."

He was still troubled. "What shall I reply to their message? It sounded most sincere ...perhaps I should still try to talk with them."

No, this will not do, she thought. *If we let them go, they will try again. We must fight them now while we outnumber them three to one -- destroy them once and for all. --I am so weary of this constant threat.*

She turned to a squire and instructed him, "Have their herald return to his masters and tell them that their King will meet with them -- on the field of battle! Go, now."

Henry raised his hand. "Wait."

The young man stopped, looking from the King to the Queen, confused about whom to obey. Tension taut as a drawn bowstring could be felt. Margaret stared at Henry, silently willing him to pursue the battle as she wished, while he, with unaccustomed stubbornness defied her. "I do not intend to send any guiltless man to death. I cannot know their hearts, but all shall be given a chance to amend. I shall issue a proclamation offering free pardon to all who leave these rebels and rally under my standard."

York did his best to keep the amnesty offer from his men but word of it spread throughout the camp. In every tent, around every campfire, men discussed the King's offer. The whole camp was on edge. An angry buzzing grew as the men became ever more sullen. There were dark looks for the leaders. An unwise word, an empty rumor, the least unforeseen occurrence would make York's troops melt away. It was plain; his men would not fight the King.

The Duke had not worried about the odds; skill and spirit were more important than numbers. But his men had no stomach for this fight. If the King were dead, not only York's soldiers but all England would rally behind the White Rose to cast out the Queen and her minions ... but Henry lived. *If the King were dead ... how could he make it clear that Henry might die at any time? Make them see that the country should not be in such mindless hands? ... If Henry were dead ... or if men thought he was... If the King were dead* ...It ran through his head like a refrain.

Dirige, Domine, Deus meus, in conspectu tuo viam meam ...the song rang clearly, sweetly, over the river on the cold autumn air. Henry, recognizing the sad, immemorial notes, sank to his knees and breathed a sincere prayer. As he rose, he said, "I pray the poor soul did not go unshriven to his Lord."

Exeter, who stood nearby, said, "You may rest assured, your Grace, he did not."

Startled, Henry demanded, "You, my captains, always seem to know all things, but how, pray can you know this?"

"Because, my Lord, it was ... or is ... you."

"What nattering is this? What do you mean, it is or was or whatever ...I?"

"Just that. The Mass is for you."

"But it is the Mass of the dead!"

"That I cannot help. I mean..." he reconsidered and tried to better phrase his words. "I mean, at all times we try to protect your Grace, but we cannot help it if the Duke of York puts out that you are dead. Or, we would help it if you would allow. We would see that my Lord Duke could never again bruit such a thing."

The Mass is for *me?"* Henry was aghast. He began to tremble just as his wife came into the royal tent. She knew that Henry would be upset at this new development but she had underestimated his reaction. He flew into such a rage as had not been seen at court since an early Plantagenet forebear chewed the rushes on the floor.

"For sweet Jesu's sake," she cried to Exeter. "We must calm the King or he will injure himself. His manner has always been sweet and gentle. This is not like him."

It took four strong soldiers to hold Henry. Always before, his madness had manifested itself in a complete withdrawal. This time, he struggled to lash out at everyone and everything. When the spell passed as rapidly as it had come, Margaret said, "It is obvious that Richard of York has called up devils to aid him, but our King Henry, in Christian love, has prevailed against ungodly hatred."

Henry, although no longer manic, was still upset. Never since the witchcraft of Eleanor Cobham had he been so wrought up. To sing the offices of the dead for him!

Oh, my poor dear, cried Margaret silently, *could I save you from the constant specter with which you confront yourself, God knows I would. What it is that speaks to you, that guides you, I know not, but as long as I have breath, I shall fight for you and our son.*

The next morning, King Henry, in all his royal panoply, appeared before his troops, in plain sight of the enemy lying across the River Teme. First there was a low murmur as York's forces caught sight of him. It grew to a shout and here and there could be heard, "The King." "King Henry." "He lives!" "God save the King!"

His surcoat was emblazoned with the arms of England quartered with those of France and Lancaster. His visor was up so that all men could see his face. A simple gold coronet encircled his helmet which flashed as he moved. Though his wont heretofore had been peaceful, he now rode back and forth before his men, haranguing them in most martial and kinglike tones to gird themselves for a battle against the foul forces of evil and treason. A dozen times as he sat his nervous horse, he was within range of Yorkist guns and bows, but there was no one in all that company who would have fired upon him.

"Poor soul," they said, or, "The Queen works her will on him," but there was not a one of them who did not love him and wish him well. If God caused a man, aye, even a King, to be simple, it was not their part to question His will. As for the right line of descent, that was for those whose concerns were with charts and all. For Jesu's sake, all these soldiers wanted was a little foreign war so that they might get honest booty and plunder. They had no wish to kill their fellow Englishmen.

There were more than Henry who thought that Mass an evil business. When the chill October darkness closed in and the great barons planned their next day's action, preparing finally for a sally, Sir Anthony Trollope, disgusted with York's double dealing, led his Calais garrison over the river and submitted himself to Henry, his true liege lord. Close behind him came Lord Powys, then others ... by dawn, half of York's army had melted away.

Duke Richard, his throat thick with anger and tears, released the soldiers who had remained loyal to him and bade them save themselves. He peered toward Ludlow Castle, where lay his family, Cecily and the younger children. He spoke to his older boys, "We must ride now, and ride hotly, for our lives."

"Do you mean to leave our mother and brothers?" asked sixteen-year-old Edmund of Rutland.

"Aye, that I do, for it will not help your mother should we lose our heads."

"But will not the King and Queen demand *their* heads?" persisted the young boy.

"No," said his brother Edward, the seventeen-year-old Earl of March, York's heir. "The King is too good and the Queen ...well, I remember her from a long time ago... it is almost like a dream. I know she is evil now... but I remember her ...she was like a fairy princess and she played with me... No, I do not think she will hurt our mother or Dicky and George."

"I marvel that you remember it," said York, gathering together a few things for the flight. "God knows it was a long time off ... a happier time. But I think you are right. Of all the people in the world I could wish the Lady Margaret dead, but still I do not think she will harm your mother or brothers."

The three magnates, along with York's sons, rode westward all the night. At dawn they parted; York and Rutland headed for

Ireland, while the others turned south for Devon. In Ireland, the Duke was welcomed with fervor for the Irish held him a fast friend.

Meanwhile, at the camp, Henry had been unable to restrain his unruly troops. They poured over the river and fell upon Ludlow Castle which they sacked and robbed to the bare walls. The men dared not harm the proud Duchess, but called upon their Queen to know what should be Cecily's fate. Margaret was strangely averse to setting any penalty. For a while she spoke of letting the soldiers have their way with the Duchess, but in the end, the wife of the greatest traitor in the land, along with her sons, was merely given into the custody of the Duchess of Buckingham, her own sister. In this matter, at least, York had well read the Queen.

CHAPTER TWENTY-TWO

June 1460

Margaret lay on her back in the middle of the great bed, staring up at the velvet canopy. The only light in the room came from the glowing embers in the fireplace where a small fire hissed and snapped. Though it was nearly July, the castle was damp and chill. Men said it was the worst summer in memory. Tears welled up in her eyes, slid down her temples and wet her hair.

They probably blame me for the weather, too. Why not? they blame me for everything else. Now they are saying it is my fault that York and the Nevilles have been attainted; that I am responsible for their treason. Why shouldn't the Yorkists petition Henry for redress of wrongs, they ask, even with arms if need be? Why can't they see that that is anarchy?

What can I do to win the people's support? And Henry -- is he going to be sick again? Those same old signs ... he has been so troubled lately. Is he slipping away from reality again because of the pain and worries that beset him? Or is he just avoiding me -- like tonight?

The royal couple had supped with their friends and then played for a short time with little Edward whose seven-year-old antics made his parents laugh. It was such a happy evening that Margaret had been optimistic that her recent fears for Henry were groundless.

When they prepared to retire, Henry, as was his custom, lightly brushed his lips over Margaret's cheek. She turned her face toward him and kissed his mouth.

"Well," he said, smiling. "Well."

"Well what, my Lord?" She smiled at him in turn.

"Well, I think I shall visit your bed tonight."

"You are most welcome there." Her tone was playful, but she was serious. How long had it been since he had been a guest in her bed? She was glad she had been bold enough to make the small advance. Sometimes Henry ignored her kisses.

As Katherine helped Margaret undress and get ready for bed, they gossiped like two young girls. There was little privacy so it was no secret to Katherine that Henry and Margaret seldom spent the night together. Indeed, Margaret had confided in her lifelong friend her concern over Henry's lack of interest in her, reaching back to Edward's birth and Henry's first illness.

"However can we get more heirs when Henry beds with me so seldom?"

"Have you spoken with him about it?" ventured Katherine.

"I tried to broach it -- but it is so delicate -- especially with him. He says that although he would dearly love to have more children, I should not fret -- he says we have done our duty already."

She had been puzzled and hurt by her husband's attitude. *Duty* had seemed such a strange word to use for making love.

"Am I not attractive?" She pulled Katherine over close to her where her friend could not avoid looking her in the eye. It was a foolish question. Margaret was thirty now, past the easy beauty of youth, but not yet aging; her body was firm, her skin clear, her teeth undiseased. She knew from her courtiers that she was appealing. She could tell that their words were sometimes more than chivalrous flattery. Only Henry seemed not to desire her. Why? She knew he had no leman ... maybe it would be better if he had. She wondered if all those hours in chapel were good for him.

Well, she would not worry now. Tonight, at least, she had attracted her husband. Perhaps they would recapture some of their earlier pleasures in each other. She climbed into the great bed and waited, naked, her pulse quickening with anticipation.

Before Henry got into bed with her, he knelt and said a *pater noster*. By the time he stretched out beside her she was warm and moist with expectation, and her nipples were hard as she put her arms around his neck and strained to him.

Though Henry held her and stroked her back, nothing happened. Margaret wound her fingers in his hair and pulled his face down to hers. She kissed him passionately, her head swimming with longing. Slowly, Henry pulled away from her. "I am sorry," he faltered.

"What is the matter?"

"Oh, my dear, I do not know...I wanted ... for you ... I know you wanted to make love..."

"Do I displease you?"

"No, no. Never ... it's just that I am tired. There are so many worries and nothing goes right. I am sorry...I have failed you ...I guess I have failed most everyone."

"There's nothing to be sorry about ...you haven't failed me ... or anyone." She had detected a note of panic in his voice. She tried to comfort him. "Like you say, you're tired ... another night, my dear, when you are better."

...But he was so much happier tonight than usual; if it isn't going be tonight, I won't put him such a position again. If he wishes it, all right, but I won't be the one to approach him.

"Now just relax and try to sleep."

"Forgive me, my dear, but I think I shall sleep better in my own bed." He got up, drew on his night robe and left her room.

Margaret wept in frustration and fear ...*what is happening?* She knew the sorrows of the past ... what would be the sorrows of the future?

Worry about the ever-looming threat from Yorkist sympathizers overrode Margaret's personal anguish. Warwick was using Calais as a base of operations to harry Lancastrians. Back in January, he and Wenlock had boldly sailed into Sandwich and pirated away the King's fleet. To compound their villainy, they had taken Richard Woodville, Lord Rivers; and his son Anthony, prisoners. Now her spies brought word that Warwick had recently returned to Calais from Ireland where he had met with York.

"I fear they were plotting mischief there," she confided to Exeter, upon whom she leaned more and more. They spoke quietly at one end of the audience chamber while Katherine and her other ladies, as well as several pages, came and went about their business at the other end of the room.

"Can you not dismiss your damsels?" asked Exeter. "There is no telling in these days who carries information to York."

"I know, but if we are circumspect and in the open, the news carried will hurt us less than evil surmises that might arise should our talks be held in private."

"Does that really worry you? Do you care if simple people give credence to easy lies?"

"Of course it worries me. Any hint of lightness on my part reflects on the Prince."

"Don't you think you're being over sensitive on that? From what I see, he is well accepted and popular. Did Parliament not grant him his petition for the towns and lordships of Kerry and Kedowen?"

"Yes. But why should he have had to petition for them? These possessions have always been granted automatically to Princes of Wales. I've had to fight for Edward's rights every step of the way and I will not put them in jeopardy."

Exeter's voice was low. "Am I never, then, to see you alone? We used to speak ... I know a place where we could meet in utmost secrecy and safety..."

Why not? How she wanted to be alone with him. Surely it couldn't hurt and she had much need of comfort. What guilt could there be--? She knew very well what guilt. Never before had she been tempted more than momentarily, but now, more and more, she felt the ground shifting beneath her feet when she was with Exeter.

Her marriage vows had brought ...what? Nothing but grief-- except for Edward. Why should she not have a little pleasure? Who would be harmed? Henry? Not if he didn't know ... and obviously his feelings toward her were no longer those of a husband. Henry would probably be happier without the strain of her importuning him. Herself? It would be a grievous sin, but was there not absolution? Forgiveness?

Edward? Ah, there was the problem. She could not risk hurting his cause. Someday, perhaps, his situation would be less precarious, but now she dared not compromise his inheritance. She wanted love -- with Exeter -- but more than that, she wanted to protect her son. She would *protect him.*

Her voice gave no hint of her struggle. "I am sorry, my Lord."

"Madame ... Margaret ..." There was an urgency in his tone. "Please, I need to talk to you ... to be with you for even just a little while alone. I promise there will be no shred of gossip."

She shook her head. "No, I cannot."

"Why not? Why not?," he insisted.

"For Edward's sake."

"But I swear --"

"No." She looked straight at him, pleading. "Oh, my dear, please cease your entreaty. Do you not understand me well enough to know I cannot ...dare not ...?"

"You, Queen, and *dare* not?"

"Oh, Exeter, not because I'm Queen ... but because I am a woman and I care for you too much."

The Duke took her hand most gently and bowed over it. From all the others in the room could tell, he was taking formal leave of her.

Softly he murmured, "You give me hope and snatch it from me all at once. I shall obey your orders, for as my Queen, you have my loyalty and as ...a woman...my love."

She pressed his hand and said with deep feeling, "I thank you, for I have need of both."

They moved toward the door. "A final commission, my Lord," she said. "You have long been jealous of your title of Admiral. If it ever meant anything to you, show us now. The back of York's rebellion will be broken if you can but arrest his arrogant nephew, Warwick."

"Though I fain would stay here, this is a commission I accept most willingly."

CHAPTER TWENTY-THREE

July - October 1460

Despite a liberal oiling of its double thickness, the royal tent oozed water. Outside, the King's standard hung sodden, while soldiers, mounted and on foot, grumbling and cursing, slogged by in ankle-deep mire. The rain had fallen steadily for three days and showed no sign of letting up. The sky looked more like November than July. Inside the tent, Henry sat slumped over, his thin hands between his knees, twisting, ever twisting his rings. Margaret, a surcoat of chain mail over her gown, looked out at the constant drizzle.

"When is all this bloodshed going to end?" cried the King. "When? It's like a bad dream ... less than a year since Ludlow and here they are, back again."

Margaret turned and raging, gripped his shoulder. "This time when we win, the story will be different. Earl Richard won't get away ... back to his safe Calais harbor. He'll be left moldering here in this Northampton mud."

"Margaret!" Henry was horrified at her savage words and steely tone.

"Can't you see? It's Warwick more than anyone else who's stirred up this trouble. Every time you send Exeter or Somerset, or anyone, to make him yield his command, he refuses them as if his word were of more import than yours. He turned your own guns on Exeter, your Admiral. And now this *demand* that you dismiss your loyal friends and put York's minions in their places. It's all Warwick's idea. Why, York himself hasn't stirred past the Irish border yet. Once overweening Earl Richard is dead perhaps we can have peace. I think I could slit his throat myself!"

Henry shuddered. "You mustn't speak of killing, you, who are but a gentle woman." He reached up and clasped her hand. "Nor do I like that armor you wear."

She laughed mirthlessly. "Have you not heard that our

enemies say I have a *tiger's heart wrapped in a woman's hide?* The armor is to protect that tiger's heart for if one of their arrows pierced it, who would care for you and our Prince?"

Henry sprang up and put his arms around his wife. "Do not say such things. No, do not. I could not bear to lose you, but there is not a man in all England who is either hateful enough or cruel enough to slay a woman. Besides, they love you; I know they do. No, I forbid you to say it."

She hid a grim smile and leaned her head briefly against her husband's breastplate. "I am sorry, my Lord. No doubt you are right. I am probably overwrought from this waiting and this miserable weather. There are several things in England I would change if I could and the weather is one of them. I sometimes think the very heavens are against us."

Henry crossed himself and replied, "It rains on them as well as on us."

"I know, but Buckingham said that his captains fear our powder is so wet that those cannon they labored to place will not fire. If so, it will be a harder fight than we thought, for there is no question that the Yorkshire bowmen excel all others."

The King marveled at how much more his wife knew about warfare than he did.

When it was time for her to leave, they embraced briefly. Then she mounted and rode to the top of a nearby hill where, hunched over in the steady rain, she watched the battle.

It lasted a scant two hours. The guns did prove useless in the downpour but as far as Margaret could tell, the Yorkist arrows were having little effect, either, for the bowstrings were soon wet and lost much of their deadly power. It began to look as if the royalist forces, safely drawn up behind the water filled ditch, must be victorious. Men who charged slipped helplessly back down glass-slick mud and mire. Just as she thought the Lancastrians would carry the day, the men of Lord Grey deRuthyn suddenly threw down their weapons, hoisted Warwick's banner of the ragged staff, and reached willing, traitorous hands to the enemy who clambered across the slippery ditch to cut a way for Warwick's men. Panicked by this treachery, the Lancastrian wings gave way.

When Margaret saw the way the battle was going, with a shout of anguish and anger, she turned her horse and gave him rein northwestward toward Coventry where Prince Edward lay. Henry's life would depend upon his son's safety. Little use to York's followers to strike at Henry while Edward lived.

Margaret and her attendant rode steadily, but the news of the Lancastrian defeat reached Coventry before them. The King had been taken and three hundred of his men lay dead, among them Egremont and Shrewsbury, who fell close to Henry's tent, trying vainly to protect his retreat.

The worst blow of all was the death of loyal Buckingham who had so many times tried to mediate between the opposing factions. Next to Henry himself, Buckingham had been the most peaceful lord in the kingdom, tied to both parties by blood and love; yet at St. Albans he had seen his son slain in the King's cause and now he lay dead in the same cause.

Margaret dared not linger at Coventry. She collected Edward and fled westward to Harlech Castle, a loyal stronghold in the northwest fastness of Wales. Jasper Tudor, Earl of Pembroke, and half-brother to Henry, held the castle and was able to guarantee the safety of the Queen and his royal nephew. From here, Margaret sent out letters and messengers to her adherents, trying to rally them to the King's cause. Never would she give up, she vowed ... never.

Exeter soon joined her and then, risking his life, went to the north of England to gather forces. Somerset and Trollope made their way to Harlech to join the Queen who was forced to bide her time while her enemies undid all the work accomplished at Ludlow and Coventry the year before.

And undone it was. Henry had been taken by Warwick and York's son, Edward of March, under guard to London and lodged in the palace at Westminster. On October 10, three days after the opening of Parliament, York arrived in London with three hundred armed men, preceded by heralds and trumpeters. A sword of state was carried before him in royal style, and he bore the undifferenced arms of England upon his surcoat and banners. He strode into Parliament -- to the throne which stood vacant. When he laid his hand upon the throne, the great murmur which had risen at his appearance suddenly ceased. York turned and looked about the hall, awaiting a shout of acclamation. The only sound that greeted him was the sharp intake of breath from the shocked onlookers. Slowly, his hand dropped to his side, and he moved away from the throne. He had gambled and lost ... this time.

The crown was almost within the Duke's grasp; he need reach only a little further. He laid his claims before the Lords. Not only had he defeated Henry in battle, but his right by descent was clear. Henry's grandfather had illegally deposed Richard the Second; Henry had no lawful right to be King. York demanded that the Lords tell Henry to step aside. Instead, they *asked* him. After all, he was usually generous and amenable to reason. He might even see this as a heaven-sent opportunity to be eased from an arduous burden.

Henry was indignant. "My father was King; his father was also King. I have worn the crown forty years from my cradle; you have all sworn fealty to me as your sovereign, and your fathers have done the like to my fathers. How then can my right be disputed?"

A delegation waited upon York and told him of Henry's refusal. The Duke shook his head, raised an eyebrow and said it would be a pity if he had to arm himself again to secure his lawful rights but --. He did not finish the sentence. The men were faced with a dilemma. They dared not depose Henry; the people held him in too much affection. Besides, the Lords themselves preferred Henry -- after all, they held their lands from the Lancastrians. But York's threat was real. He controlled the government; his party held all the London and court offices. England was at an impasse. Civil war loomed.

Finally they hammered out a compromise. Henry would remain King but name York as his heir. Upon Henry's death the crown would pass to York and his line. The only mention of Prince Edward was to bestow his titles upon York.

At the very moment the promises were made, a great crown, part of a chandelier in the Parliament, fell to the ground with a resounding crash, shattered.

Her confessor brought Margaret the news, for none other, even Katherine, dared tell her. The men and women of the castle stood about in little clusters, whispering anxiously and glancing sideways at the Queen to watch her reaction.

"Surely the messenger is mistaken," she whispered hoarsely. "Surely he ..." her voice rose, "he lies!" Her clenched fists pounded at the rough arms of the great hewn chair where she sat. "He lies!' she screamed. "It is a trick."

"Peace, daughter," admonished the priest. "It is a heavy blow which you must bear with Christian fortitude. There is no reason to doubt his word. The poor man has ridden long and hard to bring you the news."

"Better his horse had dropped in his tracks; better the fellow had his tongue torn from his mouth than bring such news," she raged. She rose abruptly and paced back and forth, trying to collect her thoughts -- to plan what she must do next -- and all the while the old churchman tried to calm her with platitudes of meekness and mercy. "Meekness? You speak to me of meekness who of all people is made most miserable just because of the meekness of the King? Of mercy to me who has seen the mercy shown to my enemies turned against me and my son?"

"My daughter," chided the old man, "your words are sinful and ill advised. We must pray to the gentle Lord Jesus that your heart will repent of this foolish sinfulness."

Margaret whirled on him. "Father, were you not a holy man, I trow you would be made to rue your words. I tell you, I would sin a thousand times, yea ... and burn in Hell, rather than give up a jot of my son's rights. I repent me only that I have been *too* meek and merciful, and from this day forth, my thoughts and deeds shall be as bloody as to make men blench! I swear that while I live never shall proud York sit upon the throne of England. When Henry ceases to reign, he shall be followed by Edward!" With that she swept from the room, leaving the attendants to gabble excitedly and the priest to sink to his knees in horrified prayer.

CHAPTER TWENTY-FOUR

December 1460

Edward's future now lay entirely in his mother's hands. She prepared to leave Wales, keeping her forces there under the care of Pembroke, Henry's half brother and Jamie Butler who had been accepted into the royal circle once more.

"Bess," said Margaret, after Wiltshire's latest escapade, "How often do you expect me to forgive your Jamie?"

The young woman knelt before her. "Madame, I know I ask a great deal. I don't know what makes him act like he does ... mayhap his hot Irish blood. If I could change him, I would. But even as he is ... and I know it is not good, I cannot help it. I love him. And I know he loves the King and you and the Prince, and he wants more than anything to work for you."

"All right, Bess. I guess we cannot know always what makes those we love act as they do. I shall receive him again ... for you. God know we have need of all who will espouse our cause. You may tell him he is forgiven."

Margaret took Edward and went to Scotland to beg help from the widowed Mary of Gueldres, mother of eight-year-old James the Third. But the English regarded Margaret's pleas to her son's Scottish relatives as outright treason. There had been too many border clashes, too much bad blood to ever look northward for help.

While Margaret tried to talk the Queen Mother into sending Scots men-at-arms across the English border to help her, her friends were busy marshaling their troops in the north of England. Exeter, Somerset, and Devon were gathering men in the west country. With over a thousand men, they marched north to a rendezvous with their friends at Hull where they were to be joined by Margaret. By December, she had a host of 15,000 men and was ready to move against her enemies.

The stewards on York's and Salisbury's estates sent their masters appeals for help against the marauders, and Cecily at

Sandal Castle added her plea that her husband and brother come to see what was happening to their holdings. When Parliament adjourned at the beginning of December, York and Edmund of Rutland, his second son, marched north along with Salisbury and one of his sons, Thomas. Warwick stayed in London to watch Henry. Edward, York's eldest son, went to Wales to raise a force to harry Margaret's friends in the marches.

On the Feast of St. Thomas the Apostle, York and Salisbury had a happy homecoming at Sandal Castle, two miles from Wakefield, where they joined Cecily. Cecily's joy at having her husband, son, brother and nephew with her once more was but little dampened by news of a gathering of armed men under young Northumberland only six miles away at Pomfret. They heard, too, that Margaret had moved from Scotland and was at the city of York where she was visited constantly by lords friendly to her. Despite growing restlessness, an uneasy truce was arranged to extend over Christmas so that all could keep the Nativity in peace and good will.

December 30, which dawned brittle cold and crisp, put an end to Christian peace. The Lancastrian horde, swelled by men brought up by Devon and Somerset, marched to Sandal and jeering and shouting outside the walls of the castle, challenged York to combat. Despite his wife's pleas, he decided to fight.

Cecily turned to her brother. "Richard, can you talk to my lord? I can do nothing with him. He has it in his mind that I am counseling cowardice ... he is so cross with me ... I cannot bear to anger him...Please, please, try to talk some sense into him."

Salisbury cautioned his brother-in-law, "I marvel that you have taken leave of your senses. Do not be so foolhardy as to think you can fight with this rabble. Let them rage without. Good Lord, man, they outnumber us three to one."

York countered, "We have beaten them before and can again. I will put an end once and for all to this harassment and this jangling."

"It will be more than jangling if we meet with this host today."

"Call it what you will, I'll fight."

"Hold then, but a few days till Edward comes from Wales with his men so that we can be more evenly matched," begged Salisbury.

Seventeen-year-old Rutland was impatient. "My father need not always rely upon my brother. I daresay my own right arm will wield many a weighty blow against that Frenchwoman's rabble."

"Well said, my son," exclaimed York with pride. "The lad has true York mettle, and will prove himself a worthy whelp today, I doubt not."

"I fear it will take more than mettle to win this day," said Salisbury. "Do not fool yourself, Richard, that they are only rabble. Look down there. There are the banners of Clifford, Northumberland, Exeter, Roos, yes ... and my own kinsmen, the other Nevilles. They are mighty lords with strong right arms of their own."

"Perhaps then, you had rather keep the castle than venture forth against such a host."

"Aye, brother, that I had ... would you, too, keep the castle. But never have I lagged a battle and it ill becomes you to speak so to me," said Salisbury sadly.

"Pardon, Richard, my words were ill spoken. You know I did not mean them ... why, you are my other self. It is just that I am wroth at being cooped up here. I know our forces are outnumbered, but I am ashamed to refuse to fight for dread of a scolding woman whose only weapons are her tongue and nails."

"York, look out there. Those swords and pikes and arrows are not mere tongues and nails."

York was adamant. "This is one battle which I am going to fight. You cannot convince me otherwise."

All the while they argued, the two men and their sons were donning their armor and preparing their weapons. Now the heavy portcullis was slowly raised with a great rumbling and creaking, and the four rode out side by side to marshal their forces.

As the men marched around the castle hill, trying to keep the advantage of the height, the Lancastrian wings came up on both flanks and swiftly closed around them. The Yorkists were caught in a trap. In half an hour, two of England's greatest warriors, veterans of scores of English and French battles, were beaten. Great Richard of York, second man in the kingdom, heir to the throne, was slain in vicious hand-to-hand fighting. Salisbury was captured. Thomas Neville lay dead of an arrow. Young Edmund of Rutland, whose horse had been cut from under him, tried to flee by foot, but Clifford overtook him at Wakefield Bridge.

"I yield me, knight," panted the lad. "This day has won you great booty, if no honor, for I am a Duke's son and my ransom will be large."

Clifford pushed back his visor with a short, breathless laugh and said, "Behold me. Your father slew my father and I shall slay his sons, every one of them. What care I for honor when I can have the blood I thirst for?" Then, with a shriek, he struck Edmund so hard that the point of his sword entered the boy's chest and came out through his back.

This was the start of the slaughter; few prisoners were taken, either nobles or commons, and at the end, 2500 Yorkists lay bloody on the field. The next day, Salisbury, who had been taken at Pomfret where he had fled, was dragged from the castle to have his head struck off.

The victorious Lancastrians rode to Margaret who waited in the freezing cold at the city of York for news. Clifford was foremost of the army to tell her of the terrible victory. Silently, grimly hiding a smile, he rode up to where the Queen waited by Micklegate Bar. In his hands he held high a pike. He lowered it and presented it to her.

"Here, Madame," he laughed. "Your war is done; here is your King's ransom." Impaled on the end of the pike was York's head, garlanded in derision with a paper crown.

With difficulty, Margaret suppressed a cry. She feared she would be sick. She wanted to turn away but she swallowed and forced herself to look at the grisly sight.

Clifford said, "I shall have his head set upon York's gate so that he may overlook the town. When she turned to leave, he said, "Wait, Madame, I have a further prize for you." The soldiers shouted for her to stay.

Clifford and Exeter rode back into the crowd. Then, swiftly

wheeling, returned, each bearing another pike. Horrified, her eyes swimming, Margaret made out the bloody features of York's son Edmund and Thomas Neville. Clifford signaled that the heads of the son and nephew should take their places beside York. Tomorrow they would be joined by Salisbury. She turned her own horse then and made her way blindly through the shouting throng of soldiers and townspeople.

Her attendants followed close behind and tried to help her when she came to her apartment, but she roughly brushed aside their willing hands and hurried to her chapel where, still not speaking, she thrust the great door closed behind her. Through the rest of the day and into the night, she knelt on the cold stone floor. A hundred pictures appeared to her: York riding out to meet her at Mantes when she was a bride; York and Cecily entertaining her; playing with the children; the laughing Edmund in his cradle ... but ever the inward vision of the happy baby was blotted out by the gory head with its filmy, sightless eyes. She saw a Princess who lived when the world was sunny and full of promise, when there was no hate and war and blood. She saw young knights prancing to tournaments with blunted swords and pikes, but the weapons suddenly sharpened and slaughtered. Over and over, she saw Edmund's bright, happy face turn into a moldering head for crows to peck.

She shuddered and wept. Finally, she prayed. Every once in a while a priest timidly approached to see if he could help, but always Margaret nodded him away. She heard one murmur to a fellow, "No doubt her Grace prays for the souls of those who died this day."

No, no. I pray for a Princess who died long ago, and I pray for Cecily, the Rose of Raby.

CHAPTER TWENTY-FIVE

January - February 1461

With all the older leaders dead now, there were sons burning to move into their places. Just as young Northumberland, Somerset and Clifford had snatched up the bloody banners of their Red Rose sires, so now Edward of March and Richard of Warwick vowed to avenge the heads on York gate. Nineteen-year-old Edward, a young giant of a man who stood six foot three, inherited along with York's title and lands, his claim to the throne of England.

Warwick, who had been keeping the New Year on his estates, thundered back to London to take charge of the Yorkist party there and to rally his men against the coming of the Queen's hordes. Edward was still in the west, keeping an eye on the Welsh borders when he learned of the death of his father at Wakefield. He feared Margaret's victorious army would join up with the Welsh troops of Pembroke and Wiltshire and advance on the capital, sweeping all before them. Indeed, had Margaret taken that action immediately, she would probably have succeeded. Ten days after Wakefield, when she could have been at the gates of London, she was back in Scotland to treat once more with the Regent, Mary of Gueldres.

During her journey to Dumfries, Margaret outlined her plan to Exeter. "If we can obtain a force of Scottish soldiers, those added to our own should easily give us a victory over Warwick. That is the only way I see to rescue Henry."

Exeter argued, "We have enough men already. I'd rather push on toward London than parley with the Scots."

"That isn't all I have in mind. I'm sure part of our trouble has been those Scots sitting on our northern border, sometimes friends and sometimes enemies. Either way, they keep the north uneasy. I would like to be friends with them."

"How do you propose to make the Scots mend their fractious ways when they pride themselves that contention is bred in their bones?"

"I intend to try the same course I did before; only now they may listen. Now that we are victors they may see an advantage to be on our side. A marriage agreement would bind them to us by ties of love and kinship."

"A marriage between whom? The same ones? Northumberland's daughter and the young King James? Mark me, they'll never agree."

"Why not? It would keep a peaceful border."

"The rulers would rather have them fighting -- keeps the clans from bothering the government."

"I can't believe that."

"Well, they'll want to save their King for a higher alliance than the daughter of an English border Lord, anyway." Suddenly he laughed his sardonic laugh so familiar to the Queen.

"Something has amused you. Tell me so I may laugh, too."

"I was just thinking ... the widowed Queen Mother is what her people call a *bonny lass.* By now she must be tired of an empty bed. What say we suggest young Somerset to fill it? He's no more than seven or eight years her junior and he's always been precocious. I warrant he'd like to be Regent of Scotland."

Margaret joined Exeter in laughter, but then she sobered. "You know, that's not a bad idea at all ... if Somerset controlled Mary and the boy James we'd have a dependable friend on our northern border."

In private, at Lincluden Abbey, she broached this idea to Mary who said, "I would be willing for such a match ... only to keep the peace, of course ... but I tread such a narrow path, trying to keep the clans satisfied, as well as our friend France and my uncle Burgundy, that I dare not so favor one faction over another. Were I to wed now, there would be a war over the Regency."

As Exeter had predicted, she would not consider betrothing the ten-year-old King to any English girl ... now, if only Margaret and Henry had a daughter ...

This was what Margaret had been waiting for. She had one more offer, one which she didn't think the dowager Queen would refuse.

"Could we not seal a pact of betrothal between the Prince of Wales and your daughter, the Princess Mary?"

Mary of Gueldres' eyes glittered. This was more like it. Her son already a King and one of her daughters to be a Queen ... a good prospect, but the children were young yet and much could happen. Even with Scotland's help the Frenchwoman might not be able to keep the crown for her son. Scotland ought to get something definite...

"Berwick," said the dowager.

"What do you mean, *Berwick?*"

"Berwick -- on the border. It really belongs to us, anyway. It's a shame there's been so much bootless quarreling over it. Let England recognize our right to Berwick and we will seal the marriage agreement."

"You to supply us men, arms, and horses to help us root out the traitors?"

"Yes."

"Agreed."

Returning to York city with her new troops, Margaret exulted. "Berwick," she said, "such a small place; a tiny price to pay for this aid. Henry's people will be pleased that we have found a way to reach accord over this troublesome old matter."

But Exeter was silent and glum for he feared that Margaret had misjudged the English. He was right. The people said it was a shameful dishonor. The Queen had betrayed them. The loss of Berwick was one more thing they held in their hearts against her.

"My old grandfer fought the Scots," said one. "And his grandfer before him, since time out of mind."

"Aye, and now this woman comes givin' away our own hard won town without so much as a *by your leave.*"

"And for what? So's a troop of Scots bullies can ravage her own country."

"Like Sandwich in '57 with the French raid."

"Like Sandwich ... I mind as how I didn't really think the Queen was back of that, but now I don't know."

"Seems as how the King ought to keep her in hand."

"Oh, him, poor natural ..."

"Well, if he can't mayhap we need someone on the throne who can, before she gives the whole country away."

"Well ..."

"Maybe ..."

"Aye..."

Worse for Margaret's cause than the rancor bred by Berwick was the delay. While her troops fretted and fumed, waiting to march southward, and growing more impatient and unruly, many frightened people rallied to Warwick. He issued commissions of array in the King's name, ordering his friends to gather their troops and join him against the *misrule and outrageous people in the north parts of this realm, coming toward these parts to the destruction thereof, of you, and the subversation of all our land.*

While Warwick collected his army, Margaret's men began slowly to move toward London. The soldiers lived off the land, pillaging and plundering as they went. Neither she nor her captains could control them. The Lancastrian troops sacked all the towns along the way as they poured down Ermine Street, the old Roman road that led from York to London. Nothing was safe from them: they robbed churches and homes, raided and then burned shops, raped women, and slew when they pleased. Margaret, who traveled with Prince Edward in the van, was appalled. She pleaded with young Somerset, the leader, with Clifford, Northumberland, and Captain Trollope to control the men.

The latter was blunt. He admitted, "I cannot."

Somerset tried to reassure her. "The men will soon tire of their madness."

"Cannot you punish the worst of the evil doers? At least a few of them, as a warning to others?"

"Their temper is so touchy, I dare not," he confessed. "It is hard enough to keep them in any semblance of order by banter. Sometimes a fractious horse is better controlled by giving him his head a little."

Clifford, asked to curb the growing unruliness of the mob, laughed derisively and advised, "Let them go, my Lady. Let them go. Those they pillage and kill are probably our enemies, anyway. Just be thankful our soldiers are with us and not against us."

As they moved toward the capital, their ranks grew. They were joined by beggars, thieves, vagabonds, by cutthroats and old soldiers, men who had lost their occupations and now looked forward to quick wealth and plunder from the sacking of London and the countryside.

While Margaret's rabble swept southward, the Earls of Pembroke and Wiltshire, bottled up in Wales by Edward of March, tried to break out and join her. On Candlemas Day, February second, the Welsh troops, about eight thousand men, were stopped by Edward's larger force at Mortimer's Cross, not far from Ludlow. On that morning, the sun rose cold and white, outlined behind a thin veil of clouds. The battle lines were drawn up opposite each other and coming together when an archer shouted, "Look up. Look up. The sky! Look at the sun!"

The men on both sides of the line looked skyward. There, shining like white molten gold was the sun and about it a halo, and at the edge of the halo, another sun with a second halo; at its edge, a third sun.

In the forefront of his troops, the giant young Edward, who bore upon his shield and surcoat the cognizance of the sun, took this as an omen. He thrust forward his sword and charged the enemy, on his lips the cry, "A sign, a sign! The sun for York!" Before his furious charge, the Lancastrians faltered, broke, then turned and fled in superstitious terror. The sun of York had won the day for York.

Although Pembroke and Wiltshire escaped with what men they could gather, to fight another day for Lancaster, two thousand of Margaret's Welsh army had been killed, among them, Owen Tudor, Henry's step-father, who was captured and beheaded.

When Margaret heard of her loss at Mortimer's Cross, she noted with a chill that even the heavens were against her.

CHAPTER TWENTY-SIX

February 1461

Could the Queen's army reach London before Edward, moving as fast as he could from Mortimer's Cross, joined Warwick? It was no use for Margaret to try to delay her men any longer, waiting for her experienced Welsh troops, for a rider had brought her word that a quarter of those troops were dead, the rest fled westward. Now it was a race against Edward.

Margaret's swollen mob pressed south. At Dunstable, less than fifty miles from London, she learned that some Yorkists waited at St. Albans with Warwick, blocking her road to the capital.

"The King is with them," reported a spy who had talked with men from the enemy camp.

"What do you mean - *with them?* Does he command any troops?"

"Oh, no, your Grace. He may even be a prisoner. The men told me that the King is not armed. They'd heard he'd refused to arm; says he has no need to protect himself from his own subjects."

"Is he a prisoner?"

"I couldn't learn. The soldiers I talked to said they never saw him, that the captains said he was with Warwick. The soldiers thought that the Earl thinks that if he has his Majesty men will believe the King is on his side -- but no one really knows."

"How many men does the Earl have?" asked Somerset. "And what is their mood?"

"Not enough to withstand an attack -- yet. Warwick waits for Duke Edward. Their mood? Uneasy."

Everything they heard gave them hope. Margaret and her captains decided to push their advantage. They sped out of Dunstable to outflank Warwick's lines at St. Albans.

The Earl, who had won fame and honor at the first battle of St. Albans almost six years before, in this second battle, was outnumbered and overwhelmed. Henry was a problem. Warwick dared not delay his flight long enough to force Henry to accompany him. After the first battle, the Yorkists used the King as a pawn; now, after the second battle, he would be a Lancastrian pawn.

Margaret's soldiers found the King in his tent, guarded by Lords Bonville and Kyriel who had promised to protect him in return for clemency.

"My dear, my dearest dear," cried Henry when he and Margaret met. There were tears in his eyes. "How good it is to see you ... you can't know ..." He wept openly, clasping his wife in his arms.

"And your son, my Lord," said Margaret, reaching out and drawing to her the young Prince who had been brought to the royal tent. Henry joyfully lifted the lad and hugged and kissed him. "How I have missed you two," he said, "but now we are together again. May the good Lord grant we stay that way." He crossed himself.

The Queen was tired and cold, her back and joints ached from the long days of riding; her nerves were raw from the pressure of trying to control her undisciplined throng. She was weary from the constant calls on her to advise her captains, to make decisions-- decisions which could influence all of Prince Edward's future. She looked at her husband with a new, and cold detachment, trying to appraise him. She admitted finally that he was weak-willed. How much mischief had he permitted -- nay, compounded -- in the seven months since she had fled with Edward from Coventry?

God, I'm tired, but I can't rest now. Henry will have to help us whether he wishes or not --

"I'm glad to hear you say that, Henry, that you want us to stay together, for we and your loyal subjects have been at some little trouble to accomplish our reunion. We weren't sure you desired it, either."

"Weren't sure I desired it? Why, Margaret, how could you have such an idea? I don't understand you...you know my every thought, saving of our Savior, is of you and Edward."

"You mean, then, that the word that reached us was false?"

"What word?"

"That you had disinherited your own son, the true Prince, and proclaimed York your heir."

"Oh, that ...well...you see...it meant nothing...I was forced..." He began twisting his ring.

"Forced? The King forced?"

"I thought it would be better."

"Better?" scoffed Margaret. "For York or Lancaster? Henry, were I King I trow I would not be forced."

"No, I don't suppose you would be ... but my poor people -- all this bloodshed. I thought I might stop it, but I guess I only made it worse." He shrugged his shoulders hopelessly and some of the new, glad light went out of his eyes.

"Well," said his wife, softening toward him as always, "What's done is done. Now, anyway, you are in a position to revoke the agreement -- his disinheritance."

"Yes, yes, of course. I'll do it right away."

How could he explain to her that he had hoped to save their Edward from the trials of being a King? He, himself, had no choice; he'd been anointed and consecrated to this heavy duty ... now it looked as if someday their son would have to take up this burden.

Margaret wondered *...will Henry's revocation be enough? Men may say I coerced him. He must do something positive to reinstate and reinforce Edward's position as rightful heir.*

She said, "You must do something special for Edward to show to all men your favor toward him."

Henry thought and then said, "I know. I shall knight him -- right here."

The following day, Prince Edward, dressed in a purple velvet brigandine, was blessed and knighted by his proud father. The seven-year-old Prince then, in his turn, knighted thirty Lancastrian soldiers, including Anthony Trollope who protested that he did not deserve such an honor because, he said, "I slew but fifteen men, for I stood still in one place and they came unto me, but they bode still with me." He had stood still in one place because his foot had been impaled on a caltrop.

After the ceremony, some of Margaret's men who had won

no honors decided they would show their own power. They dragged up Sir Thomas Kyriel and Lord Bonville and summarily struck off their heads with Margaret's approval.

When Henry learned of this he was aghast. "Margaret, what have you done?" he cried in horror. "What have you done?"

"They were traitors -- Warwick's friends."

"But I'd promised them their safety. I told them I would give them safe passage if they stayed with me. I promised them. I gave my word."

Margaret was chastened. She had no excuse except that they were Warwick's friends. She knew that would never be enough for Henry. All she could offer was, "I did not know."

CHAPTER TWENTY-SEVEN

February - March 1461

Better for Margaret's cause had she loaded Bonville and Kyriel with gifts and set them free, for Henry was so upset by this bloody act that he turned stubborn. When Margaret purposed to take her troops and storm London, Henry, with unaccustomed firmness, flatly forbade it. A rapid advance by the successful army, accompanied by their King, would surely have won London which remained undefended. Warwick had gathered his fleeing men and was headed west to look for his cousin Edward and his army.

"Madame," counseled Somerset, "Let us consolidate our gains and take London now."

"While we yet can," put in Trollope, now Sir Andrew. Still limping from his wound, he warned, "Wait and it may be too late. I know the Earl; he's but taken a little setback. First thing you know, he'll rally his men and be on us again."

Margaret clenched her fists. "I know. All that you say is true, but the King has forbidden us to enter London without the consent of its citizens."

Clifford smiled and said softly, "We all know that the King is a noble and ...good...Lord, but not exactly...well, you know... Perhaps it would be better not to bother him with this just now. Let him consult with his priests while you, my Lady, consult with your captains."

Margaret turned away from them. "I dare not. You have not seen the King these past hours. He rages in his tent. I have seen him in such wise only once before. He has been much shaken by the deaths of Bonville and Kyriel.

She rounded on Clifford. "You, too, have done that which has saddened the King. He mourns that while his father had a soldier hanged for stealing a pyx in France, an enemy country, he is forced to stand idly by while his men wantonly pillage their own churches. The Abbot has complained of how your men have sacked his Abbey and desecrated the holy altar, with never restraining hand of yours to stop them."

"It is not easy to hold men in check when they get excited, as you know; and this King is not like his father," countered Clifford.

"Yes, I know, and the King is excited, too. I dare not go against him - if I do, I fear for his sanity."

Clifford was about to retort when Somerset interrupted. "For God's sake, let's not quarrel. The Queen is right. It is not meet, nor wise, to upset his Majesty further."

"What shall we do, then?" asked Trollope.

They all looked to Margaret who was trying to calm herself, to think. Finally she spoke. "As I see it, we have two problems. First, to reassure the King and pacify him. Remember, he has not had an easy time lately, held as a virtual prisoner, and now ..." she looked steadily at Clifford, "Upset by unruly soldiers. Second, we must hold London."

"How, if we can't force them?" asked Somerset.

"Persuasion. Surely we can treat with the Common Council or the merchants or someone. After all, we do have the King on our side."

Persuasion was not as easy as Margaret had hoped. No one in the city wanted to venture out to treat with her hostile army. The Londoners were agog with fear of the northern marauders and hastened to shutter their shops, hide their belongings, and pray for their wives and daughters. On every side, men sharpened weapons grown rusty since the days of Cade's invasion. The Lancastrians among them went in almost as much fear as the Yorkists. Margaret tried to get the city to let Somerset enter with a limited number of men. The city refused, but countered by sending a few aldermen out, accompanied by the Dowager Duchess of Buckingham, Prince Edward's beloved Godmother; and Jacquetta Woodville, the Countess Rivers, to plead with the Queen for leniency toward London. The aldermen wore their robes of state but rather than striding purposefully and importantly as was their wont in city processions, they made themselves as small as possible, hiding their ample frames as well as they could behind the women. They had no wish to further anger the already wrathful Queen.

The Duchess of Buckingham spoke first and to the point. "Madame, the London Council has sent us to extend their full welcome to you and our King, provided only that you give them your solemn promise that you will guarantee the safety of the city; that there will be no pillage."

Margaret's heart sank. Neither she nor her captains had been able to restrain the men outside the city; inside, the mob would only do worse. She dared not let the aldermen realize her weakness. So, in her sternest manner she said, "We shall bide a while without the gates. But the men are tired and hungry and have long been unpaid. They fought hard for their sovereign at St. Albans and deserve some reward for loyalty ... for hardships suffered while others sat at home in comfort." She waited. One of the aldermen nudged Jacquetta who spoke then.

"We have been commissioned to promise you a sum of money and a cartload of food, but only on the understanding that some of your troops depart. The Lord Mayor says we cannot supply all of them."

"All right. To show our good faith, part of the army will be sent back to Dunstable. But in return, we expect to send a small force into London to talk with the Council and make arrangements for you to receive King Henry and the Prince of Wales."

The aldermen spoke with the women, then agreed with Margaret's proposals. She felt better. With part of the army at Dunstable where they would not frighten the Londoners, yet could be recalled if necessary, and the others placated with provender, she and Henry might yet hold London in peace. Whoever held the capital, held the key to England.

Before the delegation returned, the women drew aside to speak privately to Margaret.

"Madame," said the Duchess, "You know I love you and the King ... my son and husband died in your cause ... but because I love you, I feel that I can say, 'Please, let there be no more bloodshed.'"

Jacquetta added her earnest voice. "You know my loyalty; my husband and my son are still Warwick's prisoners in Calais, and I have no love for the Yorkists; yet, I, too, plead for peace. There has been too much of grief."

Margaret drew back. "Since your plaint is to me, no doubt you think this bloodshed is my fault. Aye, there has been grief on grief, but caused by whom? By those who make a mockery of their anointed Lord and thrust their trueborn Prince out of his rightful place. Do you think I like to see my friends slain? Or close mewed up?"

"Then can't you stop the battles?" asked the Duchess.

"When we win, the battles will stop." Margaret turned to Jacquetta. "You speak of grief. Do you think I want to add to any man's or woman's tears? And yet before you go, I'll add to yours."

"What now?" Jacquetta was frightened. "Have you news from Calais?"

"No. Closer home than that. At St. Albans ... John Grey, your daughter's husband..."

The color drained from the older woman's face. "Wounded?"

"Dead."

The Countess crossed herself. "Jesu, how shall I tell her ... with two small sons ...?"

Margaret stood unmoving. "Tell her he died with honor."

The women, and the aldermen who had remained warily silent throughout, mounted and rode slowly back toward London. Margaret watched them. The tears welled in her eyes. *This was not what she wanted -- the fear of her people, the grief of her friends, but if this is what it took, she would do it -- and more.*

While these negotiations were going on, word reached Yorkist sympathizers in the city that Warwick's men had joined those of Edward's and that ten thousand of them were making double time toward the relief of the capital. This gave the Londoners such hope that a band of them under Wenlock's leadership plundered the wagons of provisions and money which the Lord Mayor sent out in reply to Margaret's demands. At this, the furious Queen determined to storm the city gates despite everything, but before she could prepare to advance, she was warned that Warwick and Edward were but a few miles off. The Lancastrians would be caught between the Yorkists and the enraged citizens fighting for their homes. She dared not stand and meet the advancing forces where she was, for many of her men had deserted and were on their way to their northern homes, plundering the countryside again as they went. There was nothing left for Margaret to do but fall back to Dunstable and thence northward.

On February 27, just ten days after he had been forced to retreat from St. Albans, Warwick, with his cousin Edward of York, rode victoriously into London to happy shouts from the throngs who lined the streets to welcome them. Warwick well read the temper of the rejoicing crowds. Where a few short months ago they would have none of York's supplanting a beloved Henry, now they cheered wildly for York's son Edward who had saved them from the northern hordes. And Henry? Well, he was back under the control of his wife whom they hated, back in the control of the old court party. *Why should there not be a new court party* thought Warwick...*with him in control?* He moved swiftly to take advantage of the new mood in the city.

The very next day, the Earl assembled his troops in St. Johns Fields. When they were in position and a large crowd had gathered, Warwick's brother, George Neville, the Chancellor, read to them the old agreement made between the King and the Duke of York. He said that Henry had not kept his part of the pledge and had forfeited his right to the crown. Then he asked the assembly if they would accept Edward as their true King.

"Aye, aye!" rose the shout. "Long live the King! Edward! Edward!"

On March 4, dressed in royal robes, and preceded by Warwick carrying the sword of state, Edward rode to a Mass at St. Paul's, then on to Westminster Hall where he took the King's seat upon which his father had so fruitlessly laid his hand. Next, he walked to the Abbey where the Abbot placed in his hands the scepter of Edward the Confessor. He offered at the high altar and at the Confessor's tomb. Then he took his seat on the royal throne and received the acclamation of all present.

While the handsome young giant, nineteen-year-old Edward of York, was proclaimed Edward the Fourth, King of England, Margaret, with Henry and Prince Edward, was in flight northward toward York.

CHAPTER TWENTY-EIGHT

March 1461

Palm Sunday night, March 29, was cold and bright; the moon shone like a weak sun on the day's snowfall. Henry and Margaret, with Prince Edward riding pillion behind her, accompanied by a handful of friends, quitted York Castle and gave their horses head toward Scotland and safety. They stayed neither for goods nor baggage for it meant death to any of them caught by the advancing Yorkists. At dusk, Somerset and Exeter had pounded up to the castle with news that half the Lancastrian army had been slaughtered at Towton Field, only ten miles away, and that Edward and Warwick were on their way to take the city of York.

Not till later when they stopped to rest their tired horses did Margaret hear the full story pieced out by Exeter and Somerset.

When they had arrived at York on their flight from London, Margaret and Henry had rallied over 25,000 men to their cause but Warwick immediately started north and was joined by many who flocked to the banner of the recently proclaimed Edward. The new King and the Earl were determined to scotch the Lancastrian claims once and for all. Soon the two sides stood ranged for battle, each confident of victory. The Yorkists had eight thousand fewer men than their opponents, but they marched in tight, well disciplined order in contrast to the unruliness of their enemies. Edward and Warwick were spurred on by desire for revenge; each had a father and a brother to avenge. Margaret was driven, as always now, by her fierce love and ambition for her son.

The huge Red Rose army was drawn up a little south of Towton, not far from York. To the right and behind, lay Cock Brook, crossed by a small bridge. The usually shallow brook was swollen by winter rains. To the left, a road led south to Ferrybridge on the Aire River.

On Saturday, the 28th, Lord Clifford had ventured to Ferrybridge where he destroyed the bridge in an attempt to keep the Yorkists south of the river. As he returned, he was ambushed. Caught completely unawares, thinking himself in safe territory, his helmet off, the bloody Clifford fell, pierced through the throat by an arrow. Most of his men got back to their own lines but they were disheartened by the loss of their fierce leader.

The Yorkists had repaired the bridge and crossed over it while the northern lords were arguing with Henry who said he would under no circumstances do battle on Palm Sunday.

Not all the Lancastrians were sorry to see Henry refuse to take the field. Those who loved him were worried, not only about his safety but also about the state of his mind. Margaret had confided to Somerset and Exeter that the King had been brooding over the murder and rapine done by his unruly troops, that he slept fitfully on their march north, and that he was more and more troubled by evil dreams from which he would wake shrieking. The worst dream, the one that recurred most frequently, was a bloody nightmare in which a father unwittingly murdered his son in battle while another son slew his own father.

"Do not insist that the King fight," warned Margaret, and so they had let him be to attend to his beads and prayers.

By Saturday night, the Yorkists were drawn up on a small hill across from the Lancastrians.

The battle began about four in the morning of Palm Sunday. A light snow which had been sifting down all night increased and the wind began to gust. Once more, the heavens worked against the Queen. Suddenly the wind veered and drove a blizzard of snow and sleet straight into the Lancastrian faces so that they were blinded and could scarcely see their opponents. The Yorkists quickly seized the advantage. The archers advanced, let loose their arrows, and immediately pulled back. The first volley of arrows did great damage to the Queen's men. They, thinking the enemy still in range, let fly with their own arrows only to have them fall short. Thrice more the Yorkists shot, picking up Lancastrian misspent arrows as they went. The

Lancastrians ran short of arrows. Still the Yorkist missiles rained upon them, wreaking havoc. Blinded by the icy blizzard and cut down by enemy fire, their position which had seemed so favorable, became untenable.

All morning the battle continued. Despite the trouble with the archers, the Queen's army began to push back Edward's line. But then, Norfolk came swinging up the road to throw his forces against the Lancastrian left flank. Norfolk's men, fresh and untired, slowly drove back their weary enemies who had been fighting for almost seven hours. Two more hours of constant pressure drove the exhausted men off the hill. Back of them was no place to flee but Cock Brook. Some soldiers got across the narrow bridge and some waded the flooded waters at shallow spots, but many fell into the deeper holes or slipped from the wet and slimy stones. Once down, a man never rose, for his armor weighted him. Even the leather jackets of the foot soldiers were cumbersome, and the icy waters of the Cock proved the grave of thousands that day. Eventually the bodies were piled so high that some luckier men escaped over them. By dusk, the brook was full and ran red. The snow of Towton Field had turned from white to crimson. Ten thousand English men and boys died there that Palm Sunday, and most of them were Lancastrians.

Margaret, stunned, learned the full extent of her losses: Clifford, Northumberland, Stafford, Trollope, and a host of other brave men. Most of the nobility had been left on the red snow of Towton Field. Exeter's brother and the Earl of Devon were taken, to be beheaded the next day. And Jamie Butler, the handsome Earl of Wiltshire, so often her despair, was captured on his way to join Margaret and Henry. He was beheaded by Edward at Newcastle, his head sent to blacken on London Bridge. The horror of so many battles, of St. Albans, Wakefield, Northampton, Towton, piled one on another, the old friends lost to bloody death, now followed by young friends -- it was too much. The tears refused to come.

Edward's first victorious act was to remove the drying heads of his father, brother, uncle, and cousin from Micklegate Bar and give them Christian burial. While Margaret and Henry fled northward, almost alone, toward Scotland, Edward kept Easter with regal dignity at York and then set off northward himself to try to overtake the royal fugitives.

Towton Field had swallowed Margaret's hopes.

CHAPTER TWENTY-NINE

June 1461 - December 1462

It was late June, and while the youthful Earl of March was being crowned Edward the Fourth in Westminster, Henry and Margaret lay at Edinburgh Castle, partaking of the hospitality of Mary of Gueldres, Queen-Regent of Scotland. Margaret had sent Somerset, Hungerford and Whittingham to France to ask aid from her uncle, King Charles. Her ambassadors landed in France only to learn that Charles had died and that his son, Louis the Eleventh, was King. The men were sent to cool their heels in Dieppe, waiting an audience with the new ruler.

When Edward in London heard of the accession of Louis, he was encouraged for as Dauphin Louis had shown his party favor. Louis as King would be another matter. He, who was to go down in history as the Spider King, was a devious man, utterly ambitious to unite France under his firm hand. Louis decided to help his cousin Margaret, only because he realized that young Edward with his friend Warwick was stronger than Margaret and Henry, and Louis wanted a weak England.

He sent Margaret's emissaries home with many apologies for their troubles...*it was an unsettled time...the changeover in government...such an unhappy misunderstanding.* He gave them a few gifts and vague hints of possible aid for their mistress. It was enough, though, to hearten her who had no other straws to grasp.

In April 1462, seventeen years after she had bid farewell to her childhood home, Margaret left Henry and Prince Edward in Scotland and sailed back to France, accompanied by Somerset and Jasper Tudor to seek aid from her cousin.

First they went to Angers where she was welcomed by her father, Rene, and his wife, Jeanne de Laval, whom he had married nine years before, after Isabelle's death. The two women greeted each other stiffly. When Rene gathered his daughter into his arms she surprised herself and her father by bursting into tears with unexpected emotion.

When she calmed down, Rene held her at arm's length and exclaimed, "You are as lovely as ever." Privately, he thought she had not aged well. She was still lovely, only thirty-two, but few of the seventeen years since her marriage had been happy or peaceful.

Rene, ever a showman, played the loving grandfather but his heart was not in it. He listened politely while Margaret bragged about little Edward -- what a good child he was, how smart, how brave! But Rene patently wasn't very interested in a far off grandson -- nor in his daughter's troubles.

"Perhaps your cousin King Louis can help you. You know there is nothing I would like better than to give you all my possessions if it would put your husband back on the throne, but -- you understand -- I have problems, too."

Margaret realized she was being dismissed.

She had not expected much help from her father so that was no great surprise, but she was hurt, just the same. She did not know exactly what she expected of him but it was more than she had received.

She would go on in her quest for succor from France. She could not afford to give in to disappointment.

The King was at Chinon so Margaret and her friends went to Chinon to plead her case.

Louis received her in his audience chamber. "You need help and *Le Bon Dieu* knows that above all things we would like to give you that help ...but we would be remiss in our new duties as King if we did not think first of our poor people. Naturally they must have first call on any funds from our meager coffers, my dear Cousin, is that not so?"

Naturally, your Highness."

"Naturally. Ah, it is hard to go against the desires of the heart ... but duty ... we are sure you, as sovereign, yourself, understand. *Hein?*"

She nodded, her heart sinking, her pride galled at his condescending tone. But she *must* enlist France's aid. It was her last hope.

Somerset stepped forward, "Could not your Highness look upon aid to her Grace's cause as an investment? For your people? It is plain that the usurper Edward grows closer daily to the house of Burgundy and throws the lucrative English trade toward them. Would it not rather profit France were Henry, the true King, on the throne -- grateful to his kinsman and more likely to increase English trade with France?

King Louis drew his lips into a thin line, then pursed them. He fingered a religious amulet he wore on his shabby hat. He considered. There was not a sound in the hall other than the heavy breathing of Louis and those who waited. Finally, he looked up.

"Perhaps. But an investment should be secured. What have you to offer? You forgive us ... you understand this is merely to protect our poor people ... to whom we stand in the place of a father..."

Margaret admitted, "Nothing, except the chance to ally yourself with friends and discomfit old enemies."

"Ah," he remonstrated. "But Burgundy had long been our friend. He gave us sanctuary when our late, beloved father, whom God forgive ... misunderstood us."

Margaret persisted. "But now you are the father -- to your people, as you said."

"Yes ...and?"

"And I believe their interests lie with England -- and Henry -- rather than with Philip of Burgundy."

"You may be right. But we have been thinking ... if there is no security, it makes it a gamble rather than an investment, doesn't it?"

"A sure gamble. We have it all worked out. Money, men, and ships from you and we mount an invasion from the east. At the same time, we still have loyal troops in the north, and Pembroke here," she indicated Jasper Tudor, "will bring men from Wales, from the west. This time we cannot lose."

"All the same," said Louis dogmatically, "It is a gamble."

"For high stakes."

"Then you, too, should risk something."

Somerset broke in. "We do risk something. We risk much -- our lives."

Louis laughed softly. "You do, you do ... but these hardly help our people."

"Your children," muttered Somerset under his breath, but Louis either did not hear or disdained to notice him and, making a peak of his fingers, continued, "Say we loan you 20,000 livres ... and a body of men... and some ships ... not too many, but sufficient to carry the men...Let us set a fair reward for this investment, or gamble ..." He trailed off while they waited impatiently for him to finish. He nodded his head thoughtfully and went on, "Yes ..." Then his voice hardened. "In return for this, you turn over to us ... what is our rightful property, anyway -- Calais!"

The English were horrified. Somerset forgot himself and cried aloud to Margaret," No, you can't! You can't!"

"Ah, I see that we have upset you," said Louis sadly. "Perhaps it was not a good idea. Let us forget it."

"No, no!" cried Margaret. "Wait!" she tried to collect her thoughts. Calais was a nuisance, a stronghold governed by her arch-enemy, Warwick, from whence came only trouble. Her friends did not share her feelings toward Calais. but whatever they thought, she could not afford to lose Louis' help.

"Double the money," she said desperately. "Within a year of the King's restoration, I guarantee that we will pay you back double your 20,000 livres."

"And if not -- then Calais?"

"Y-yes," she said.

Louis furnished Margaret a body of one thousand men-at-arms with their attendants and placed over them her old friend, Pierre deBreze. They tried to keep the bargain secret but the news, as always, leaked out. Edward's fleet patrolled the Channel on the lookout for the Queen. When everything was ready, she with her men, eluded the English ships and landed at Tynemouth. There she waited but the troops she had counted on did not come. The Northumbrians, fearful of Edward's army, kept to their homes.

In despair, Margaret turned to Breze for advice and made him commander of her forces. She told Somerset, "Breze has had much experience in warfare -- many more years than you and my other English captains. Besides, the French soldiers are used to him and will more readily obey his commands. You understand, don't you?"

Somerset sulked. "Oh, I understand, Madame, and I realize, too, that you would hardly want to rely on us when we did so poorly at Towton."

, "That's not fair! Surely you can't believe that I have anything but the greatest trust in your skill ... I know your bravery is second to none."

"Then put me in charge," challenged the young Duke.

"You shall be in charge --" She raised her hand to silence him. "Not of the French troops, but of one of the castle strongholds we intend to get and keep so that we will have a northern base from which to move. Pierre says this is most important."

The tall French soldier nodded his head. Then he took a stick and drew a few, quick lines in the dirt to indicate the English coast. "Now, here we are. We move north along the coast and take Alnwick first ..."

And so they did. Here they left Hungerford and Whittingham in charge, along with Breze's son. Next, they moved to Dunstanburgh where Margaret installed more men. On from there they went to Bamborough which she placed in the hands of Somerset and Ralph Percy, brother of the dead Northumberland. They were still hopeful of Scottish and Northumbrian reinforcements when they learned of approaching Yorkists. Margaret left garrisons at each of the three castles and took the rest of the troops and set sail with them, under Breze, headed for Berwick and safety. Her last words to Somerset and Percy were that she would be back as soon as possible.

Margaret's fleet of fifty-odd small ships, with sails partly furled, ran before a near gale. It was a motley armada, no two of the ships alike in size or shape.

The Queen, with Breze, was aboard the largest of the vessels which belied her name, the *Belle Dame*. Designed as a merchant ship, she was broad of beam and stubby of mast. Her makeshift conversion to a vessel of war did little to improve her appearance. A few cannon protruded through hastily cut openings in her gunnels; her decks were crowded with men, horses, ammunition, and supplies, placed at random.

Their plan, outlined by Breze, was simple. The fleet would stay together and within sight of land until they reached Berwick. Their fastest ship, the *Sans Souci,* a small caravel, used as often for smuggling as for fishing, had been ordered to lie off the coast to bring warning should Edward's fleet appear. Her captain and crew had sailed together for years and had joined this venture in hope of booty. Confident of their ability to outsail any craft they might encounter, they were an ideal rear guard.

The *Belle Dame's* captain was apprehensive. This undertaking was not to his taste. The confusion galled his sense of order and he was in strange waters with an unskilled crew and no charts worthy of the name. During the first day, they sailed at hull speed with sails partially furled. The wind had risen until there was spindrift on the surface of the sea. As darkness approached, the fleet cautiously felt its way toward shore, hove to, and anchored.

At first light they were underway again. During the night the wind had shifted to the south and continued to rise ominously.

"Berwick cannot be far," said Breze. "With this wind we should soon be there."

Just then, the lookout cried, "Astern, astern! The *Sans Souci!*"

The latter, under full sail, rapidly overhauled the *Belle Dame*. Her captain shouted that he had sighted three English ships headed north toward them. The captains called back and forth with Breze joining in. Then the Frenchman reported to Margaret, "The English are coming, and in better ships than ours so there is no question of fighting. We are disbanding the fleet. Each ship will sail for Berwick as fast as she can. Some of us --

perhaps all -- can outrun the English. If we once make the river, their larger ships won't be able to follow us."

Margaret watched the smaller ships pull ahead and out of sight. The captain of the *Belle Dame* sent his sailors scrambling aloft to set the sails, and a froth of foam appeared at the ship's bow as she picked up speed. Coming about smartly, the *Sans Souci* began to beat back toward their pursuers, to look and to flee again, if necessary.

Quiet followed the frenzied activity aboard the *Belle Dame*. There was nothing to do now but wait and pray that they could reach Berwick before they were overtaken. With the wind at her stern, and pushed ahead by the rising swells, the broad beamed merchant ship sailed as she had never sailed before. Margaret and Breze exulted in their speed and the feel of the wind in their faces. Surely they would outrun the English. But the captain shook his head with foreboding. Only he realized the fearful strain that the ever rising gale put on their masts and rigging.

Suddenly there was a cannon-like report as the mainmast snapped at deck level and crashed into the sea amid a tangle of lines. The ship braked and turned until it wallowed helplessly. The captain and his crew worked frantically to cut the mast free as the ship rolled sickeningly. Two of the French cannon which King Louis had given them tore loose from their lashings and smashed heavily into a mass of terrified, rearing, neighing horses and screaming soldiers. As the ship rolled, water from the boiling sea poured over all of them.

At this moment, the *Sans Souci* reappeared. With mainsails furled and storm jibs flying, she slipped skillfully into the lee of the *Belle Dame* and hove to. Quickly, the captain set some of his crew to launch a small boat as he summoned Margaret and Breze.

Holding to ropes and capstans, and over and over losing her footing on the wet, pitching deck, Margaret finally, with Breze's help, reached the side and was lowered into the boat as it pulled away to the *Sans Souci* where they were hauled aboard, wet and shivering. As the *Sans Souci* fell away and headed for Berwick, Margaret, her soaked dress plastered against her shaking body, her drenched hair loosened and down to her waist, was taken to the captain's room and made as comfortable as possible. She was safe, but where was the rest of her fleet?

When they reached Berwick, she learned that the *Belle Dame* and others of her larger ships were lost. Besides this, six hundred of her French soldiers had been driven aground on Holy Island where they had been forced to surrender to their English pursuers. The main part of Margaret's new army and her French loan were gone.

Worse was yet to come. While she had been battling the storm at sea, the forces she had left under Somerset put down their arms and marched out into the hands of Warwick. In her safe harbor at Berwick, Margaret was stunned to learn that Somerset, her staunchest supporter, had been pardoned and taken into favor by Edward.

CHAPTER THIRTY

January - July 1463

Margaret brooded over Somerset's betrayal. Could it have been for jealous anger? She knew he had disliked her old friend, Breze, considered him a sly Frenchman, resented the long, intimate talks -- they were merely laughing over and reliving the days when she was carefree and young in Anjou and he and a dozen others bore her girlish favors in her father's tournaments. *Such a silly thing to be cross about!* Too late she remembered Somerset's anger at being left in charge of Bamborough Castle -- *mured up, he* had complained -- while she and Breze sailed to Berwick. But never, never would she have thought he would turn traitor. Wenlock, Grey deRuthyn, the others: these defections had grieved and embittered her, but none to severely as Somerset's.

And still another blow. Sir Ralph Percy, brother of the Northumberland slain at Towton, and head of the Percy family during his nephew's minority, had also lined up with the usurper. In return for his treason, he was made Governor of Bamborough by a grateful Edward. She shook her head and then laughed at a sudden thought. *I wonder how they'll get along, the Nevilles and the Percies...what an odd group the usurper has gathered about him. Perhaps they will tear each other apart ...like wild dogs...*

Dunstanburgh also surrendered; the whole north was now lost. Only the besieged Alnwick Castle, garrisoned by Breze's son, stood, now in an untenable position with Warwick a few miles south.

Margaret had been deserted by old friends but it was far from her intention to leave any of her own loyal soldiers at the mercy of enemies. At five o'clock in the morning of a cold January day, Pierre deBreze, at the head of a small Lancastrian force, marched up to the gates of Alnwick, almost under the very nose of Warwick. Before Earl Richard could muster his sleepy troops, the castle garrison poured out and swiftly fled, some of them riding pillion with their rescuers. Soon the men, once considered hopelessly trapped, were safe over the border in Scotland.

Now only Harlech Castle in Wales held out for Lancaster.

Warwick felt no further need to stay in the north and went to London to enjoy a more leisurely life. His wife and daughters Anne and Isabel joined him there. The only thing that disturbed his sense of well-being, of peace and good will, was a small but nagging worry that King Edward was becoming soft and luxury-loving. The Earl tried to remonstrate with his cousin but Edward laughed good naturedly and chided him for a Lollard.

In May, while Warwick and Edward were in London, Margaret was heartened by word that Ralph Percy had become disenchanted with the usurper and the Nevilles and wished for a return of the old government. At the same time, news came that Sir Ralph Grey, a Yorkist, was also willing to change sides. He had been promised the governorship of Alnwick Castle by Edward who then reneged on his pledge. Margaret, Hungerford and Breze hurried south with a band of Scots and received both Bamborough and Alnwick back into their hands.

In July, over Henry's objections, Margaret took the nine-year-old Edward with her on a foray into northern England to try to capture Norham Castle on the Scots border. Young Prince Edward was already being taught the arts of war. Margaret said, "I am determined that he be a strong ruler once the reins of government are secured for his hands. The only way to learn is to do."

Henry, his feelings wounded, let her have her way. He understood the unspoken rebuke.

The Queen expected the capture of Norham to be simple, but even so, after the Prince's presence had stirred up her forces' patriotic fervor, she insisted he remain well behind the active lines to insure his safety. It was lucky that she did, for instead of the small band of armed retainers she expected to encounter, the enemy turned out to be Warwick and his brother Montagu who had hurried north on getting word of Margaret's approach. Her company was broken up and scattered and in the confusion she and the Prince were separated from the rest.

They galloped along a narrow, rutted road which turned into a forest. Soon they came upon a fallen tree where the road disappeared completely.

"We'd better turn back," said the boy.

"No, we dare not. If the Nevilles learn we were at Norham -- and surely someone will tell them -- they'll be on the lookout for us. We'll have to go on and trust the road takes up again."

"Wait here a moment," said Edward, dismounting and handing the reins to his mother. "I'll walk around and see if I can find any sign of a path."

"Don't go out of sight of me," she cautioned. "The trees are dense and you could easily get lost."

"Don't worry. I won't go far and I could break twigs or mark the tree trunks with my knife to show me the way back. My father and Exeter showed me how when we were hunting."

Margaret smiled at his serious manner and his pride in knowing what to do, but she said, "If you get lost whole hunting you can always sound your horn; here, we'd better be as quiet as possible. Right now we don't want the wrong people to find us. Hurry, now, and see if you can find a path."

He was back in a few minutes. "No good, but it's not very thick on ahead. Maybe there was a road that's grown over."

He mounted and they continued, their horses stepping carefully over downed trees and avoiding heavy undergrowth and brambles. Soon the trees became denser than ever and Margaret received many a sharp and painful sting when a branch that Edward had pushed aside snapped back and whipped across her face. However, she kept on silently.

The horses were tired and lathered from their hard gallop and now the added labor of picking their way through the woods. Margaret became more and more worried but hid her uneasiness so as not to frighten her son. He was big for his age, and competent, but he was still a child and she knew that their situation was truly precarious. The enemies behind would give them no quarter. She thought of York's young Edmund and his terrible fate. Ahead lay, she knew not what. *Could the dead watch them? Were York and his son's spirits hovering near? Bonville? Kyriel?* She pressed the crucifix she wore about her neck and breathed a prayer. Surely Edward would be protected by Heaven ... but if not by Heaven, then by her.

Suddenly Edward's horse caught his foot in a hole that lay hidden under some brush and crashed down heavily, pinning the boy's leg under him. Margaret stiffly dismounted and ran to her son.

"Edward," she cried in a low voice. "Are you all right?"

"I think so, but my knee hurts."

Pulling with all her strength, she managed to free him and helped him to his feet. His knee ached terribly, he said, but when she pressed it she could feel nothing unusual.

"Here, lean on me and see if you can put your weight on that leg."

He did, wincing, and said, "I guess it's all right, but something's the matter with Sorel."

The horse had not risen and was nickering painfully. Margaret ran her hand down the horse's leg. She was dismayed. "Dear, I fear his leg is broken."

"But it can't be ... are you sure? It wasn't a bad fall."

"Yes, I'm sure. Feel here."

The boy's eyes filled with tears. "But ... but ...what can we do? Where can we get help?"

Margaret was feverish and near exhaustion and filled with apprehension for her son, but she tried to comfort him. As kindly as she could, she told him, "Dear, there's only one thing we *can* do -- we must kill him."

He began to cry harder and she was afraid he would break down completely so she forced herself to be stern though she wanted to hold him and weep with him. "Edward, you must not. Remember who you are. This has to be done. When a horse breaks his leg he must be slain. He cannot get well and he is in pain ... soon his neighing will become louder and may bring our foes upon us. I will show you where to press with your sword and Sorel's pain will be over."

He took his sword of which he was so proud, with its jeweled hilt, the sword his father had knighted him with, and pressed where Margaret pointed, just behind Sorel's shoulder, forward of his ribs, but he could not drive it in.

"You must hurry."

"I cannot, Mother. I cannot!."

"Give it to me, then. And go over there." She took the sword and as soon as Edward turned to limp away, she clenched her jaws, closed her eyes, and plunged the weapon deep into the spot she had indicated. Sorel gave a great shudder and was still.

As she pulled out the sword and wiped the blade on some leaves she wondered how soon it would be bathed in human blood. She went over to Edward and gathered the sobbing boy into her arms and stroked his hair."

"I am so sorry, Dear, but there was no choice. Now we must decide what to do. We dare not linger."

As she released him she saw she had left a great red streak of blood on his forehead. She shivered and looked at her hand. Sorel's blood was already drying to a dirty brown. She wiped her hand on her gown and went over to examine her own horse.

"She can go no further," she observed. "We'll have to walk. Help me take off her saddle and bridle so she doesn't get entangled in the bushes. When we find our way out, we'll send someone after her." She wasn't at all sure they would be able to find their way out and if they did it might be into enemy hands, but at least she would give the poor beast a chance.

The two set out, not sure of their direction, but determined to try to reach Scotland and safety. It was nightfall when, numbed with fatigue, they stumbled on a cave. They were hungry, thirsty and tired, their clothes ripped and torn by brambles. Their faces and arms were scratched and caked with dried blood and sweat. Edward's knee pained him more than ever but he bore it bravely while he leaned on his mother. The heat of the day had turned to a night chill so they huddled together for warmth, Margaret curling around her son, trying to protect him from the cold. Exhausted as they were, he fell asleep immediately in spite of hunger and his throbbing knee, but she lay thinking and worrying, unable to sleep. They would have to be on the move in the morning.

*Will we be able to find a house? Will the people be friendly? Surely no one will dream two such ragged and dirty creatures as we are could be the royal family...*Sometime before dawn she fell into a fitful, uneasy sleep. They were wakened by the sound of loud, rough laughter.

"Come, see what we have here," cried a tall, unshaven man.

Margaret pulled herself up to a sitting position and Edward moaned a little and opened his eyes. Then he, too, sat up. Two other men came running. They were dressed in soiled and torn homespun and their shaggy heads were unkempt and matted. One, who was fat, bent over Margaret and jerked her to her feet. Edward sprang up, wincing with pain, and hurled himself at the man who had pulled Margaret up.

"You let my mother alone!" he cried.

The tall man reached a dirty, ham hand and held him at arm's length. "Mettlesome wight, ain't he?"

"Who are you and what are you doing here?" demanded the fat man who held Margaret by the wrist.

Edward started to reply, "My mother is--" when she cut him off abruptly.

"I am a lady of Scotland. We were in a hunting party and became lost. If you will direct me to my home, you will receive a rich reward."

The man dropped her hand and stepped back so that he could see her better.

"You don't sound like a Scotswoman," he said.

She caught Edward's eye with a warning look. "Oh ...well, I was born in France, but my husband is in Scotland."

The men looked Margaret and Edward over, appraising them. Their clothes, although tattered and stained, were of good quality. The man who was holding Edward spied the boy's jeweled sword hilt. "God's, blood, look at that, will you." He dropped his hand from the boy's shoulder and pulled the sword from its scabbard.

"It has writing on it...what's it say?"

Again Edward started to answer and again Margaret broke in. "It says *Edward*. His father is a squire and a gentleman gave it to him."

"Must be worth more than a sovereign," said the man.

"I'm not sure the stones are real," said Margaret matter-of-factly.

"I think I'll keep it, anyway," snarled the man.

The third man, shorter and leaner than the other two, stood back, watching. Behind him, a rope around her neck, stood Margaret's horse, looking as well as ever, evidently rested during the night. By now, the fat man had noticed Margaret's hands. She wore the fair ruby which Henry had given her for a wedding ring, and three other rings besides. She wore, too, a gold, jeweled crucifix. He grabbed her hand and tugged at the ruby. It would not come off though he hurt her finger so that she cried out despite herself and Edward started toward her so that the ham handed man slapped him. The fat man avidly wrenched Margaret's other rings from her fingers and snatched the crucifix and chain from her neck.

"Guess I'll have to chop your finger off to get that ring," he threatened.

She would not quaver or let him see her fear. She repeated, "If you take us home, my husband will reward you."

"I'll wager," scoffed the man. "I can just guess what kind of reward an outlaw'd get ... most likely the block -- or the scourge, at least. I'll take my own reward here." He held her hand tightly and tugged at the knife in his belt. Margaret could not help but cower.

The third man who had been holding the horse and who had said nothing, stepped closer. "Just a minute. There's no sense in harming the lady ... yet. I've a mind to use her. Look you," he went on, "you've got three rings and that cross and Gil's got the sword. Let me have the woman with her ring."

"But you've got the horse. It'll fetch a good sum."

"Maybe, maybe not. I'll have to find a buyer."

"The ring, the woman, and the horse ... it's too much."

"Yes," agreed Gil. "And I ought to have more than the sword ... she said maybe the stones ain't real."

The third man edged closer to Edward, and Margaret thought he signaled to her to move nearer her horse. She didn't understand his intent but he seemed less hostile than the others. *Can he be trying to help us?* It was worth a try. She felt between the folds of her skirt where the small purse hanging from her girdle remained hidden. She pulled the purse loose and flung it

237

behind her into the cave where it fell with a thud and the sound of jingling coins. The fat man and the one who had hit Edward pushed past her and scrambled for the purse while she ran to the horse. The third man picked Edward up and swung him onto the saddle, then mounted himself and pulled Margaret up in front of him. With Edward clinging to his waist, he dug his heels into the horse's flanks and the three rode off.

They neither spoke nor stopped for a mile. Then they paused at a stream where they let the mare drink.

"What are you going to do with us?" asked Margaret. "Will you take us to Scotland and receive your reward?"

"Madame, I'll take you to some people who will take you to Scotland, but I don't figure to show my face far outside this forest. There's a price on my head."

"Why?" asked Edward.

"For several reasons. Long ago I ran off from my master... that was the second wrong thing I did. Since then, I've robbed a few people and I've killed the King's deer ... all crimes in England."

"You say *the second thing*...what was the first?" asked Margaret.

"I let my daughter marry off the manor ... but that was paid off." He peered at the Queen.

"Why, just such a thing happened --" Margaret stopped ..."You're the man, aren't you ...? It was such a long time ago ... I don't even remember quite where ... but I gave you ...a wedding present for your daughter ...Margery? Yes, that's it! Margery! ...But then, you know who we are?"

"I do."

"You'll hold us for ransom, then? From King Henry, not Edward, the usurper?" she asked, suddenly apprehensive. "King Henry will pay you well."

He shook his head. "No, Madame, I'll take no pay from either. It's few people who get a wedding gift from a Queen, but it's fewer still, who give a gift *to* a Queen. I give you your life and your son's. Now we'd better be off before my friends catch up with us."

In a house at the edge of the forest, the outlaw turned the

Queen and Prince over to Lancastrian sympathizers who promised to get them safely to Berwick.

Margaret said, "When King Henry comes to the throne again, come to ask your reward. You'll find that under the rightful King you won't have to be an outlaw."

The man laughed bitterly at this before he disappeared into the forest. "'Twas under King Henry that I became an outlaw and it's been no different under King Edward. Seems to me it doesn't matter much in the lives of common folk who sits on the throne."

CHAPTER THIRTY-ONE

August 1463 - May 1464

Warwick stayed in the area so there were no more Lancastrian forays over the border. With his brother, Montagu, the Earl sped past the troublesome castles and on a short way into Scotland. The fearful Scots repudiated Margaret and signed a treaty with King Edward. Margaret felt her welcome grow cold. What if the Scots decided to turn the royal family over to the usurper? Anything was possible.

"There is only one thing I can do now," she told Henry. "You must stay here, ready to take advantage of any chance that comes to increase your strength in the northern counties."

"What do you mean ... I stay here? You're not leaving me, are you?" Henry was miserable. "You know I need you more than ever."

"I know that more than you need me here, you need me in France. It is common knowledge that Burgundy is trying to arrange a peace between Louis and the usurper. They are planning a meeting of ambassadors."

"What has that to do with you?"

"Don't you see? We've lost Scotland as an ally. If we lose France, too, we shall never win the throne again.

Henry objected. "I still don't see what you can do."

"Oh. neither do I ... really." There was desperation in her voice. "Once I am there, perhaps it will come to me. There has to be *some* way to win Louis' support. It is our only chance!"

In August, with tears on Henry's part and loving promises on Margaret's, she and Edward set sail for Flanders. She was determined to prevent a meeting of the French with the Yorkists. Henry paced up and down in the royal cabin, bestowing kisses and blessings on his wife and son. He cautioned her time and again to guard her health and Edward's, to go daily to prayers, and to be sustained in all her endeavors by the gentle Lord Jesus. "Surely in our hour of need He will not forget us."

"No," she agreed humbly while the Prince, almost ten, raced about the deck, prying into all the new and interesting things he saw. He disappeared and then came back carrying a tabby cat he had discovered, to find his father and mother kneeling in prayer. Excited, he rushed into the room.

"The captain says she is to catch the mice and rats but I may play with her."

At a sign from his smiling mother, he broke off. His father was intoning Latin, and the young prince sank to his knees, too, the cat squirming in his arms.

With the tide, the ship moved slowly off. Margaret and Edward waved to Henry even after they could no longer make out his figure on the dock. It was the last sight of him they were ever to have.

In view of her last encounter, Margaret thought that a meeting with the cold and calculating Spider King, Louis, would be fruitless. She had no more towns to mortgage. Still beautiful, and pitied all over Europe as a tragic Queen, she decided as a last chance to appeal to the chivalrous Philip, Duke of Burgundy, who was supporting Edward. When the Duke learned of her approach, he fled to St. Pol, for a meeting with the deposed English Queen was the last thing he wanted. If he received her, he would have to show her his famed *politesse* and that did not fit in with his plans to ruin forever her chances to regain the English rule.

When Margaret arrived at Sluys, none of the officials could or would tell her the whereabouts of their Duke. She went first to Bruges, where she left Edward safe in the care of his tutor, Sir John Fortescue, and his squire, Sir William Vaux, Katherine's husband. Then, with only Katherine, two other women attendants, and the ever faithful Breze to accompany her, riding in a farm cart, dressed as a simple peasant to prevent word of her approach, she set out to track down Philip and force the meeting he so devoutly wished to avoid.

The jolting, dusty ride was lightened by her amusement at the thought of the Duke's chagrin at her arrival. At Lille, Philip's unfilial son and Margaret's friend, the Count of Charolais, entertained her lavishly, loaned her five hundred crowns and, with a satisfied grin, turned her cart toward St. Omer where the Anglo-French conference was soon to be held.

When Philip's friends brought him word of the cart with its riders, he decided he might better intercept the determined Queen rather than have her arrive at St. Omer to mar the negotiations. He sent out a party of archers to meet the cart and accompany Margaret to St. Pol where, he said, he would be most happy to receive his royal cousin. It was a splendid meeting despite Margaret's peasant clothes. At thirty-three she was still beautiful, although evidence of the years of strife and worry could be seen in the lines on her forehead and a tenseness around her mouth. Everyone was agog to catch a glimpse of her for her misfortunes were widely known and she wore an aura of romantic tragedy in the eyes of the common people.

Margaret carefully planned to appeal to Burgundy's famous chivalry, while he did his utmost to keep relations on a cold and formal level. When Philip appeared, Margaret ran to meet him, taking advantage of her air of *dishabille* to throw herself as a distressed woman on his vaunted courtesy and generosity. He held Margaret at arm's length and only with difficulty kept her from kneeling abjectly at his feet to plead for help for Henry.

"Madame. Your Grace. I implore you. Please," he hissed as she feigned deafness. He was a man well gone in years but he kept her on her feet.

"Wicked men who seek to set kindred at enmity have told you slanders about King Henry and myself," she told him. "We have only wished to be your friends."

"Oh, I believe you, your Grace," he assured her. "Never have I been impressed by these tales."

But try as she would, she was unable to move Philip from his resolve to reconcile France and Yorkist England. Although he gave a splendid banquet in his guest's honor -- in keeping with his reputation as a host -- and presented gifts to her, her women, and Breze, about the truce he remained adamant. "It is better for all Christendom," he explained. Neither stern arguments nor soft entreaties moved him. All her trouble to seek him out had been in vain.

A month later, France's Louis agreed to withhold any further aid to the Lancastrians. Hard on the heels of this came word that Mary of Gueldres had died and the other Regents of Scotland had signed a truce with Edward, promising to give no sanctuary to Margaret. Now she could not return to Henry in Scotland. Her presence at the court of either Burgundy or France was unthinkable. She had little choice but to accept her father Rene's rather reluctant invitation to spend the winter as his guest in the Duchy of Bar.

The long winter melancholy, lightened only by the growing promise of the young Prince, suddenly blossomed with hope as spring approached. Letters from Henry brought the almost unbelievably good news that Somerset was back. His jealousy of Breze had not been enough to sustain him in friendship with the usurper, although Edward had showered him with honors. Somerset had slept in the King's chamber and eaten with him at the high table, but such nights were unrefreshing and such food stuck in his throat. Honor was not something to be thrown away lightly in a pique or a fit of ill temper.

Somerset joined Henry who had fled to Bamborough Castle when the Scots signed the truce with Edward. There they spent the first three months of the year in safety. But the coming of spring also brought news that the Scots planned to extend their truce with Edward and to help him against the Lancastrians. Bamborough would not be able to hold out against a combined Scottish and Yorkist force.

News from England to Bar was maddeningly slow. The only letters from Henry asked her to form an alliance with Charolais of Burgundy, with Brittany. She was begged to obtain food, artillery, money from her father, from Louis, anyone. Henry did not seem to realize that she was powerless to arrange anything. Since Edward controlled England, no one on the continent wanted to become involved with Margaret.

Unfortunately, we have no money for this.
The time is not ripe.
Later, perhaps.
We cannot antagonize France.
We dare not provoke Burgundy.
Surely you understand.
Wait just a bit.
Wait.
Only wait.

And so she waited, helpless, wondering what was happening at Bamborough. The only thing that occupied her besides vain entreaties was Prince Edward's education. She saw to it that Exeter, who had joined her in exile, gave the young boy military training to fit him for the life of a soldier knight, while his main education was entrusted to Sir John Fortescue who had been Lord Chief Justice and Henry's Chancellor. Margaret trusted that his wisdom would combat some of the silly notions that Rene was apt to put into his grandson's head. She was determined that when her Edward finally became King he would be fitted in every way for the throne.

When the long awaited packets came from England, Margaret tore at the cords and seals with nervous, eager fingers. As the read, her face drained of color.

"What is it, Madam?" cried Katherine.

"Read it aloud," begged Exeter.

Margaret shook her head angrily and said only, "Hush!" She read on, skimming each sheet rapidly to get the gist of matters. Later, she would read the pages over and over until they became worn and hardly legible. A few times she gave a low cry of anguish. When she finished the letters she thrust them at Exeter.

"Somerset ... the others ... read it," she said hoarsely.

Somerset, in order to break out of the net that was slowly strangling the Lancastrians garrisoned in the northern castles, had decided to move against the enemy. At Hedgely Moor, Margaret's adherents had attacked Warwick's brother Montagu who was trying to get to Scotland for a peace parley. Most of the outnumbered Lancastrians fled, but Ralph Percy stood his ground and, swinging his battle axe, finally went down, overwhelmed by the enemy.

Hard on the heels of this, at Hexham, on May 13, the Lancastrian lords fought their last field. To a man, they were slain in battle or captured and executed.

Less than an hour had told the story. Among those captured were Somerset, Roos, Hungerford, Wentworth, and a score more. The rest lay dead on the field. Somehow, Henry, almost alone, escaped. The men who had been taken were condemned and beheaded forthwith. Margaret mourned for her young knight, Henry Beaufort, Third Duke of Somerset, who had followed his father, Edmund, the Second Duke in bloody death in the service of his sovereigns.--*How long ago had it been when he had made Henry grumble with his hounds in the chapel? How long ago had it been when hearts were light and laughter had rung through the halls of England's true rulers? ...*

Margaret's grief at the death of still more old friends was overshadowed only by her frantic worry over Henry. No man could say where he was or whether he even lived.

CHAPTER THIRTY-TWO

May 1464 - December 1467

With the battle of Hexham, news from England just about dried up. Some of the Lancastrians who survived the battle defected to Edward and others crossed to France to join their Queen's little group to await a turn of fortune's wheel.

The turn came sooner than Margaret expected, and from a far different source than she would have dreamed.

Warwick had been courting the French King's favor by trying to arrange a marriage between Edward and Bona of Savoy, Louis' sister-in-law, with Louis doing his best to advance the alliance. Rumors flew that Louis had promised Warwick the appanage of Normandy once a firm and lasting peace was made with England, sealed by the betrothal. But the prospective bridegroom dragged his feet. Edward allowed Warwick to make proposals in his name but he constantly refused to take the final step of a formal betrothal.

When September came, the King's Council met to approve the French negotiations. They prayed to Edward to hasten his marriage to Bona.

"My Lord," urged Warwick, "Your people earnestly wish that you will give them a Queen, and that as shortly as possible so that your own happiness and theirs may be increased and so that the true line of Kings will ever be maintained."

Edward leaned back in his chair and looked slowly about the room. Finally he spoke. "Of a truth, I entertain a wish to wed ... none more ... but perchance my choice of a wife might not be to the liking of all of you."

Chancellor George Neville, Warwick's brother, said, "You know that we have thought the Princess Bona, sister-in-law of the French King would be a most appropriate match --"

"And one which seemed pleasing to you," cut in Warwick. "But if your Grace has someone else in mind, please tell us who she is so we may hasten the proceedings."

They all waited for Edward to speak. He laughed and said, "You ask, so I shall tell you. I would take to wife the lovely widow, Elizabeth Grey, daughter of Woodville, Lord Rivers."

The councilors stood amazed, their mouths agape.

"Surely you jest, Sire," said Warwick.

"Indeed no. I find her exceeding fair and pleasing to me."

Then they all objected at once.

"Fair she may be, but she is no match for a high Prince."

"Her father is but a knight."

"Bona of Savoy is a royal Princess and far more meet."

"The Woodvilles are only ambitious climbers--"

Edward struck the arm of his chair. "Silence! Whether it pleases you or no, it is I who am to marry and I shall have no other wife than the Lady Elizabeth Grey. That is my pleasure."

Warwick stepped forward. "Mayhap we have been too importunate in our desire to settle this matter. Let us speak further of this another time."

"Well," drawled Edward, smiling again. "I don't think that will help. You see ... last spring ... at Grafton Regis ... the lady Elizabeth and I were wed!"

This stifled Louis' hopes for an Anglo-French alliance. Word had it that Warwick was chagrined and extremely wroth. He had been made to look like a fool over the proposal and his pride was sorely wounded.

Margaret's hopes rose. Edward had done what she couldn't -- insulted Louis, ruined the French-English peace, and driven a wedge between himself and his chief prop, Warwick.

"What a fool the usurper is," Margaret said. "To throw away so much for a woman, one older than he, with children, and a Lancastrian to boot."

"I rather imagine she's a Yorkist now," observed Exeter.

"Like her father, she was ever ambitious, but I little thought she looked as high as the royal throne. That she did may be a stroke of luck for us and perhaps we shall the readier topple both her and the usurper from it. I wager the people of England will show little favor toward her or her horde of greedy brothers and sisters."

"Her father Rivers and brother Scales were already enemies

of Warwick's. I'll warrant this marriage won't make them any friendlier," said Exeter.

"This headstrong action of Edward of York has been good news to me. The Woodvilles, even though they have gone over to the White Rose, are still helping the Red. And anything that annoys Warwick gives me added pleasure."

Margaret's hopes, nourished by news of Edward's unwise marriage, were soon blasted by the next news from England. In July, 1465, Henry was taken in a wood beside Bungerly Hyppingstones, removed to London by Warwick, and placed in the Tower. Edward kept him closely guarded, but allowed him to have visitors so that all could see that though Henry's body was whole, his wits were not.

Margaret was sure that Edward would not dare actually do harm to Henry who had always had the affection of his subjects but she feared he would suffer neglect. As long as he had a modicum of care during his *good days* he probably would be reconciled to a quiet captivity. She wondered if he ever heard word of her and Edward. Did he even know if they lived and where they were?

She knew that as long as Prince Edward was alive Henry was safe for what good would it do the usurper to remove poor muddled Henry if his son was alive to take his place in Lancastrian hearts?

Tragedy piled on tragedy. July had brought not only the capture of Henry, but also the death of her trusted Breze who fell in France at the Battle of Montlhery.

With Henry in Yorkist hands and Yorkist hands firmly on the reins of the English government, and himself embroiled at home, Louis was in no mood to give more aid to Margaret. Despite her supplications, all he would do at the time was to give her permission to stay in France and grant her a pension of four thousand francs a year. As for any further help, she would have to wait until it suited some new policy of Louis. Wait, always wait, and keep an eye on what was happening across the Channel.

Warwick was apparently reconciled to the Woodville faction for he stood Godfather to the newborn Princess Elizabeth. But then Edward refused to let his brother George, Duke of Clarence, wed Isabel, the elder of Warwick's two daughters. Woodvilles were being raised up while Nevilles were slighted. Warwick fumed at Edward's ingratitude. Had not he, Earl Richard, worked and fought to put Edward on the throne? He had made Edward King. Was this the reward for faithful service? An angry Warwick retired to his castle at Middleham.

Margaret, always waiting, exulted at the rumors of a rift between her enemies. Louis, also waiting and watching, had an idea how to benefit from the rift. His plans for a peace with England had come to naught and he was worried when his spies brought word that Edward had offered his sister Margaret to Charolais, Burgundy's son. It did not sort at all with his plans. If Charolais, who any day now would inherit Burgundy, were to turn and look with favor upon the Yorkists, perhaps it was time for France to aid the Lancastrians and replace Henry on the throne. His friend Warwick was just the man to help accomplish that.

Surely no one but Louis, the Spider King, was crafty enough to dream of an alliance between Warwick and Margaret -- Warwick, who had insulted Margaret, labeled her son a bastard, and driven her from England, and Margaret who had caused the deaths of the Earl's father, brother, uncle and cousin. What a strange alliance that would be; perhaps not possible at all, but Louis would keep it in mind.

CHAPTER THIRTY-THREE

January 1468 - July 1470

Word of Warwick's amazing break with Edward reached Margaret and her friends, closely countered by more news that the Earl was once again back in the King's grace. Margaret could only guess what was going on in England. She heard that the usurper was negotiating a treaty with the new Duke of Burgundy, Charolais, or as men called him, Charles the Rash. The treaty was to be sealed with the espousal of Edward's sister, Margaret of York, to Charles. It was said that Warwick stoutly opposed this marriage. What was the Queen to think, then, of the report that when Margaret of York left England on her journey to her new home, Warwick led the train?

Margaret desperately wanted to know what was happening in Burgundy. There were too many conflicting rumors.

"I must have someone there whom I can trust to plead Henry's case," she said to Exeter.

"Edmund Beaufort is there," he pointed out. Beaufort had assumed his dead brother Somerset's titles and duties.

"I know, but he doesn't seem to make much headway. Besides, he is a negligent correspondent. This uncertainty about what is going on is driving me frantic."

"Fortescue?" ventured Exeter.

"No. He is a good man, and judicious, but too cool and aloof. He is an excellent counselor for the Prince but I need a man with fire and enthusiasm to convince Burgundy of the merit of our cause."

"A hard task."

"And a thankless one, too. If he should fail, for his pains he will have nothing but our love and thanks."

Exeter sighed and said, "Please, Margaret, don't ask me to go."

"Was I that transparent?"

"To one who knows you as well as I."

"Why don't you want to go? There is no risk -- you are kin to Burgundy. At the worst it will be a bootless trip. Or is it that? Are you tired of mere love and thanks?"

"You can be cruel. You know that isn't why."

"I'm sorry. Yes, I know that isn't why ... but I still don't know the real reason you don't want to go."

"I guess I'd like to stay here. I've fallen into a way of life that pleases me."

She broke in. "Here? To sit here month upon month? Doing nothing? Is this your pleasant way of life?"

He shrugged his shoulders. "Seeing you ... yes. And while it isn't what I might have asked for, these peaceful years away from the wrangling, jangling time of England have had their merit."

"But Exeter, this isn't what we were born for!"

"We? What we?"

"We ... all of us ... Prince Edward ... I ... you."

"I wasn't born to be King -- remember?" He smiled his lopsided smile.

"No, not yourself, but you can help to make a King."

"You really want me to go, then?"

"Yes."

"All right. For you I will. But I'll make a sorry ambassador, I fear. I'll have to walk to Burgundy, and you may have noted that my clothes have grown shabby. I hope it won't put Charolais off."

Margaret reached into her purse and then handed Exeter some gold coins. She smiled with pride. "Here ... enough for a mount and decent apparel. Plead England's case in style."

His mouth fell open in surprise. "Where --?"

"I sold my ruby." She held out her bare hand. "Henry was consecrated King of France with that ring and then he gave it me when we were wed. What better use could I put it to than this? Mayhap it will help win him back his throne. Now listen; if it is not too late, do anything you can to block the marriage of Burgundy with the usurper's sister..."

King Louis was mightily disturbed by the projected English-Burgundian alliance. Moreover, the way King Edward had led him on and insulted his dear sister Bona rankled. If he could repay Edward while protecting his own cause, it would be two blows with one thrust. And if he could give a little joy to his unfortunate cousin, Margaret, well, *le bon Dieu* loves a cheerful giver. He chuckled and sent ambassadors to Margaret at Bar.

Margaret did not know what was going on in England, but Edward, right there, scarcely knew more. He knew that there were uprisings, but not that Warwick had a hand in them. The mighty Earl was determined to pay back the slight he had received from the ungrateful man he had boosted to the throne. He secretly vowed to topple Edward and the greedy Woodville clan. He would replace them with Edward's brother, George of Clarence, and the Neville family. Warwick was still set on marrying his daughter Isabel to Clarence though the King had absolutely forbidden the union. If the Earl could not control Edward he would replace him with the weaker, more amenable Clarence, and would eventually see a Neville grandchild on the throne of England.

In July, Clarence slipped across the Channel to Calais and joined Warwick. There, on the 11th, George, Duke of Clarence, brother of Edward the Fourth of England, wed Isabelle Neville, daughter and heiress of Warwick. They kept but a hasty marriage feast for the next day the men were back, raising a strong force in Kent.

Margaret received the astounding news that Warwick had taken Edward and had executed the usurper's father-in-law, Earl Rivers, and his son, John Woodville.

Hard on the heels of this was word that Warwick had released Edward after securing pardons and even new offices for himself and his son-in-law, Clarence. She thought *it must be an uneasy truce ... if only Edward and the Earl could be divided...*

She had not long to wait. In March of 1470, there was

another uprising against Edward, and soon there were 15,000 men in arms, shouting for King Henry. When a captured leader admitted on the block that Clarence and Warwick were behind the rebellion, those two fled for their lives to Calais where the Earl had left Wenlock in charge. With them they took Warwick's Countess and his daughters, Anne and Isabel who was over eight months pregnant. To Warwick's consternation, Wenlock, under the watchful eyes of some of Edward's officers, refused to let the party land though Isabel was by this time in painful labor. While they lay off Calais under the fire of Wenlock's cannons, aimed over their heads, Isabel gave birth to a still-born son, a crushing blow to Warwick's hopes. He had no choice but to weigh anchor for Honfleur. In France, he was welcomed heartily by Louis' emissaries.

With Warwick now irredeemably alienated from the man he had put on the throne, Louis seized on the idea of using him to help Henry regain that seat. In July, the French King sent for Margaret to join him at Angers.

When she arrived with her small company of supporters, she was angered to learn that her arch enemy was installed in one of Louis' apartments. She made every effort to avoid meeting the Earl so when she found herself in the audience chamber with him she was deeply chagrined.

"My Lord," she said to Louis, sinking into a deep curtsy while trembling with rage, "You must forgive me ... I am unwell. I must leave."

"We are most sorry to hear it," said Louis with a smile, raising his hand to signal Warwick to draw closer. The Earl scowled but obeyed as the King continued softly, "However, stay a while, for we have that news that should make you well. We intend to place our cousin Henry back on his rightful throne. Would that please you?"

She straightened. "You know it would, my Lord. I have been asking such aid these many years."

"The time has not been ripe before. Now it is. On our part it will take much work ... and money. From you, we ask in return for this help but a trifle ..."

"And that is?"

"Yes, really a trifle. It has long distressed us to see our friend Milord Warwick and you, my dear cousin, at enmity. It is necessary now only that you make friends."

"Never!" exploded Margaret, her blue eyes blazing, glaring at Warwick, the chief cause of all her past and present griefs. "Rather had I stay in exile a hundred years than treat that traitorous villain as a friend. You do me great wrong to ask it. Now you must excuse me." She swept from the chamber.

"You see," said Warwick, "I told you."

"Nonsense." Louis was undisturbed. "She will come around. You will see. It is *we* who tell *you.*"

CHAPTER THIRTY-FOUR

July - September 1470

Margaret returned to her own rooms, trembling. How could Louis think that she could possibly ever be friendly to Warwick? Warwick, who had twice driven her from England, who had with his own hands led Henry to the Tower and had, worst of all, tried to stigmatize her son as a bastard? She clenched her hands into fists and beat them against her sides, repeating, "I will not do it. I will not do it."

"Madame, I know it is difficult to imagine," ventured Sir John Fortescue who had accompanied her. "However, it is the duty of Princes to do many difficult things. Do not reject King Louis' plan out of hand without finding out more about it, without examining it fully."

"Never!"

"Please, your Majesty. You have good cause for your enmity against the Earl, none better, but if you could use him to attain your own aims, would it not be wise?"

She did not answer immediately but paced back and forth. Finally she stopped, facing Sir John. "What do you mean?"

"Your desire is to regain the throne, is it not?"

"You know it is."

"King Louis, with Warwick's aid, can help you do it."

"Why must it be with Warwick's aid?"

"The King is a practical man. He knows that Earl Richard can draw off a large part of Edward's supporters. He can raise a mighty army and that, plus the loyal Lancastrians who will come out at your call, should be enough to overbalance Edward."

"I do not trust the Earl," she countered.

"But King Louis does and he is the one on whom you must now rely. Face it, your Grace; without Louis you are helpless and Louis will not join the venture without Warwick."

"You may be right, but I would never consent to owe the throne to Warwick. It is Henry's by right and there is no reason he should be beholden to any man."

"You would not need to owe him anything. He would merely be righting the wrong he committed when he helped Edward seize the crown. Besides, he is fulfilling his own desires in revenging himself on Edward. You would be helping him as much as he would be helping you."

"I do not want to help Earl Richard."

"Not if it's the only way back to the throne?"

Katherine Vaux said, "My William doesn't like Warwick any more than you do, but he says the Earl is a good captain, that the men will follow him." She lowered her voice and said earnestly, "I have been happy here with you and the Prince; happier than in England. But this idle time has galled my husband. He doesn't understand our French ways and he grows bitter and short of temper. He wants to go home. He swears that with the Earl's help you can win. Madame, let's try it ... I have seen you, too, grow bitter during these years. Pretend it isn't Warwick ... use him as a stranger."

Prince Edward added his plea. Margaret was shocked.

"You ask your own mother to forgive the knave who insulted her? Who keeps you from your rightful inheritance?"

"Yes, if now through him I can get back my rightful inheritance. As for the insult, how better could the Earl retract it than to show the world by his new friendship that his old claim was false?"

"You really want me to throw our lot in with Earl Richard?"

"Yes, Lady Mother, I beg it of you."

"I can scarce believe my ears to hear you speak so."

"Why should I not? My father is the rightful King of England and I am Prince of Wales. You, yourself, have told me over and over that we live but to regain the crown; yet almost since I can remember, we've hidden here at Grandfather's. I am no longer a child. It is time to go home and if we need Warwick's help to get there, I say let's take it."

When Margaret finally agreed to join with her former enemy, Louis had a further suggestion -- just one more -- that the alliance should be firmly cemented by the marriage of Prince Edward to Anne Neville, Warwick's younger daughter.

"God's blood!" stormed the Queen. "What have they cooked up now? Such an idea is beneath our very notice. The Earl overreaches himself to think his daughter a fit match for Prince Edward."

Fortescue reminded her, "The Lady Anne will someday share with her sister the vast holdings of the Nevilles. It is an inheritance not to be considered lightly."

"Wealthy she may be, but she still is not of the blood royal. If my son is to wed an enemy's daughter, why not the usurper's? I warrant Edward of York would be relieved to have such an alliance. It is no stranger an ideas that the other ... indeed, it has some merit. The usurper has no sons and unless we oust him, *his* daughter will inherit a kingdom!"

"Mayhap," said Fortescue, "But his wife is fecund. She had two sons by her first husband and has already borne Edward three daughters and men say she goes with child again. She may yet have many sons."

"Nevertheless, I do not propose to wed Prince Edward to the Lady Anne. Let us see first if Warwick can topple the usurper."

Warwick was adamant. The marriage would be a surety that Margaret would not turn against him once he put Henry back on the throne. Louis pointed out to the stubborn Queen that the Earl would be much more firmly bound if his daughter would one day be Queen. Prince Edward added his voice, declaring himself willing. He had seen the Lady Anne.

Margaret, still reluctant, finally agreed to this, too, but she insisted that Anne should live in her household and that the marriage should be consummated only after Warwick had won back Henry's kingdom for him. Nor would Margaret allow Prince Edward to cross the Channel till Warwick's forces were successful.

The midsummer sun shone brightly through the narrow

windows of the castle at Angers. Warwick knelt humbly before the exiled Queen who stood regally before him. He had been kneeling for fully fifteen minutes before she signed for him to rise. Margaret had been forced by political expediency to accept her former enemy but she was not going to do it easily. It went hard with her, against her inmost feelings. At last she spoke. "We understand you wish to do homage to the house of Lancaster, your true liege lords?"

"Yes, your Grace."

"Prince Edward, as his father's representative, will receive your vows." The Prince stepped forward and the forty-two- year-old Warwick knelt before him and placed his hands between those of the seventeen-year-old lad and said, "I, Richard, Earl of Warwick, do become your liege man of life and limb and earthly worship, and faith and truth will I bear unto you to live and die against all manner of folk."

Before he rose, he swore fealty also to King Henry and promised that he would free him as soon as possible.

Then, under Louis' watchful eye, they discussed the details of the alliance. Warwick was to go to England, accompanied by Jasper Tudor, who would raise a Welsh force, and the Earl of Oxford, who could count on many Lancastrian friends. For his part in the struggle, Warwick demanded that he have sway of government during the Prince's minority should Henry prove incapable. Also, he won the concession that should no issue be born to Anne and Prince Edward, then George of Clarence, his other son-in-law, was to stand next in line to the throne. Thus, whatever came, Neville descendants would one day be Kings of England.

But one party was not consulted and to him the new alliance was anything but agreeable. Clarence, who, for his earlier treason, had fully expected to replace his brother Edward on the throne, now found himself further than ever from it. Secretly, he sent a message to Edward, begging his forgiveness, and promising to go over to his side and away from his father-in-law when the time should prove propitious.

Warwick, with a fleet supplied by Louis, was to go to Valognes, there to mount an invasion against England as soon as conditions allowed. Margaret would retire again to Bar to wait with Edward and Anne. As soon as Warwick was in control, they would follow across the Channel. Wenlock, who had earlier stolen away from Calais to join the Earl, was sent to accompany the Queen and the others to Bar. She had never been able to abide her former chamberlain since his defection after the first battle of St. Albans, but she supposed there was little use to strain at his presence when she had swallowed so much more. He was there ostensibly to protect her but she was sure his real purpose was to spy upon her for Warwick. Such was the trust the Earl and the Queen had for each other.

After a long wait for the weather, Warwick and Clarence with their men crossed the Channel and landed on the coast of Devon. As soon as they touched shore, Jasper Tudor rode hot for Wales to raise his followers. Oxford called out his retainers. Warwick marched through the south of England, once more gathering men to his banner as he went. The levies poured in. He issued a proclamation that all men, whatever their past loyalties, would be pardoned if they now joined him in restoring Henry to the throne. When they reached Coventry with their ever growing ranks, they learned, glad news, that Montagu, with a force much larger than Edward's own troops, had come over to his brother Warwick's side. At that news, Edward's army had broken and run and Edward himself with his young brother Richard and a small company had been forced to flee for their lives. They had crossed to Holland. The country was in Warwick's hands.

When the news, fast for once, reached Margaret, she had a *Te Deum* sung and prepared to sail to England.

CHAPTER THIRTY-FIVE

October 1470 - April 1471

The Yorkists were in a panic. In the dead of night, Edward's Queen, Elizabeth Woodville, and her daughters and mother, Jaquetta, fled to sanctuary at Westminster. There, scarcely a month later, she gave birth to a son whom she named Edward. Other Yorkists in London either took sanctuary, too, or went over to Warwick's side. Warwick and Clarence entered London unopposed in triumph on October 6th, their ears ringing to shouts that had only recently been raised for the popular Edward. The Earl entered the Tower and released Henry. He, poor man, slightly dirty and ill kempt, blinked at the unaccustomed bright sunlight and docilely allowed himself to be exhibited to his people. With a sweet smile and a gentle nodding of his head, he accepted the apologies of his liberator. Warwick publicly humbled himself and asked pardon not only of Henry but also of God and the English people.

Well could the Earl afford to bow in supplication before his King; it would win him English hearts. Besides, it was a great deal easier to kneel to holy Henry than it had been to humble himself before proud Margaret. He had never been able to control Edward whom he had made King; but he would be able to control this shadow whom he now made King again...and later, his seed to sit upon the throne of England in their own right ... Yes, it was easy to kneel humbly before Henry of Lancaster while his heart swelled with pride and his ears were filled with the people's acclaim.

A week later, Henry, dressed in royal robes of blue velvet, and wearing the crown, led a solemn procession to St. Paul's to give thanks for his deliverance. His claim to the title was reiterated at a Parliament on November 26th. Maybe now there would be peace. There, at Westminster, in the name of Henry, Warwick and Clarence were constituted governors of the land, but the grasp of the reins was Warwick's and he did not intend to yield it. Clarence was slightly mollified by being recognized as legal heir of the house of York whose vast holdings were now all his, for both his brothers were attainted, their estates forfeit. He was declared Henry's heir if Henry should die without male issue; but Prince Edward lived, a healthy young man, betrothed, and no doubt soon to have issue of his own. The only sure winner was Warwick whose grandchild would, one way or another, York or Lancaster, some day be King.

In France, Margaret, once so eager to return to England, had second thoughts. It might be wiser to keep Prince Edward safe in France until she saw how Warwick intended to act. She still did not trust him. If he once had the Prince in his hands, might he not destroy him, depose Henry, and claim the throne for George of Clarence, his other son-in-law ... or even, since he was ever a man of overweening ambition, for himself? The whole situation would bear examination. As she pondered, she began to see the betrothal as a fruitless relationship, binding her to her erstwhile enemy with little advantage to her and her house. She who had been opposed to an early consummation of the marriage, now urged it.

"It is all right with me, Mother, said Edward, "For it is what Anne and I desire most. It is tedious to be kept ever apart, but I marvel that you have changed your mind so readily. We thought the marriage was not to take place until we landed in England."

"Believe me, I have not changed my mind readily but we must think of what is wisest. My original plan was to wait but I have thought better of it. We must always be ready to change with the times and conditions. I do not trust the Earl overmuch. In the back of my mind is the fear that he might go over to York again. But if Anne bears within her the heir of Lancaster, then indeed we would have surety of Neville's loyalty."

"Mother," he laughed, "your thinking is almost too devious for me, but devious or not, it sorts well with me if it will hasten my wedding to Anne. And most willingly will I get her with child."

While Margaret delayed in France, Edward was working to wrest the throne from Henry once again. He sent secret messages to England: to his old retainers in the north; to his sure friends in London; and to his brother Clarence. He did his best to bring Burgundy more actively over to his support. Burgundy's wife, Margaret of York, was pleading her brother Edward's cause both at board and in bed and her arguments were very strong. Burgundy had always disliked Warwick, that new Lancastrian partisan, so that, all in all, Duke Charles was ready to increase his help to Edward despite his friendship for both Somerset and Exeter. He gave them handsome gifts of money and sent them home to work what mischief they could. Loyal to Henry and Margaret, they accepted Burgundy's gifts, determined to use the money in the royal cause. Then, they swore privately, they would do their utmost to free the King from Warwick's influence.

As soon as they reached England, Somerset rode to the northwest to claim his family estates, and Exeter went to Westminster to repledge allegiance to Henry and give him news of his years with Margaret and Prince Edward.

Warwick waited impatiently for Margaret. He dared not leave the land unguarded lest Edward return. Rumors of a hostile fleet in the Channel kept Margaret hesitant, fearful to risk her son's life in a crossing that might bring Burgundian ships down on them. So, while Warwick daily searched the eastern horizon for the Queen's sails, her ships rode uneasily at anchor in the French harbor. It was a fatal delay. When Margaret decided that she must risk the venture, the weather had changed and the winds turned against her. Each time the ships put out, they were buffeted mercilessly and forced to return to harbor.

Further to the north, in the Lowlands, other ships also waited to sail. There the weather broke first and Edward of York, with sixteen hundred English and Burgundian soldiers weighed anchor for England. Edward made the crossing easily and landed unopposed at Ravenspur, while his younger brother, Richard, landed four miles away and quickly joined him. Warwick quitted his fruitless vigil and turned northward to cut off Edward's forces.

Edward met almost no resistance on his way inland and was soon at York. That town's citizens had little stomach for either battle or siege and threw wide open their gates which had once displayed the heads of Edward's father and brother. People were tired of battles. It didn't seem to matter too much who was King. Either way, it was more taxes and bad government with the nobles, who should have protected them, at each other's throats. Let Lancaster and York fight it out between them, just so they left the common people in peace. Now it was time to plant their crops and tend to the new lambing.

The Earl was by now garrisoned at Coventry from whence he issued a call for his retainers and partisans to ride to him. His brother Montagu held Pomfret Castle which lay between him and Edward. Something went wrong, though, and almost before they knew it, Edward had marched safely around Pomfret and was in Wakefield on his way to Coventry.

"Let him come,' cried Warwick. "I shall hold him here while my brother comes down from Pomfret and my son-in-law Clarence comes up from the south. Edward will find he has marched into a trap. He was ever wont to be rash."

Once more, Edward's rashness served him well, for Montagu's troops moved slowly and Clarence tarried. As March drew to a close, while many a Lancastrian noble with his followers, unwilling to fight for Warwick, waited stubbornly in London or Wales for the coming of Queen Margaret, Edward reached the gates of Coventry and challenged his former friend to battle. The Earl, hoping desperately for reinforcements, delayed, refused to fight.

On April 1, Edward, determined to linger no longer, continued on his way toward London. As he marched, declaring himself King, he was joined by Clarence who was happy to be reconciled with his brother when he was in the ascendant. At full speed, the scions of York: Edward, George and Richard, marched toward the capital. Now Warwick left Coventry and hotly pursued them. It was his last chance. He dared not let them reach London unopposed. He sent a hasty message to his brother, George Neville, the Archbishop whom he had left in charge, to hold the city and to hide Henry until he, Warwick, should arrive. If only, he prayed, Margaret would land, then King Edward would be caught between two hostile forces.

But on April 11, Maundy Thursday, it was Edward the Fourth as King and not Henry who ceremoniously washed the feet of twenty-nine poor London beggars, one for each year of his life. He had entered the capital easily, for no one had the heart to stand against him. Archbishop Neville, hearing the joyful shouts of the citizens as they lined the victor's way, was one of the first to pledge allegiance to Edward and sue for mercy. The Yorkists who had taken sanctuary six months before poured out of churches, and thronged around their triumphant young leader. The Lancastrians who had not already fled the city now took their turn in sanctuary, and docile Henry was led once more back to his grim apartment in the Tower.

CHAPTER THIRTY-SIX

April 1471

Warwick had been joined by his brother Montagu and was now at St. Albans. On Easter Eve, his army moved to Barnet on the way to London where they took up a position along the crest of a hill. Edward, pushing his men as close as possible, stopped after dark only a few yards below the enemy.

Easter dawned wet and grey. A thick pall of fog rose from the ground, chilled the armor, and made clammy the leather leggings and vests. The men could scarcely see a bow's length ahead of them. Warwick, with his brother, both on foot, commanded the main force. To Warwick's left was his former enemy, now his ally, Exeter. To Warwick's right was Oxford. Because the lines were slightly askew, when the trumpets signaled the advance, Oxford's troops thundered by the foe in the dense fog. As soon as he realized his mistake, Oxford turned and fell upon his enemies' flank and rearguard. The Yorkist line broke and the soldiers fled in panic back to Barnet with Oxford's horsemen pursuing them.

The rest of the battle raged back and forth with both sides trading blows, the edge with Warwick who had the larger force. It looked as if the day would go to the Lancastrians when suddenly a force of cavalry came looming out of the mist from the Yorkist side with banners hanging limp in the fog. The Lancastrian archers let loose a volley at this new threat when from the advancing line rose and anguished cry of "Treason! Treason!" The advancing men were Oxford's returning from the rout of the enemy. They had become lost in the dense murk and had regrouped to return to the fight. Oxford's banner bore a blazing star which the Lancastrians had mistaken through the fog for the sun of York. In that tragic moment, they fired upon their own comrades. The long fostered enmity between the Lancastrians and the followers of Warwick now rose to destroy them and turn the battle for the Yorkists. Oxford's men, old enemies of Warwick's, repeated the cry of "Treason," wheeled and fled pell mell. The Earl's men, hearing the cry and fearing themselves betrayed, faltered, then ran, too. Montagu was cut down. Great Warwick stumbled, righted himself, and fought savagely, hewing away with his war axe, his eyes blinded by blood streaming from his head. Suddenly, he, too, as the others, threw down his weapon and ran toward the horses. He never made it.

That same Easter Day, in Weymouth, 150 miles away from where her great captain lost his life on Barnet Field, Margaret stepped onto English ground again. The voyage which should have taken only a day or two, was not completed for a full sixteen from when she had first tried to set sail. The Queen, as well as the other royal passengers, the Prince and Princess of Wales, was sick, sore and hungry. She had left France as Queen of England; now she learned that Edward had again claimed the throne, that Henry was once more in the Tower. England's Queen was Elizabeth Woodville, recently come out of sanctuary with her infant heir, another Prince Edward.

"Where is Warwick?" asked Margaret, losing no time in planning her next move despite the strain of the arduous voyage.

"Warwick?" repeated a guildsman. "I am not sure, your Grace. Some say he is at Coventry, but I do not know. We are out of things down here and do not keep up with the happenings in London and in the north. But I heard he was in Coventry."

The royal party moved on to Beaulieu Abbey in New Forest where they joined the Countess of Warwick and others whose ships had become separated from them. There they were soon met by Edmund Beaufort. The young man, disheveled and bemired from a long, hard ride, rushed into Margaret's presence without stopping to wash or refresh himself. He knelt in sorrow before the Queen whose coming he had so long awaited.

"Your Grace ..." He faltered. He looked at the stone floor instead of up at Margaret.

"Edmund," she said, "it has been long since I last saw you and of all men, saving my Lord, the King, I had most hoped to look upon your face again, but I have a sudden fear that you bring not the hope we have looked forward to, but some bad news. Even so, give us your news directly."

Prince Edward put in, "Yes, my Lord, speak -- and if it is that you fear to tell us that the usurper is back in power, do not worry. We know that already and we shall not be long in gathering a force to drive him out once and for all."

The Duke shook his head. "That is part of it -- but only part...the Earl of Warwick ..." He stopped, looked over at the two Annes, the Countess and her daughter, the Princess of Wales, who stood leaning forward slightly to catch his every word. He moistened his lips with his tongue, tried to frame his words, then blurted, "The Earl of Warwick is dead."

His Countess shrieked and Princess Anne reached to support her. Margaret rose, a low cry on her lips, "How?"

"In battle, your Grace."

"In battle?" exclaimed Margaret and Prince Edward together.

"Where?" demanded the Queen.

"Who was with him?" asked Edward.

"Were you there?" put in Wenlock whose eyes were filling with tears. Warwick's most trusted captain, he had chafed at having to stay behind with Margaret. Now he faced Somerset, his and Warwick's hated enemy, and repeated, "Were you there?"

Somerset ignored the old soldier, directing his answers to the Queen and Prince.

"There was a battle at Barnet ... Sunday ... Edward has won. Besides Warwick, Montagu, too, is slain. No other of note. Oxford and Exeter have escaped, though the latter was sorely wounded ... but now that you have come we can regroup and --"

She cut him off. "No."

"No?" exclaimed Somerset and the Prince together.

"Do not parrot me like ninnies," she snapped, her nerves frayed by the terrible news. "I said *No* and I meant it. I am through with fighting, for it seems as if the Lord Himself is against us. We shall leave this Godforsaken land while we still can ... while you still live, my son."

The Prince and Somerset spoke at once.

"This is unlike your Grace."

"Mother, you can't mean it."

"I do mean it. And who is to say what is unlike me? Is it unlike me to show some sense and refuse a bootless fight? Do you think I like to hear the weeping of widows and orphans?" She flung her hand out toward the two Annes who stood sobbing together.

"God's blood! I have had all I can take. I have had my hopes raised only to be dashed too many times. I have had enough. My son and I shall return to France. He can govern my father's Anjou. Let Edward of York have his accursed throne!"

"But my father?" argued the young Prince.

His mother shook her head. "Ah ... Henry ... I had almost forgotten him; Jesu comfort the poor man. I do not think he ever cared over much for being King, and he is so gentle and peaceable that I do not imagine captivity sits as hard upon him as it would on another. It is not a question of him any longer -- there is little we can do for him -- it is you now whom I must save."

The young man struck his fist upon the table in a movement of impatient anger. "You say your decision is for me... Well, I do not choose to scurry back to France to sit at Louis' feet, to someday govern my grandfather's few acres. England, all England is mine! You have always taught me that I was born to be England's King. Well, I intend to claim my kingdom!"

"Edward, Edward, we have lost our foremost champion, the man on whom I relied."

"There are others, my Lady," Somerset reminded her.

"None so good as Warwick," said Wenlock, the tears openly streaming down his broad face. "I think you are right to go back home, Madame."

They looked at him.

"The Queen's home is here," said her son.

"York, too, would doubtless like her Grace to return to France," said Somerset.

"What does that mean?" asked Wenlock, coloring.

For the second time, Somerset ignored him. "As I said, there are others ...Oxford, Exeter, Devon, myself ... Why my men are ready to fight now. There are many who would not fight for Warwick will fight for you, my Lady."

"I thought as much," mourned Wenlock.

"There's my brother John, and Audeley, and Langstrother whom you brought with you, as well as Sir John, here. And all who have been waiting for your return ... and ..." He was getting excited. "There's Tudor. He can raise half of Wales. Madame, you cannot pass up this chance. You must fight now."

Edward begged, "We cannot leave with victory in sight. Mother, give me my chance."

They argued the rest of the day. Even the two Annes urged Margaret to stay and fight. The Countess wanted her husband avenged and the Princess was sure that Prince Edward would be victorious. Margaret was finally won over or worn down. She could not hold out against her son's eager pleading. She could remember, even now, how bright the future had looked when she was his age. She was wiser now ... or was it just that she was tired?

She knew now that most hope fades and that those who are most exalted have the farthest to fall from Fortune's wheel. But she knew, too, that she had rather been herself with her yearning, aching, even destroying ambition than to have been like Henry, so gentle and saintly that he never reached out for worldly glory. She could not deny the Prince. He would have his chance.

The candles guttered, the servants slept, even Somerset dozed in his chair when Margaret finally yielded.

"All right, my son. We shall stay and fight."

CHAPTER THIRTY-SEVEN

April 1471 - August 1482

As soon as Margaret made up her mind to stay and fight for Edward's rights, she moved. She sent out calls for adherents and pushed on north, raising an army in Prince Edward's name as she went. King Edward set out to overtake her. While she was at Bath, his army reached Malmesbury, a little over twenty miles away. Margaret moved to Bristol. To the west lay Wales and Jasper Tudor with a mighty army. To reach him and safety she would have to cross the Severn. The nearest crossing was at Gloucester so she turned her troops northward. Edward, who knew he must keep her from joining Tudor, sent messengers racing to Gloucester with the command to hold the city.

When the Lancastrian army reached there, they found the city barricaded against them and Edward close behind. There was no time to parley; there was no safe place to camp. She had to urge her footsore men on northward to the next river crossing, the ford at Tewkesbury. At four o'clock in the afternoon of May 3rd, the Lancastrian army, exhausted by their night and day forced marches, reached Tewkesbury. Galled by their armor, some with raw and blistered feet, all hungry and tired, they were in no condition to ford the swift river. If Edward came on they must fight. But the King's men were just as tired so he was content to let them rest for the night. He camped nearby, and at that first light which precedes sunrise, was on the move again, to draw his lines up in battle formation half a mile south of the Lancastrians.

Margaret and Anne and their ladies, at the insistence of Prince Edward, had been hurried across the river and into a simple house where they anxiously awaited news of the battle. When their hostess brought them food and drink, Margaret, in an agony of fear for her son, could not eat. Anne took but little. Her fear was mixed with excitement and pride at the way her husband had taken command, had ridden up and down the lines, directing the building of the defense, and his easy handling of the men, from raw country recruits to grizzled, hard-bitten knights, veterans of a score of past fights. Margaret would a hundred times rather have stayed in the van with the baggage where she would have been closer to the battle, but her son had declared, "You have had your battles. This one is mine."

Still she wanted to stay and probably would have had her way, for there was little time for argument, but Edward had added, "Please go with Anne -- and take care of her if anything should happen, but it won't --" He crossed himself. "She will need you."

Again, she could not deny him. She had no stomach for this fight. She was old and tired. If it would make him easier if she went with Anne, then she would. There was so little she could do now. Dry-eyed, with a prayer, she watched him as he reined in his horse, turned, and galloped back to the line. Her heart alone cried after him, willing him to be careful, to be safe, *"My son, my son ..."*

The battle itself did not take long. There had been a quarrel over who would command the main force. Somerset asked it, arguing his experience, but Margaret had sided with her son and he took the center against King Edward and George of Clarence. Somerset took the left flank against Richard of Gloucester. Devon, on Margaret's side, was opposed by Hastings. Despite his experience, Somerset, always impetuous, drove too hard, penetrating to a dangerous, untenable position. When he was inevitably repulsed by the superior generalship of Richard of Gloucester, he rode back to camp in a fury to find Wenlock with his men still drawn up, inactive. In his rage he accused Wenlock of treachery. It was, he said, common knowledge that Warwick's old captain preferred the Yorkists ... It was too much for his hot blood. In blind anger, Somerset fell upon Wenlock and slew him. Thereupon, Wenlock's men simply melted away. On the other flank, Devon and Dorset were slain. Somerset, hot for more blood, returned to the line and was taken by the calmer Gloucester.

In the center, Edward fought Edward. The younger man was no match for his experienced Yorkist cousin. Prince Edward, his once glorious dreams dissolving in a melee of screaming, cursing men, of hacked and butchered bodies, slipping in the red gore of his country's sons, finally went down, crying vainly for help to his brother-in-law, Clarence.

It was over. The heir and hope of Lancaster was dead with a thousand others, friend and enemy, on Bloody Meadow, outside Tewkesbury. The Wars of the Roses were ended.

But when, within the hour, word came to Margaret that the Red Rose, her Rose, was dead, she who had been meekly willing to give up all and return to France to keep him safe, steeled herself for one final effort. She turned and faced the now wailing Princess Anne. "Stop that bootless noise and come. We have but a few minutes at best."

"For what?" the girl managed to get out.

"To flee to safety."

"There is no safety and I am too tired." She broke down once more.

While Margaret directed her ladies to gather together their few necessities, Anne calmed long enough to say, "Look ... I know Edward ... I mean King Edward ... and Richard of Gloucester. Richard spent his boyhood at Middleham, my home ... anyway, I know we can throw ourselves on their mercy ..."

"No." Margaret was adamant. "My son is dead but I shall follow his wishes. He left you in my care."

Anne was too upset to hold out against her mother-in-law's grim inflexibility. She allowed herself to be bundled into a farm cart and they fled in haste northward, jostling over the uneven road and often mired in deep mud. When the Yorkist soldiers came shortly afterwards to seize them, their one-time hostess sent the men on a fruitless trip westward. Margaret and Anne were on their way to a loyal priory at Little Malvern where the Queen planned to hide. Anne, who knew that Margaret had little love for her, could not understand her solicitude. There was a good reason, though. Margaret had only one hope left, but it, as

277

all the others, was soon dashed. In less than a week, Katherine reported.

"Your Grace, the Princess is not with child. Just this morning her flux came upon her."

"You are sure?"

"Yes, Madame. She even has bad cramps and has kept to her bed today."

The last slim hope, which was not really a hope at all, but only a wisp ...God had never been that good to her ...that had kept her going, now vanished. If, by God's favor, Anne had been pregnant with Edward's child, Margaret, cheated of her son, the reason for her life, would have had a token of remembrance of his life ... a token that would have given her own life meaning. But now, nothing. All form, all reason for life was gone.

The disappointment, even though the hope had been small, was devastating. She crumpled. She sat motionless, staring at the road that stretched out into the distance toward Wales and safety. All feeling was gone.

When the fat, little prior hurried in to tell her that King Edward's men were approaching, searching every building for the fugitives, she did not move. There was still time to flee, he urged. Her ladies pleaded with her, but Margaret turned a deaf ear to them. Anne crept to her and reminded her of the Prince's last request. The Princess was frightened, not so much by the approach of Edward's men as by the unnatural behavior of the old Queen.

Margaret turned dull eyes to Anne, reached out and patted her hand. "He had a care for you, my dear, and so did I ... but that is no matter now. You are no longer a hope to me ... nor a threat to them. Once they might have slain you ... but not now, so you tell them how things stand with you. The King ...ah, never did I think to use that word for Edward of York ... but the King will no doubt show you mercy, as you said. You and I have no more to do with each other. You may flee ... as you will ... but I shall take what comes."

So Edward's men found out the little party at Malvern Priory. Margaret, she who had been Queen, was led away, unprotesting, unfeeling now. She was taken before Edward at

Coventry. There she was told that Somerset, Audeley, and others had been taken and executed. The Red Rose had been rooted out. *why should she care? Blood and death were an old story to her.* She listened, unheeding. She did, indeed, no longer care.

On May 21st, 1471, Margaret, a broken, middle-aged woman, was led into London, the prize of Edward's triumphal procession. For her who had once received shouts of praise there were now only curses and catcalls. They did not reach her. She did not care.

That afternoon she was placed in the Tower. The next morning, Ascension Day, Margaret learned from her jailer that Richard of Gloucester was in the royal apartments of the Tower and she begged that she might talk with him. Once she would never have deigned to speak with York, but now it did not matter ... *what can matter when all that you love is gone?* ...She asked for him and he came, although reluctantly.

"My Lord Duke, I will have little to ask of your or your brother ... there has been too much bad blood between us ... but I do ask one favor."

"Yes?" He stood quietly, one shoulder a little higher than the other, one arm held so that it did not show. He had been born a trifle deformed and he was shy about it. Tears came to her eyes. Her own son -- so perfect -- just the age of this Richard, a little under eighteen. The cousins should have been friends, not fatal enemies ... *But Richard lived and her son was dead ...forever...it was not fair.*

She asked her favor. "Might I be imprisoned in the same room with my Lord Henry? I have much need of his comfort and perhaps he can teach me to bear my fate with Christian strength."

The young man started, turned from her and stared mutely at the wall. Then he faced her again and said tonelessly, "Know you, Madame, that Henry Plantagenet died last night."

Her eyes widened. Was no one to be spared? Her voice hoarse, she whispered, "Was that needful?"

"It was." He added, "I am truly sorry."

"I believe you. Then one other boon I ask."

"I can do nothing that is not in the King's ... my brother's interest."

"The Lady Anne Neville ... she is no danger to Edward ... protect her. It was his -- my son's wish..."

The young Duke nodded. Margaret turned away and he left.

By the end of the year it was apparent that the red rose was no longer a threat. Prince Edward lay entombed in the Abbey at Tewkesbury and King Henry was interred at Chertsey. Margaret was moved from her Tower prison and given into the custody of Edward's sister, the Duchess of Suffolk.

Four years later, Edward signed a treaty with King Louis of France. Part of the treaty was an agreement to ransom Margaret for 50,000 crowns and the renunciation of any English rights she might have. They brought her the document: *I, Margaret, formerly married in the Kingdom of England, hereby assign all that I could pretend to in England by the articles of my marriage, with all other things thereto to Edward, now King of England.*

She signed it with no protest.

Upon her return to her native land there was another document to be signed, one that would strip her of her birthright. In exchange for the help which Louis claimed to have given her over the past fifteen years, she was asked to deed over to him any inheritance rights she might have from her mother's Duchy of Lorraine and from Rene's Anjou, Bar, and Provence. She signed it without protest. She did not care. She had no one to pass these rights on to. Now she owned nothing. Gratefully, she accepted a small pension from Louis and retired to her father's estates.

One more friend was to be taken from her. Shortly afterwards, she learned that Exeter, imprisoned since the Battle of Barnet, had been released from the Tower. On his way across the Channel to France he had been *found dead ... between Dover and Calais.* As to how he drowned, *the certainty is not known.*

When Rene died in 1480, his lands passed into the royal domain. Margaret lived two years longer. Faithful Katherine, whose husband had been slain at Tewkesbury, witnessed Margaret's will which was made a few months before she died at fifty-three. Margaret asked that all her worldly goods be used to pay her debts and if her belongings were not enough for this, *I implore the King to meet and pay the outstanding debts as sole heir of the wealth which I inherited through my father and my mother and my other relatives and ancestors.*

After Margaret's death, King Louis sent a squire to see what possessions she might have left. In a small chest he found a letter she had received from Rene: *My child may God relieve you in your counsels, for men seldom give help in times of ill fortune. When you think about your troubles, think of mine: they are great.*

There was also a pale and dusty garland of dried and brittle daisies which he threw away.

BIBLIOGRAPHY

Bagley, J.J. *Margaret of Anjou.* Herbert Jenkins. London

Christie, Mabel E. *Henry VI.* Constable, London 1922

Costain, Thomas B. *The Last Plantagenets.* Doubleday, Garden City. 1962. Has good maps of battlefields.

Daniel, Samuel. *The Civil Wars.* ed. Laurence Michel. Yale. New Haven. 1958.

Dictionary of National Biography.

Hall, Edward. *The Union of the Two Noble Families of Lancaster and York* ...John Day. London. 1583

Haswell, Jock. *The Ardent Queen.* Peter Davies. Lond. 1976

Hookham, Mary Ann. *The Life and Times of Margaret of Anjou.* Tinsley Bros. London. 1872

Jacob, E. F. *The Fifteenth Century.* Oxford, 1961. Oxford History of England Series.

Kendall, Paul Murray. *Warwick the Kingmaker.* Norton, NY, 1967.

Mowat, R. B. *Wars of the Roses.* Lockwood. London. 1914.

Oman, Charles. *Warwick the Kingmaker.* Macmillan. Lon.1891.

Orridge, B. B. *Illustrations of Jack Cade's Rebellion.* John Camden Hotten. London. 1869.

Scofield, Cora L. *The Life and Reign of Edward the Fourth.* 2 vol. Octagon Books. NY. 1976 reprint of 1923.

Strickland, Agnes. *Lives of the Queens of England.* Vol. 1. Lea & Blanchard. Philadelphia. 1850.

Wright, Thomas. *Political Songs of England.* Camden Society. London.

About the Author

Mrs. Perot graduated from Lawrence University in Appleton, Wisconsin, with a major in English literature. She earned an M.A. from the State University of New York at Buffalo where her thesis was on Shakespeare's History Plays. Her research showed that Shakespeare had misrepresented Margaret of Anjou.

This sparked her lifelong interest in the Queen that carried on throughout a career of commercial writing and her business in out-of-print books. This interest has culminated in a highly accurate and sensitive novel.

The author now lives in Fairhope, Alabama, with her cat, Sally.

9 781587 212338